Larry Brandtberry

INTRODU

D0769612

September Sonata by Andrea B
Kristin and Blaine Robinson
as she raised the kids and he was away a lot on his job as a
fireman. When an injury forces Blaine into early retirement and Kristin faces new obstacles at the school where
she had been working, these two must rediscover the joy
they once knew in their marriage.

October Waltz by DiAnn Mills
Abby Martin is ready to sell the western clothing store
she has operated in Cypress, Texas, for twenty-five years.
The buyer is Ron Bassinger, who needs a place to invest
some money and wants to rekindle an old flame with Abby.
Has anything really changed between them when Ron still
refuses to acknowledge her God?

November Nocturne by Dianna Crawford
Jack and Jill ran up many a hill together as children. Jill went
on to marry, have children, be widowed, and start a career.
Jack dedicated his life to a medical career and service to the
Lord in Third-World hospitals. He adopted two Asian boys
but never married. A chance reunion for Jack and Jill could
spark new love. But are the challenges of grown children
and long-distance romance too much?

December Duet by Sally Laity
Life for Cora Dennison has consisted of caring for five
younger siblings. Suddenly she is no longer a caregiver and
her youthful years have slipped away. Finding new ways to
help others and revitalize her old home brings her in contact with a building contractor. Michael Burgess has committed to living solo after a broken heart. Can these two
become one?

AUTUMN
Crescendo

*Four Novellas Celebrating
the Changing Seasons of Life*

Andrea Boeshaar
Dianna Crawford
Sally Laity
DiAnn Mills

BARBOUR
PUBLISHING, INC.
Uhrichsville, Ohio

September Sonata ©2001 by Andrea Boeshaar.
October Waltz ©2001 by DiAnn Mills.
November Nocturne ©2001 by Dianna Crawford.
December Duet ©2001 by Sally Laity.

Illustrations by Mari Goering.

ISBN 1-58660-228-4

All rights reserved. No part of this publication may be reproduced or transmitted in any form or by any means without written permission of the publisher.

All Scripture quotations, unless otherwise indicated, are taken from the HOLY BIBLE, NEW INTERNATIONAL VERSION®. NIV®. Copyright © 1973, 1978, 1984 by International Bible Society. Used by permission of Zondervan Publishing House. All rights reserved.

Scripture quotations marked KJV are taken from the King James Version.

Published by Barbour Publishing, Inc., P.O. Box 719, Uhrichsville, Ohio 44683 http://www.barbourbooks.com

 Member of the
Evangelical Christian
Publishers Association

Printed in the United States of America.

AUTUMN
Crescendo

September Sonata

by Andrea Boeshaar

Dedication

To Norma Z. with love.

Prologue

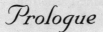

Milwaukee, WI
May 2000

I cy fear gripped Kristin Robinson's heart as she raced down the emergency room's stark corridor.

A dark-haired woman in blue scrubs stepped into her path. "Can I help you?"

"I. . .I'm looking for my husband," Krissy panted, halting in midstride. "His name is Blaine Robinson. He's a fireman, and he was injured—"

"Yes, I know who you mean. Follow me."

The nurse led her into a bustling area where doctors, nurses, and secretaries conducted business matters around an island containing desks and computers. Reaching the last room in a row of six, the woman opened a sliding glass door. There, right before Krissy's eyes, lay her husband, stretched out on a hospital gurney. His face had been blackened with soot and his hair and skin smelled singed by the hungry flames that had obviously sought to devour him.

"Blaine," she choked, rushing to his bedside. She noticed the blue and white hospital gown he wore, and the lightweight blanket covering him from the waist down. "Are you all right? I came as soon as I could."

"I'm okay, Honey." He peeked at her through one open eye. "I fell through the roof and injured my back. Looks like I might have cracked a couple of vertebrae."

"Oh, Blaine, no!"

"Now, don't worry. It's not as bad as it sounds. Could have been worse. I'm praising the Lord that my spinal cord is intact. I can move my feet, wiggle my toes. . .sure hurts though." He winced as if to prove his point.

"Blaine. . ."

With tears pricking the backs of her eyes, Krissy lifted his hand and held it between both of hers. In all their twenty years of marriage, this is what she'd feared the most: An injury in the line of duty. How many endless nights had she lain awake worrying that he'd never come home again to her and their two daughters? She knew too well that firefighters faced the possibility of death each and every time they responded to a call and by now, Krissy thought she'd have become accustomed to the ever-present threat. Today, however, when she'd received the phone call informing her that Blaine had been hurt, it was like living the nightmare.

"Hon, I'm going to make a full recovery," Blaine assured her, his eyelids looking heavy with whatever the nurses had given him for pain. "The ER doc said the orthopedic surgeon on call is coming to speak with us. I'll probably have to have surgery to help my back heal, and after a few months of recuperation, I'll be as good as new." He paused, grinning beneath the filmy soot covering his mouth. "Maybe even better. . ."

Chapter 1

Three Months Later

A re you sure you're up to driving?" Krissy asked Blaine as they headed north in their minivan. They'd dropped their twin daughters off at a Christian college in Florida and had been traveling most of the day. According to Krissy's calculations, they had another seventeen hours to go before they reached Wisconsin. Since Blaine was still recovering from his back surgery, she didn't want him to overdo it. "Would you like me to take the wheel for awhile?"

"I'm fine," he replied, "but I think we'll stop at a motel in Knoxville."

Krissy nodded, knowing her husband wasn't all that "fine" if he intended to stop for the night. Not Mr. Drive-'til-we-get-there Blaine Robinson. His back was most likely aching from all the activity that week. He'd loaded and unloaded the girls' belongings in and out of the van and carried items into their dormitory that he probably shouldn't have lifted.

Krissy glanced over at the profile that, in the past two decades, had become as familiar as her own face. Blaine's chestnut-brown hair was tinged with just a hint of gray above the ears, and in the last five years, he'd developed a bald spot at the crown of his head that the girls liked to kiss just to irritate him. His skin was tanned from the summer sunshine since he took advantage of convalescing outdoors. His neck and shoulders were thick with muscles he'd developed lifting heavy fire hoses and other equipment while he'd been on the job, although his midsection was getting awfully thick these days. Krissy didn't want to mention it, but she figured he'd put on about twenty pounds in the past three months. Worse, it seemed to her that he'd gotten lazy and slack when it came to his appearance. All these years, they had both tried to take care of themselves and keep fit, but lately Blaine seemed to have let himself go. It was rather disappointing.

Still, she loved him. He was the man with whom she would spend the remainder of her life. . .but why did that suddenly sound like such a long time?

"It's kind of weird without Mandy and Laina around," Krissy stated on a rueful note.

"Yeah, I think the girls chattered the entire way to Florida."

Krissy grinned. "They did. . .and now it's too quiet in here."

Blaine apparently decided to remedy the matter by turning the radio on to a syndicated talk show.

"Must you really subject me to this?" Krissy complained. "You listen to this guy every day."

"Yeah, so?" Blaine took his eyes off the road for a moment and looked over at her through his fashionable sunglasses.

"I don't care for some of his views," Krissy said.

"Well, I do, and with the presidential election coming up in November, I want to stay informed."

Krissy gritted her teeth and leaned back in the seat, closing her eyes and trying not to listen to the male voice booming conservative credos through the stereo speakers. While she considered herself a conservative Christian, she simply found the popular radio talk show host, in a word, annoying. In the last twelve weeks, while Blaine recuperated, Krissy had tolerated his penchant for the program. But now, as a captive audience, she felt resentful. Trapped.

She opened her eyes and leaned forward abruptly. "Blaine, can't we compromise? Surely there's another news station we could listen to."

"Relax. This show is only on for another hour and then I'll change the channel if you want."

Won't be any reason to change the channel then, she silently fumed.

Krissy turned her head toward the window and watched the scenery go by. It was only late August, but already some treetops were turning gold, orange, and russet. Autumn had begun in the Smoky and Appalachian Mountains. And next week Krissy would be back at school, teaching third graders. She mulled over everything she had to do in preparation. This year would be much different than the past twelve since Grace Christian School, the elementary school in which she'd taught, had merged with a larger institution due to financial constraints. Krissy expected changes, but she tried not to worry about them. Monday would come soon enough.

The minutes ticked by and finally the ragging on the liberals ceased. Blaine pressed the radio buttons until he found classical music. Krissy's taut nerves began to relax.

"Better?" Blaine asked, a slight smirk curving his well-shaped mouth.

"Much. Thanks." Krissy couldn't seem to help the note of cynicism in her reply. Then she paused, listening. "I don't recognize this piece."

Blaine gave it a moment's deliberation. "I believe it's one of Mozart's sonatas, obviously for the violin and piano."

"Obviously." Krissy quipped, smiling. She had acquired a taste for classical music over the years but hadn't ever learned to discern the various artists' styles, let alone the titles. "And tell me again how a sonata differs from, say, a waltz or serenade."

"A waltz is basically dance music written in triple time with the accent on the first beat."

"Ah, yes, that's right."

"A sonata is written in three or four movements."

"It's coming back to me now," Krissy said.

Blaine chuckled. "After hearing this music for twenty years, you should be an expert."

"Yes, I suppose I should."

"Well, after another twenty," Blaine stated in jest, "you're bound to be a fine critic of classic music."

An odd, sinking feeling enveloped Krissy. Symphonies and overtures were Blaine's forte, not hers. He was an accomplished musician himself and played the piano, although he hadn't practiced in years. Regardless, she had developed knowledge and respect for the art because of him and had to admit that Brahms, Beethoven, and Mozart did have a way of soothing her jangled nerves after a long day at school. Nevertheless, she enjoyed other types of music as much or more. In fact, she and the girls liked to attend musicals, both in Chicago and Milwaukee. They had seen *Show Boat* and *Phantom of the Opera*. . .

But the girls are eighteen years old and in college now, Krissy thought. *Blaine and I have the rest of our lives. . . together. Alone.*

The reality of her situation suddenly struck with full force. There were no more children to care for, fret over, shop with, or cook for. No more parent-teacher conferences to attend, basketball and football games to watch as her lovely daughters cheered on their high school's team. Although Amanda and Alaina were twins, they weren't identical, and each had her own fun personality that Krissy now realized she would sorely miss.

Tears began to well in her eyes and spill down her cheeks. She sniffed and then reached for her purse to find a tissue.

"What's the matter?"

"Oh, nothing."

"What?" Blaine pursued. "It's not the talk radio show. . . ? It's over now."

"No, no. . .it's the girls. They're gone." Krissy's tears flowed all the harder now. Her babies. Grown up. Living far away from home. Why, she'd been so preoccupied with helping them prepare and pack for college, not to mention nursing Blaine back to health, that she hadn't realized the impact the girls' departure would have. "They grew up so fast," Krissy said, blowing hard into the tissue. "Where did the years go?"

"Oh, for pity's sake. . ." Krissy heard the exasperation in her husband's voice. But then he reached across the built-in plastic console in the center of the two front seats and stroked the back of her hair. "Sweetheart, the girls'll be back. In just a few months it's Christmas. A few months after that, they'll be home for summer vacation. . .and you'll never have the telephone to yourself again."

Krissy managed a smile. "You're right," she said with a little sniffle. "I'm being silly." She thought it over, then sighed. "I just wish we would have had more children."

"That's a ridiculous wish, and you know it," Blaine said, removing his hand and placing both palms on the steering wheel. "We tried, but God didn't see fit to give us any more kids. Instead, Mandy and Laina were a double blessing. Still are. Always will be."

Krissy couldn't argue. Their twin daughters were a special gift from God.

"Think of it this way," Blaine continued, a smile in his deep voice, "we're still young. You and I have the rest of our lives together."

Krissy winced, and fresh tears filled her eyes. How could she tell Blaine that the very words he just spoke to cheer her up depressed her? She wasn't exactly feeling like the godly, submissive wife of which the Bible speaks, yet her feelings were real, and she didn't know how to handle them. True, she and Blaine had the rest of their lives, but what would they do with all those years together? She loved him, but somehow that didn't seem like enough. In the past twenty years, Blaine had been gone more than he'd been home, and Krissy had been a busy mother and schoolteacher. Of course, she and Blaine would continue to have their work. But was that all their lives together amounted to? Separate occupations? Separate lives, joined together by a vow to have and to hold, for better or for worse. . .'til death do us part. . . ?

"What's eating you?" Blaine asked later as he lay on one of the double beds in the motel room. He was clad in a white T-shirt and navy-printed boxers, and beneath his knees, Krissy had placed three pillows to ease his back discomfort. Unfortunately, she couldn't do anything about the atmosphere. Coupled with her melancholy, the air-conditioning unit wasn't working well, and the room felt hot and stuffy on this sweltering August night in Knoxville, Tennessee. "You haven't said more than five words since we stopped for supper."

"Oh, I'm just tired." Krissy decided that had to be it. Exhaustion. Sitting in a nearby floral-upholstered armchair, she stared blindly at the newscast on television. Maybe once she got back home and fell into a routine, teaching during the day, correcting homework in the evenings, she wouldn't miss the girls so much.

"Go take a cold shower," Blaine suggested. "That made me feel better."

"Yeah, maybe I will."

She looked over at him again, noticing for the first time that his brawny frame took up most of the bed. They slept on a king-size mattress at home. Last night, they'd rented a motel room with the same size bed. But tonight, this room with two doubles was all the desk clerk could offer them if they preferred a nonsmoking environment—which they did. If Blaine weren't healing from back surgery, Krissy wouldn't hesitate to tell him to move over, but it appeared as though tonight she'd sleep alone.

Separate lives. Separate beds. What a way to start the rest of their lives together.

Chapter 2

B laine watched Krissy back the minivan out of the driveway, then accelerate down the street. He couldn't figure out what had gotten into her. She'd been glum for the past few days. He'd first concluded that it was because the girls were gone, but after listening to her talking on the telephone with them yesterday afternoon, hearing her encourage their daughters, Blaine had to assume there was more to Krissy's doldrums.

So he questioned her.

In reply she had merely shrugged and admitted she didn't know what was wrong.

Maybe after today she'll feel more like her old self, he thought, moving away from the living room windows. After today Krissy would be teaching school again.

Walking into the kitchen, Blaine smiled at the red apples on green vines that Krissy and the girls had papered onto the walls not even a month ago. They had urged him to stay out of their way while they pasted and hung the wallpaper, giggling and chattering all the while, and Blaine had no problem finding something else to do.

Females. After living with three of them for nearly two decades, Blaine still couldn't figure them out half the time.

He continued grinning as he poured himself a cup of coffee. Taking a sip, he thought over Krissy's odd mood swing, then recalled what she'd said about her new school, its principal, and the other teachers. He figured she was most likely suffering from a case of nerves. Or maybe it was getting to be that time of month. Well, whatever bothered her, she'd snap out of it.

Blaine glanced at the clock and realized he had to hurry and shower in order to make it to his physical therapy appointment. Pushing thoughts of Krissy from his mind, he set down his coffee mug and headed for the bathroom.

Krissy glanced around at all the enthusiastic faces in the conference room of Wellsprings Academy and realized she was one of the older teachers here. Surrounding her were five other women, all appearing to have just graduated from college, and three men, who couldn't be any older than the academy's principal, Matt Sawyer, who looked about thirty-something. As Mr. Sawyer detailed his plans for the upcoming year, Krissy wondered if she really belonged at this place.

"I'd like every teacher to get personally involved with his or her students' education this year," the principal said, and when his gaze came her way, Krissy noticed how blue his eyes were, how strong his jawline seemed, how tall he stood, and how broad his shoulders looked beneath the crisp, white dress shirt he wore.

I wonder if he's married, she thought. But in the next moment, she berated herself for even allowing the question to take form in her mind. *I'm married and I love my husband,* she silently reaffirmed. However, it was disheartening that she found another man attractive.

Oh, Lord, what's wrong with me? Nothing has seemed right since Blaine's accident.

Krissy sighed. When no divine reply was forthcoming, she gave herself a mental shake and forced her thoughts back to the meeting.

At the midmorning break, Krissy helped herself to a cup of steaming coffee from the long, narrow refreshment table which had been set up in the hallway. She looked over the delectable treats which were also on display and chose a small cinnamon muffin.

"Those are my favorite."

Krissy turned to find Matt Sawyer standing directly behind her. Then he reached around her and plucked a muffin from the plastic plate.

"Well, what do you think so far?" he asked.

She smiled. "I think your staff is very young."

He grinned and took a bite of his muffin. Chewing, he looked around at the other teachers congregating on either side of them. "They're all qualified educators, believe me."

"Oh, I'm sure they are. It's just that. . .well, I don't see any of the teachers I worked with last year."

"They seemed competent and experienced. I read each one's resume. Unfortunately, we only had need for one third grade teacher since Leslie Comings got married this past summer."

Krissy couldn't believe her ears. "You mean to tell me I'm the only teacher who didn't lose her job?"

"Combining two schools isn't as simple as it might appear, I'm afraid. There were no easy decisions for the board members. The truth of the matter is, the merger didn't warrant extra teachers—even with the addition of Grace Christian School's populace."

"I see." She suddenly felt very badly for all her former colleagues.

"But we're glad you're here. . .Kristin, isn't it?"

She nodded.

"I've always been partial to the name. If I'd have had a daughter, I would have liked to name her Kristin."

She smiled nervously, unsure of how to respond. "Well, thank you, Mr. Sawyer."

He grinned. "Call me Matt. We're all in this together, and I think we should be on a first name basis, don't you?"

"Sure." She'd been on a first name basis with the principal of Grace Christian School. The solidly built, gray-headed man had been a father figure to her when situations arose in the classroom and Krissy wanted advice. But somehow she couldn't imagine herself running to Matt Sawyer's office for morsels of wisdom and seasoned counsel. The guy was too charming. Too. . . threatening.

"So you, um, have no daughters?" Krissy ventured, thinking that bringing up his family life would deter her attraction to him. "You and your wife have sons?"

"I have neither a wife nor children," Matt said as a rueful expression crossed his handsome features. "My wife is dead. She died very suddenly about three years ago."

Krissy sucked in a horrified gasp.

"It's no secret around here," Matt continued, "and I find being open about the tragedy has helped me recover."

"I'm so sorry. . ."

"Thank you." He paused and took another bite of his muffin. "My wife suffered with severe stomach problems. The medicine she took caused her to feel tired and depressed much of the time. Finally, she conceded to have surgery to fix the problem but something went horribly wrong and she never regained consciousness despite the doctors' best efforts."

"How tragic," Krissy said.

Matt nodded and finished the rest of his baked treat. "Yes, but I'm comforted to know that my wife was a believer. I like to imagine that when she met the Savior, He put His loving arms around her and. . .and wiped away all tears from her eyes. He probably assured her that there would be no more death, neither sorrow, nor crying, and no more pain."

Krissy recognized the paraphrase from the book of Revelation, saw the faraway, mournful look in Matt's gaze, and marveled at the depth of his sensitivity.

"Well, I hope you'll enjoy your year at Wellsprings Academy," he said, snapping from his reverie and pulling Krissy from hers also.

"Thanks," she replied, giving him a smile.

"And I'll look forward to getting to know you better," he added with a light in his blue eyes.

"Same here." The words were out of her mouth before Krissy even realized she'd spoken them.

❧

Blaine groaned in pain as he lowered himself onto the padded lawn chair in the backyard. His physical therapy session had taken a toll on him today; he'd used muscles in his back he hadn't realized he possessed. Unfortunately, instead of feeling better, he felt more disabled than ever. Glancing around the yard, he wished he could pull out the weed-whacker and get rid of the some of the growth inching upward through the patio blocks. He wished he could mow the lawn. This summer Krissy and the girls had taken turns and, while they did an adequate job, they didn't mow it the way Blaine liked. But he didn't complain. How could he? He'd been little more than vegetation, supervising from the lawn chair.

"Hi, Blaine." The cool feminine voice wafted over the wooden fence from the yard next door. "It sure is hot this afternoon."

Lifting an eyelid, he saw his neighbor, Jill, wearing nothing but a little halter top and a skimpy pair of shorts. He closed his eyes again. "Hi yourself. Pardon me for not being a gentleman and getting up. The truth is, I can't move."

He heard his neighbor's soft laugh. "Give me a break. Even flat on your back you're a gentleman."

Stretched out in the shady part of the yard, Blaine grinned at the remark. He felt complimented.

"I wish Ryan was as much a gentleman as you."

Hearing the anguish in her voice, Blaine's heart filled with sympathy. His neighbors weren't exactly the happily married couple that he and Krissy were. During the summer months with the windows open, sounds of their feuding drifted over the property line nearly every night. Blaine and Krissy had shared the Good News with the couple, inviting them out to attend a Bible study and church, but Ryan and Jill had vehemently stated they weren't "into religion." Regardless, prayers continued on their behalf.

"Did the girls get off to college all right?" Jill wanted to know.

"Yep. They called this weekend and seem to be doing fine. They like their roommates."

"Think they'll get homesick?"

"Probably."

Jill laughed and Blaine prayed she'd quit her chatting and tend to the toddler he could hear yelping inside the house. Nothing grated on his nerves more than a bawling child. Krissy said the neighbors' bickering bothered her more than listening to their kids throwing temper tantrums. Blaine, on the other hand, had no problem tuning out the arguing, but the kids' fussing made him edgy.

"I'll sure miss Mandy and Laina," Jill said. "They were such handy baby-sitters."

"They'll be back."

"Yeah, but my sanity might be gone by then." The child's wailing increased. "Well, I'd better go. See ya later."

"Sure, Jill. See ya."

Blaine opened his eyes in time to see his neighbor stoop near the sandbox and retrieve two small navy-blue sneakers. She shook the sand off of them, then entered the house.

Left alone to relax once more, Blaine suddenly felt glad those days of sandboxes, diapers, and crying children were behind him. He recalled how he had enjoyed leaving the house for work just because he knew he wouldn't be back for thirty-six hours. Thirty-six hours without listening to kids cry. Krissy, of course, handled things much better than he; she never complained. Not once. She never seemed to get upset or impatient with the twins. They turned out to be sweet young ladies largely because of her, although Blaine had made it a point to be part of their lives as much as possible. He'd enjoyed his daughters from the time they were about six years old on up. He coached their girls' softball team in the summertime and gymnastics team during the winter months. He involved himself with the youth group at church and chaperoned outings and events whenever his schedule permitted. He had fond memories of his daughters' growing up years. But he felt glad they were over.

Off in the direction of the garage, a car door slammed shut and Blaine realized Krissy had arrived home from work. He heard her enter the house and wondered how long it would take before she found him languishing in the yard. She'd have to help him out of the lawn chair. He hadn't been lying to Jill when he said he couldn't move. Minutes later, much to his relief, Krissy appeared.

"Must be nice to lounge around all day," she quipped, her hands on her slender hips. The tepid autumn breeze tousled her blond hair, causing it to brush lightly against the tops of her shoulders.

"Hey, you're a sight for sore eyes. Can you help me out of this chair?"

Krissy wagged her head, obviously over his pathetic state, and walked toward him. When she reached the edge of the lawn chair, she held out her hand. Blaine took it, but instead of allowing her to pull him up, he tugged, causing her to fall against him. Then he kissed her soundly, albeit awkwardly.

"You're real funny," she said, working herself into a sitting position on the side of the chair near Blaine's knees. "The two of us are liable to break this flimsy thing and then you'll really have back problems."

Blaine sighed. "I suppose you're right."

"As always." Krissy discreetly tucked her denim dress beneath her.

"How was your day?" he asked.

"Not too bad. And yours?"

"In a word. . .painful."

"Sorry to hear that." Krissy stood and helped Blaine to his feet. Lightning-hot pain bolted down his lower spine and thighs, blinding him for about ten seconds.

"Are you all right?"

"Yeah." He forced a smile, not wanting to worry his wife. "What's for supper?"

"I don't know. What are you hungry for?"

"Not sure."

"We're a decisive team."

Blaine grinned, then looped his arm around Krissy's shoulders, leaning on her as they walked toward the house. He didn't inquire further about her day. Didn't need to. His wife seemed to be her old self again.

Chapter 3

Mind if I use you for a pillow?"

"Do I look like a pillow?"

Blaine grinned. "You're soft and curvy. You'll do."

Unable to help a grin, Krissy scooted over and made room for Blaine on the couch. He stretched out, his head at the far end, while he lifted his legs onto her lap.

"I've got to have something under my knees when I lie down," he explained. "I think that's why I couldn't get myself out of the lawn chair earlier."

"I'm honored that you've selected me as your cushion," Krissy replied on a note of sarcasm. "Nice to know I'm good for something around here other than cooking, cleaning, and playing nurse and taxicab driver to a convalescing husband."

"Playing nurse is my favorite," Blaine shot back with a mischievous gleam in his eyes. "I only wish I could enjoy it more."

Shaking her head at him, Krissy lifted her feet onto the coffee table and set aside her now-empty paper plate. She and Blaine had decided to order out tonight. He wanted Italian and she wanted Chinese and neither would compromise, so Krissy ended up making two stops.

"How was your supper?"

"Great," Blaine replied. "Yours?"

"Marvelous. Sweet and sour chicken is my ultimate favorite."

"The stuff gives me gas. Are you sure it's chicken that Chinese place uses? Hard to tell with all the breading and sauce."

"Oh, quiet. Of course it's chicken."

Blaine chuckled, and Krissy rested her hands on his navy wind-pants. "One of the guys at work told me this joke about a Chinese Restaurant."

"I don't want to hear it."

"Something about a cat in the kettle at the Peking Room."

"Blaine, I said I don't want to hear it!"

He laughed while she bristled. Why did he always have to poke fun at the food she ate? She would never do such a thing to him. . .not that he'd let an unsavory joke spoil his appetite.

Still fuming, she tried to squelch her irritation by allowing her gaze to wander around their lower-level family room. The walls were paneled with knotty pine and decorated with various family snapshots that ranged from Blaine and Krissy's wedding to the twins' first steps to their graduating from high school last May. As she recalled each special event, a wave of nostalgia crashed over her.

Her exasperation forgotten for the moment, she turned to Blaine. She'd intended to engage him in a match of "remember when" but noticed that he'd begun to doze. Disappointed, Krissy looked back at the television set. As she watched the handsome, syndicated talk show host, she decided he had the same strong jawline as Matt Sawyer and a little smile tugged at the corners of her mouth.

Yes, the principal of Wellsprings Academy could certainly dub for a celebrity with his good looks and charming manner. Krissy couldn't help but wonder why he didn't remarry. She imagined Matt would most likely say it was because he hadn't "found the right one." That seemed to be a standard line among single people these days. However, Krissy noticed that there were a number of unattached, pretty females teaching at the academy and she guessed it wouldn't be long before the "right one" walked into Matt's life.

Within moments, her musings took flight and she speculated on the sort of woman it would take to win Matt's heart. Obviously, he'd been devastated when his first wife died, so the next woman to enter his life would have to somehow dispel all the hurts and fears born from such a tragedy. Krissy thought she knew what she'd do if she weren't married. She'd cultivate a friendship with the man, learning all his likes and dislikes, and she would be quick to point out the interests they shared. Like reading for instance. This afternoon while Krissy acquainted herself with her new classroom, Matt had stopped by with a novel in his hands.

"Have you by any chance read this book?"

Spying the cover, Krissy recognized it, nodded, and rambled off an impromptu quote that could have come straight from the book jacket.

"Yes, that's the one." Matt grinned. "I'm enjoying it very much."

"I recall it was a very touching story."

"Quite. And this entire series. . .have you read it?"

"Every book."

"What's your take on the novels?"

For nearly an hour, they had discussed books and shared their perspectives on various authors, styles, and story lines. Krissy found the conversation refreshing, since she'd been trying for two decades to get Blaine interested in books. But he only liked to read if the topics pertained to sports or firefighting, and he couldn't appreciate anything longer than a feature article.

She glanced over at him now, expecting to find him snoozing. But to her outright chagrin, she discovered Blaine staring back at her.

"What are you thinking about?" he asked softly. His eyes seemed to scrutinize her every feature.

Krissy felt her cheeks redden with embarrassment. "Books. I was thinking about books."

"Mmm. . ."

Blaine's gaze was like a weighty probe, searching into her heart, her soul. Suddenly she felt like the wickedest woman ever to roam Wisconsin. Here she ought to be enjoying her husband's company, but instead she was dreaming of capturing another man's heart.

Forgive me, Lord, she silently prayed. *What's wrong with me?*

Krissy crawled out from under Blaine's knees, then placed a large throw pillow beneath them in her stead.

"I'm tired. I think I'll turn in."

"Sure. Good night, Hon."

" 'Night."

Heavyhearted and feeling more than just a tad guilty, Krissy made her way upstairs to the master bedroom.

That was weird, Blaine thought, watching Krissy's departure. He'd never seen such an odd expression on his wife's face. She'd been daydreaming, that was obvious. But about books? No way. If she would have said she'd been thinking about the girls and remembering some silly thing the three of them had done together, Blaine would have bought it, lock, stock, and barrel. Unfortunately, he didn't buy it at all, and a slight foreboding sent a chill up his already aching spine. What was with Krissy these days?

Time to find out.

With a determined set to his jaw, he roused himself from the couch and made his way upstairs. He walked down the hallway, heading for their room. When he reached the doorway, however, he stopped short, seeing Krissy on her knees at the side of the bed, her Bible open on the floral spread in front of her. Silently, Blaine stepped backward, retracing his steps to the living room where he decided to put off any discussion until she finished her devotions.

Nearly twenty minutes later, he heard the bathroom door close followed by sounds of the shower spray.

Great, he thought, *she'll be in there all night*.

Well, fine, he would just wait for Krissy in the bedroom. Once more he ambled upstairs and down the hallway and entered their room. Lowering himself onto the bed, Blaine threw a pillow under his knees, turned on the small television, and began his vigil.

Krissy heard him before she ever saw him. Blaine. Snoring loudly. On top of their bed. And with her pillow under his knees, no less. Had he worn those windpants all day? To physical therapy with a lot of sick people around? Wonderful. Like she really wanted to place her head on it now!

Irritation coursed through her veins as she slipped into her nightie. Did Blaine ever once think of her? Couldn't he respect her feelings on anything, be it carryout food or books or her own, personal pillow?

With a huff, she grabbed the remote from where it lay on Blaine's T-shirt encased stomach and turned off the TV. Next, she switched off the lamp and stomped out of the room, intending to sleep in one of the girls' beds tonight. She wanted to slam the door but refrained from doing so. Still, she wasn't quiet about putting clean sheets on Mandy's bed.

Regardless, Blaine never awoke.

Chapter 4

Blaine yawned and stumbled into the kitchen. "How come you slept in Mandy's room last night?"

Krissy threw him an annoyed look, then whirled around and finished preparing a pot of coffee. She had already dressed for school and Blaine thought she was quite attractive in the blue and green plaid cotton skirt and hunter-green T-shirt. The outfit complemented her blond hair and tanned skin.

"All right, Krissy, spit it out. What's up with you these days?"

She flipped on the coffeemaker and it began to brew. Turning to face him again, she folded her arms in front of her.

"Well?" Blaine demanded.

"Nothing is 'up with me.'"

"Nothing? It's hardly nothing, Kris," he said, easing himself into a chair at the kitchen table. "You've been acting so strange. . .ever since the girls went off to school. I mean. . ." He searched his mind for the right words. "Sometimes I feel like I don't even know you anymore. Like last night. I've got a feeling you weren't daydreaming about books. So what was going through your head?"

He watched as she blushed slightly before lifting her chin. She appeared almost defiant—another trait unlike the Krissy he'd married.

"I think you said it all," she stated softly, "when you said you don't know me anymore. In all honesty, you don't."

"What in the world are you talking about?"

"It's true," she said, avoiding his gaze, her voice wavering. "We never talk like we used to and when I try to discuss a topic of importance to me, you never listen. You don't even know what's going on in my life these days. You think you do, but really you don't."

Minutes ticked by as they regarded each other in silence. Then, once the coffee finished brewing, Krissy turned and poured two mugs. She crossed the room and placed one in front of Blaine.

Sipping it, he tried to think how he should handle this situation. Maybe hormones were to blame. Sometimes when she got this way it was just a matter of riding out the storm.

As if she'd read his mind, she spat, "And don't think this is just a PMS thing. It's not. This is something I've been aware of for a long time now. An intricate part of our marriage is gone, and it's never been more prevalent than it has since your accident. You and I, Blaine, have nothing in common. We're two people who are married and live under one roof, but we're not one flesh. Not anymore."

Blaine narrowed his gaze, feeling more than just a little disturbed by what he'd just heard. "Krissy, are you. . .are you thinking. . . ?"

He couldn't get himself to say the word "divorce." Thinking about it caused his gut to knot up.

"Krissy," he began again, "you and I made vows to each other—"

"I'm not about to break my wedding vows," she shot back.

"Well, that's good."

"We're just stuck with each other. . .for the rest of our lives."

Blaine felt his jaw drop slightly. "Stuck with each other?"

Krissy had the good grace to look chagrined.

"Stuck? Is that how you see it?"

"I'm going to be late." She marched quickly past him and grabbed her bagged lunch and purse.

Blaine rose from the chair. "Wait."

She didn't. "See you tonight."

She fled out the side door before he could stop her. As a feeling of disbelief enveloped him, Blaine listened to the van door slam, the engine roar to life, and the sounds of Krissy backing the vehicle out of the garage and down the driveway.

"Stuck with each other," Blaine whispered incredulously. Next came the tidal wave of hurt that threatened to submerge him in a mixture of sorrow and rage.

He didn't feel "stuck" with her. He loved Krissy—loved her with all his heart. He'd do anything for her. But she felt "stuck" with him.

First the rage. *How can she be so selfish, thinking only of herself and what she wants? And what does she want anyhow? She's got everything. A house, a job she enjoys, a husband who loves her, two nearly perfect daughters. . . .*

He fumed all the while he dressed. Then, as he drove to his doctor's appointment later in the morning, the agonizing sorrow gripped his heart. *She doesn't love me anymore. What does a guy do when his wife doesn't love him anymore? When did it happen? How come I never noticed?*

Blaine had heard of marriages crumbling once the kids were grown and gone. He would believe it'd happen to his next door neighbors, but not to him and Krissy. They were Christians. This stuff wasn't supposed to happen to godly couples.

Perplexed, he drove into the clinic's parking structure, found a spot, and pulled his truck to a halt.

"So how's the back?" Dr. Lemke asked about thirty minutes later. The man's bald head shone like a brand-new plastic toy under the fluorescent lights in the exam room. Blaine would wager the short, stocky physician weighed about three hundred and fifty pounds, and he prayed he'd never end up fat and bald in his old age.

"Back's not so good. I'm still in a lot of pain."

The doctor glanced up. "Yes, so I see from the physical therapist's report. He states you're unable to do some pretty simple stretching and bending exercises."

"True, but don't think I haven't been practicing at

home just like the therapist told me," Blaine stated in his own defense. "But the exercises aren't working."

"Hmm. . ."

Blaine watched the pen tip wiggle as Dr. Lemke scratched down what they'd discussed. Since the man was employed by the City of Milwaukee, Blaine figured he wanted to write out a return-to-work slip as soon as possible and spare further workers' compensation. In truth, Blaine wanted that too. He was growing bored at home all day.

"You're going to have to see a specialist," the doctor said at last. "Go back to the surgeon who operated. I'm afraid I can't do anything more for you."

"Sure. Whatever."

The doctor scribbled out the referral and his medical assistant made the appointment for Blaine. Sheet of paper in hand, he left the clinic and climbed into his pickup truck. He didn't care a whit about himself as he made the drive toward home. He kept thinking about what Krissy said that morning.

We're stuck with each other.

Blaine knew she meant it, too. They'd said things to each other before that they didn't mean, just like most other married couples. They'd apologized for it, then prayed together and asked for God's forgiveness, too. But given Krissy's odd behavior of late, he could tell those words had come from the very depth of her being.

Lord, what do I do? he prayed as he pulled into the driveway. Tears welled in Blaine's eyes, and he couldn't even remember the last time he'd cried. *Lord, please help* me. *Please save my marriage. I'm nothing without Krissy.*

Did you ever tell her that?

The Voice wasn't an audible one, but it had replied to his heart just the same.

Sure I told her. Millions of times.

Millions?

And trillions.

Blaine shifted, feeling uncomfortable since he suddenly couldn't recall when he'd last shared his heart with Krissy.

How many times does a guy have to tell his wife the same old thing?

Millions and trillions.

Blaine grinned and gazed up through his sun roof and the blue, cloudless sky. "All right, Lord. I get it. You don't have to hit me over the head with a brick."

Exiting his truck, he grimaced as a shooting pain blasted down his leg. "On second thought, maybe You did."

❧

"Mrs. Robinson, you have a phone call." Turning from the bulletin board she was decorating, Krissy forced a smile at the secretary. "I would have used the intercom system," the woman continued, "but it doesn't seem to be working. We'll have it fixed by the time school starts though."

"Thanks. I'll be right there."

The tall, slim, redhead whose age seemed unfathomable nodded and exited the classroom. Krissy had heard Mrs. Sterling was pushing sixty, yet she looked and acted no older than thirty-five. Secretly, Krissy hoped she'd be in such good shape at that age.

Setting the stapler down on her desk, Krissy followed the secretary through the hallway. They entered the office suite, Mrs. Sterling returned to her desk, and without even picking up the receiver, Krissy knew Blaine would be at the other end of the line. What had possessed her to throw such hateful words at him? She'd felt badly all the way to school and then Matt's morning "challenge" to all the teachers had really touched her heart.

"Hello?" she answered somewhat timidly.

"Hi, Hon, what do you want for supper tonight?"

Blaine sounded like his same old self for which Krissy felt grateful. "Um, I really hadn't thought about it."

"Well, do you mind if I whip up something?"

She grimaced. Blaine was famous for his three-alarm chili at the fire station. Unfortunately, it wasn't one of Krissy's favorites. But she'd hurt him enough for one day. "Sure, make whatever you want."

"Okay."

"And, Blaine?"

"Yeah?"

Krissy glanced over her shoulder to be sure no one could overhear. Mrs. Sterling was nowhere in sight. "Sorry about this morning. . . ."

"Honey, all is forgiven, and we can talk about it tonight if you feel up to it."

"We can?" Holding the phone several inches away, Krissy stared at it like the piece of equipment had just grown a mouth of its own. "Well, all right," she said at last. "I'll see you in about an hour."

"Sounds good. And Kris. . .I love you."

She smiled, feeling guilty as she hung up the phone. Why was Blaine acting so nice after she'd been so mean? Of course, he wasn't a guy to stay angry or hold grudges, but he wasn't always so agreeable either.

"Everything all right, Kristin?" Pivoting, she glanced across the office suite in time to watch Matt walk out of his private office. "You look like you might have had some bad news."

"No, no," she assured him. "I think the doctor just gave my husband some different pain medication. He didn't sound like himself."

"Hmm. . ." Matt gave her a curious frown. "Pain medication for what?"

"For his back. Blaine was injured at work. He's a fireman and he fell through the roof of a two-story house. Cracked a couple of vertebrae and had surgery to repair a couple of discs that ruptured in the process."

"How horrible. When did that happen?"

"This past May."

"I see. Well, I'll pray for him. It's my belief that chonic pain often leads to drug addiction. My wife nearly became addicted to her precription drugs. It's one of the reasons she opted for the surgery."

Krissy sucked in a breath, hoping such a thing wouldn't befall Blaine. But she quickly shook off her misgivings, realizing her husband hadn't been depressed a day in his life. As for an addiction to pain medication, he rarely took the stuff—even when he legitimately needed it.

"I didn't mean to frighten you," Matt said, looking earnest.

Krissy snapped from her musing. "You didn't. You just gave me something to think about."

"One thing I learned from the situation with my wife is that life is short. Too short to waste on unhappiness."

Krissy couldn't help agreeing. She'd felt dispirited for over a week and it wasn't any fun.

Matt gave her a compassionate grin. "You can talk to me anytime. I'll be here for you."

Krissy felt a blush creep up her neck and warm her cheeks. "That's very kind."

"I mean it."

"I know you do. Thanks."

Their gazes met and Krissy's traitorous heart began to hammer so loudly she felt certain Matt could hear it. She was only too grateful when Mrs. Sterling reentered the office, carrying a stack of papers.

Krissy quickly made her exit.

Chapter 5

K rissy turned the van into the driveway and groaned at the sight of her next door neighbor, Jill Nebhardt, standing near the patio wearing khaki shorts and red T-shirt. Next she noticed the cloud of gray smoke billowing into the air and guessed that Blaine had fired up the grill. Now Jill was most likely chatting his ear off while he barbequed.

Well, at least he didn't make his three-alarm chili, Krissy mused gratefully as she killed the engine. Grabbing her purse, she climbed out of the van.

As she strode toward her husband and neighbor, Krissy experienced a twinge of guilt for not feeling very friendly. She supposed she should have compassion on the poor woman since Jill was terribly discouraged in her marriage. On the other hand, Krissy felt tired, and she and Blaine had their own issues right now.

"Hey, you're home," Blaine said as a smile split his tanned face. "I didn't even hear you pull in." His gaze flittered to Jill in explanation, and Krissy understood immediately.

"I was just telling Blaine about Ryan's new work schedule. He's gone twelve, sometimes thirteen hours a day. When he comes home, he's so crabby the kids and I can't stand to be around him. Worse, he expects dinner on the table and the house to be spotless."

"I told Jill I know the feeling since that's what you expect too, right Hon?"

Krissy rolled her eyes. "You haven't done housework in twenty years, Blaine."

"With three women around, why should I?" Pointing the metal spatula at her, he added, "And you haven't changed a flat tire in all that time. Or shoveled snow."

"You won't let me use your snow blower, otherwise I would." Krissy leaned toward Jill. "This argument could go on all night."

The younger woman chuckled. "I'm so glad to see you two aren't perfect. You seem like it sometimes. I'm really envious of your relationship." She peered into Krissy's face with teary brown eyes. "You don't know how lucky you've got it, Girlfriend."

"I remind Krissy of that at least three times a day," Blaine said.

Sudden shouts from the adjoining backyard brought Jill to attention. "Uh-oh. . .sounds like Grant and Royce are at it again. I'd better scoot. Talk to you guys later."

"See ya, Jill," Blaine replied.

"Bye." Krissy watched their neighbor jog around the house before looking back at Blaine. "Hi."

"Hi." He stepped around the smoking grill and

gave her a kiss. "Have a good day?"

"Yeah, and you?"

"Okay."

"What did the doctor say?"

"He wants me to go back and see Dr. Klevins."

"The surgeon? How come?"

"Because my back isn't improving at the rate he'd like."

Krissy nibbled her lower lip in momentary contemplation. "Do you think another operation is ahead of you?"

"I doubt it. I've had a fusion, what more can the surgeon do?"

"I don't know."

Blaine looked down at whatever he was cooking.

"What are you making for supper?" Krissy asked, curious.

Bringing his gaze back to hers, he grinned. "Beef tenderloin. One of your favorites."

The news made her smile. "I've been hungry for a grilled steak. And here I had assumed you concocted your famous chili."

"You hate my chili. Why would I make it when it's just you and me for supper tonight?"

"Well, I—"

"See, I know you, Krissy. Better than you think." He raised an eyebrow as if to make his point.

"Touché." Hitching her purse up higher onto her shoulder, she couldn't help grinning. "I'm going inside to change."

"Slipping into something more comfortable, are you, Darling?" Blaine asked in a feigned British accent.

"Oh, like right." Krissy shook her head at him and walked to the side door. "I've got a mountain of things to accomplish tonight."

Entering the house, a swell of disappointment rose inside her when she realized she could sure use a romantic evening. Then, much to her shame, a vision of Matt Sawyer and his tender blue eyes flittered across her mind.

"You're not eating."

Krissy looked up from her plate. "Everything is perfect, Blaine. The steak, the salad, the dinner rolls. . ."

"But?"

"But I feel a little down all of a sudden. I can't explain it. It's just weird."

"Maybe it's the company," Blaine quipped, setting his fork down none too gently.

Krissy stared at him ruefully. How could she make him understand what was going on inside her when she didn't understand it herself? "Blaine. . ."

"You know what," he said, an earnest light in his dusky, blue-gray eyes, "I've been in love with you since we were juniors in high school."

Krissy had to smile as mental snapshots of the past flashed through her mind. "I know. . ."

"And when you agreed to go to the prom with me that year, I felt like the luckiest guy alive. I mean, Krissy Marens. . .*the* Krissy Marens, prettiest girl in school. . .going to the prom with me. . .and I wasn't even on the football team."

Laughing, she sat back in her chair and folded her arms. "I thought you were awfully cute."

Blaine's smile faded. "Change your mind lately?"

"No. . .I mean. . ." She sighed. "I don't know. . ."

She began picking at her salad again, not willing to see the pain she probably inflicted on the man she was supposed to love unconditionally. She felt guiltier now, trying to be honest, than if she'd have just stuffed these feelings in the deepest part of her and somehow tried to forget them there.

"I can't help it that my hair is thinning," Blaine said. "This bald patch on the back of my head seems to get bigger every year."

Krissy glanced at him and smiled. "I like your bald spot. And I think your thinning hair makes you appear. . .distinguished."

"Hmm. . ." He rubbed his jaw, looking perplexed. "Maybe my five o'clock shadow bugs you, is that it?"

"No, I like your five o'clock shadow. I wish you had it all day."

"Want me to quit shaving?"

Krissy rolled her eyes. "No."

"Help me out here, Woman," Blaine cried in exasperation, holding his arms out wide. "I want to please you, but how can I when I don't know what it is that's displeasing you?"

"The paunch hanging over your belt turns me off. There. I said it."

"Thank you." Throwing his gaze upward, he shook his head. "For your information, I plan to get rid of my. . .paunch. . .just as soon as my back heals up."

"That's what I figured, so I didn't want to make a big deal out of it. But you've been wearing such sloppy clothes lately."

"My blue jeans are a little snug. Besides, they're hard to pull on with my back killing me half the time."

Krissy shrugged.

"Okay, okay, okay," he said, his palms out as if to forestall further debate. "I'll lose some weight. I'm not pleased with this extra twenty pounds either."

"You'll feel better, too. That's twenty pounds off your aching back."

Blaine humbly agreed. "Now, I need to ask you something else," he said, standing and taking his silverware and half-empty plate to the sink. "Something important."

Krissy felt horrible for ruining his dinner. "What's the question?"

"I want a totally honest answer. No beating around the bush." After depositing his dishes near the sink, he turned and faced her.

She rose and cleared her place, setting everything on the counter next to Blaine's utensils. Standing in front of him, she looked up into his eyes, unsure if she trusted herself to be as forthright as he requested.

"You still love me, Krissy?" Her brawny husband wore an expression of boyish vulnerability and the sight moved her to tears.

"Yes, I love you. Of course I love you. It's just that. . ."

"What?"

"It's just that in so many ways, Blaine, we're strangers."

"That makes no sense. We've been married for twenty years. We've known each other since high school. How can we possibly be strangers?"

"Because since the twins were born we put all our energy into raising them. We did a good job, too. But, when the girls were in first grade, I went back to school and finished my degree and from that point on, I had my career, you had yours, and our home life consisted of our daughters and maintaining a house."

Krissy expelled a long breath, hoping she was getting through to him. "I don't regret any of the sacrifices we made for Mandy and Laina, except for one. Our relationship. We lost touch, you and I, and now there's a distance between us that I don't know how to bridge."

Working the side of his lip between his teeth, Blaine seemed to be considering everything she said. Then he sighed, shrugged, and gathered Krissy into his arms. "If we love each other, which we do," he stated at last, "then we can pray about these things and work on spanning whatever gap exists."

Resting her head against the lower part of his shoulder, Krissy could hear the strong, steady beat of Blaine's heart. She could smell smoke on his T-shirt from the outside grill. It was a scent she'd become well-acquainted with over the years because of his occupation. She associated the odor with an unsettled sensation and realized that, even though they'd grown apart, she'd always concerned herself with his safety. She had fretted and prayed for him during those hours following his accident. Wasn't that love? Of course it was!

Blaine placed a light kiss on her forehead. "Everything'll be all right."

She nodded and tightened her arms around his waist. "Fall always seems like a time of change and adjustment. A different school year, new students—and this year another school altogether for me, and now Mandy and Laina are gone."

"Honey, they're not 'gone.' You make it sound like they're dead. They're just away at college. It's a temporary thing."

"Like the season."

"Right. Life's full of seasons."

Krissy nodded, wishing this one would pass quickly.

Chapter 6

It was the last day of the week and first day of September. Warm sunshine spilled through the partially cloudy sky and onto the black asphalt where Krissy's third graders were at play. Shiny new equipment in bright yellows and reds beckoned children of all ages to its monkey bars, slide, and swings. The little girl inside Krissy felt tempted to join the kids each time she heard their squeals of laughter.

"I wish they would have made gym sets like that when I was growing up," fellow teacher, Erin Latrell, said. She stood to Krissy's right, observing her second graders.

Krissy laughed. "I was thinking along those same lines." Tipping her head, she considered the young woman. Krissy guessed Erin wasn't much older than the twins, with her peaches-and-cream complexion and blue-eyed innocence framed with shoulder-length, reddish-brown hair that fell in soft curls past her shoulders. "Mind if I ask where you attended college?"

"Not at all. I stayed right here in Wisconsin. I lived

at home. Still do, but I'm getting married soon. Next summer, in fact."

"How nice." Krissy smiled, suddenly wishing she would have insisted that Mandy and Laina live at home while going to school. But as she mentally replayed the conversation she'd had with each of her daughters last night, she realized the girls were happy and enjoying campus life. Besides, they truly needed this time to blossom and grow into the young women God intended them to be.

Wistfully, she returned her gaze to the children at play. *Blaine was right*, she thought, *this is just a season. . . a stormy one. And it's storming in my heart.*

The sound of hard sole shoes tapping against the pavement drew Krissy out of her reverie. Glancing over her shoulder, she saw Matt Sawyer, dressed in a light brown suit, striding toward them. Reaching her and Erin, he grinned.

"Nice day."

Krissy smiled. "It certainly is."

Erin nodded in agreement.

"I wanted to deliver these personally," he said, handing each of them a white, sealed envelope. "They're invitations to my annual Labor Day party this coming weekend. Time got away from me, and I didn't trust placing them in teachers' in-boxes." He paused, bestowing a warm smile on Erin, then Krissy. "I'd be honored if you would both attend."

Krissy glanced down at the envelope in her hand, not wanting to look up into Matt's blue eyes. She was a married woman and to flirt would be very wrong, but if she wasn't mistaken, Matt sought out her company. . .and Krissy felt more than flattered. Worse, she enjoyed it.

Oh, Lord, this is a bad situation, one I can't give in to even if I'm tempted to. . .

"May I bring my fiancé?" Erin asked.

"Of course. I'd love to meet him," Matt replied graciously. "And, Kristin," he added, turning toward her, "I hope you'll bring your spouse."

Why had that just sounded like a question? Did Matt care one way or the other?

Pushing her ponderings aside, she tried to attack the issue pragmatically. Would she bring Blaine? Or rather, would he deign to accompany her? In all probability, he'd elect to stay home. He abhorred attending social functions that included Krissy's coworkers. He said teachers were boring and tried to one-up each other as proof of their intellect. Of course, the same could not be said for Blaine's colleagues who played tug-of-war over mud pits and blasted each other with fire hoses on their company picnics. Over the years Krissy had gone to each and every one with Blaine, and she did so without complaint.

Mustering her courage, she glanced up at Matt and gave him a formal grin. "I'll pass the invitation on to my husband. Thanks."

"Great," he said, but Krissy sensed the answer lacked Matt's usual enthusiasm.

As he walked away and reentered the school, she felt her heart take a plunge from the weight of the guilt she'd been carrying around for almost two weeks. Yet, she hadn't done anything to feel ashamed about, except entertain thoughts of impossibilities. She wasn't about to leave Blaine in order to have a fling with her new principal. She was a Christian. She loved her husband. He loved her.

Krissy sighed. *So what in the world is my problem?*

Blaine wasn't sure how he felt as he drove home that Friday afternoon. Disappointed, scared, and irritated all at the same time. He'd seen the orthopedic surgeon, and after hearing the bad news, he checked in at the fire station to say hello to the guys. Next, he conversed with the captain for a long while, and at last, Blaine saw the wisdom behind taking the permanent disability the city offered, along with a compensation package the union procured for him. The surgeon had stated that Blaine would never return to work. His back wasn't ever going to be as limber and as strong as it had been before the accident. However, his physician ordered him to swim and lose weight. . .that is if he didn't want to turn into a mass of plump vegetation. Blaine knew it was sound advice, and he'd been watching his diet lately. He'd even shed a few pounds, but he had many more to lose. So, after the fire station, Blaine's next visit was to the local health club where he purchased a membership. He figured a workout would use up an hour or two, but how would he spend the rest of his days?

Lord, there has to be a job out there somewhere that I can do. A man doesn't work, he doesn't eat. . .

Blaine pulled into the driveway and parked behind Krissy's van. Climbing out of his truck, he entered the house and the aroma of sautéing garlic immediately met his senses. He followed his nose to the kitchen where he found Krissy at the stove.

"Smells great in here," he said, placing his hands on her slim hips and kissing her neck. "What are you making?"

"A stir-fry. . .with real chicken," she replied emphatically.

Blaine chuckled. "Your version of Chinese food is always tasty, Hon. It's the order-out stuff that rouses my curiosity."

"What did the doctor say?" Krissy asked in a no-nonsense tone.

He chewed the side of his lip and considered her. Was she in one of her moods again? She didn't even acknowledge the compliment he'd just paid her.

She looked at him askance. "Well?"

"I've got six months to live."

Krissy gave him a quelling look. "Don't even joke about such things, Blaine."

"Well, maybe that's what you'd like to hear," he blurted. He was getting tired of catering to her whimsical ups and downs. Didn't she care a whit about him?

Setting down the spatula, she faced him, hands on hips. "I'm not up to sparring with you, so just tell me what the doctor said, okay?"

Blaine exhaled and fought against the frustration welling inside of him. "He said I can't go back to work because I'll never be able to function in the capacity the fire department expects. So, I stopped by the station and accepted the permanent disability offer and comp package. I'm no longer a firefighter."

Krissy's jaw dropped slightly. "You're out of a job? Just like that? Can't they give you some more time to recuperate?"

"It's been three months, Kris."

"But—"

"Look, the doc said it and my captain agreed. I'm no longer physically able to perform my job. And I won't be. Ever."

Blaine saw Krissy swallow hard. "We can't live on my salary. . .and help the girls through college."

"I'll have money coming in. And I plan to find something else to do besides sit around here all day watching soap operas."

"You've been watching the soaps?"

Blaine laughed at her horrified expression. "I meant that figuratively."

She nodded, looking relieved, and began slicing the boneless chicken breasts and adding the pieces to the oil and garlic.

"Honey, don't worry. Things are going to be fine. The Lord will take care of us. He'll find me some sort of work that I can do to supplement the disability payments."

"Yes, I. . .I'm sure you're right."

Blaine folded his arms and watched his wife prepare their meal with lackluster efforts. It just wasn't like her. Up until a few weeks ago, she'd had an unsurpassed zest for life, but now a kind of dreariness clouded her eyes. He wished he could get inside her head for five minutes. Maybe then he could understand whatever it was that bothered her. . .other than what she'd previously admitted to. He had a feeling the problem was more than just his extra poundage and the girls being away, although the combination might have been the boiling point.

"Hard day at school, Kris?"

"Not exactly."

"Well, what *exactly* is bugging you right now? Me?"

"No. . .not you. It's just that I was thinking about quitting my job until you came home with your news."

Blaine brought his chin back in surprise. "Why do you want to quit your job? You don't like the new school?"

"I don't know. . .maybe I'm just tired of teaching altogether. Maybe I've lost what it takes to be a good educator."

"That's not what you said Monday night. You said the kids seemed to adore you and that they were excited about their new third grade teacher. I really thought you were starting to snap out of this depression. . .or whatever you want to call it."

Krissy began chopping celery, onions, and mushrooms. Next she tossed the vegetables into the wok on the stove. "There's just this person at school who. . ." She swallowed and Blaine sensed she was trying to carefully select her words. "Well, I don't know if it's. . .healthy for me to work near this person."

Blaine frowned. "Not healthy?"

"Emotionally speaking."

"Hmm. . ." He thought it over. "So this person is verbally abusive or threatening?"

"Threatening," Krissy replied on a decisive note.

"You're kidding? This person is making threats? Let's call the cops!"

"No, no, Blaine, not that kind of threatening. I mean, he's not threatening me, he's just a threat to me."

"Like he wants to take over your job?"

Krissy turned thoughtful. "Something like that, I guess. He wants to take over something."

"Man, you wouldn't think that kind of competition existed in Christian day schools, but I suppose it's everywhere." He paused, thinking it over. So all this was about her career? Well, that made sense. "Listen, Kris, if after bathing the matter in prayer, you feel you need to quit your job, go ahead. You'll find another one. Probably a better paying one, too." With that he closed the distance between them and kissed her cheek. "See? Problem solved."

༆

Krissy watched her husband's retreating form as he left the kitchen and entered the living room. Next she heard the rustling of the paper and knew he'd taken to reading the daily local news.

Blaine thinks the problem's solved, she thought, jabbing at the stir-fry with the wooden spatula. She then placed the cover on top of the wok and allowed it to cook. *The problem is not solved. It's far from being solved. But what do I say? I'm bored with our marriage and I'm attracted to Matt Sawyer?* Krissy shook her head. Blaine would hit the ceiling. What husband wouldn't? And here she was supposed to be a good, Christian wife.

Her spirit plummeted deeper with discouragement and shame. Not only was she a lousy wife, but she was a sorry excuse for a Christian woman as well.

Chapter 7

Krissy sulked around the house for the rest of the evening, and Blaine didn't even bother trying to cheer her up. Frankly, he hadn't the slightest clue what more to do for her, other than leave her alone and allow her to come to her own conclusions about whether she should quit her job. Meanwhile, he started his new swimming routine on Saturday morning, and after completing several laps he could tell the exercise would strengthen his back muscles. Maybe he'd take off this extra weight quicker than he anticipated. The idea encouraged him.

On Sunday morning, he and Krissy attended their usual Bible study and the service that followed. When the pastor gave an altar call, Krissy went forward, looking more miserable than Blaine had ever seen her.

Lord, I feel helpless, he silently prayed, stepping into the aisle and allowing Krissy back into the pew after she'd knelt and prayed up front. It comforted Blaine to know she, at least, communed with their Heavenly Father. God had the answers that he lacked, and the

Lord would guide Krissy's steps.

Back at home, she seemed. . .happier.

"Everything okay?" Blaine asked as they stood in their bedroom. He unknotted his tie, then yanked it out from around his neck.

Krissy smiled and nodded as she changed her clothes. "Everything's fine."

"What do you want to do this afternoon?"

She stopped and glanced at him, her expression one of surprise. "You want to do something?"

"Well, yeah. . .why is that such a shock?"

Krissy laughed softly and hung up her dress. "Because you usually like a nap on Sunday afternoons."

"That's when I was a hardworking man. Now I'm footloose and fancy-free."

"Oh, brother!" She rolled her eyes.

Blaine chuckled. "And tomorrow's a holiday, so you don't need a nap either."

"We sound like two old fogies."

"We are two old fogies. So what do you want to do this afternoon, *Granny?*" Judging from her wounded expression, Blaine instantly knew he'd said the wrong thing. "Honey, I was only kidding. The granny-thing was supposed to be funny."

"I know. . .I guess it just struck me the wrong way." She gave him an earnest stare. "I'm not ready for old age."

"Well, we're not getting any younger. I mean, think about it. We could be grandparents in the next couple of years."

"Bite your tongue!"

Blaine laughed at her incredulous expression. Then she threw one of the bed pillows at him. He caught it and whipped it back, hitting her in the shoulder.

"All right, that's it. The war's on."

"Now, wait a second, here. I've got an injured back, remember?"

"Too bad. All's fair in love, war, and pillow fights. . . even when you're wounded."

Blaine grinned broadly. He hadn't seen Krissy this feisty in months. Clad in her lacy white slip, she made a fetching sight as she gathered her ammunition. He gave her enticing curves a long, appreciative glance.

Then suddenly the phone rang, intruding upon their special moment.

"Let's not answer it," Blaine said.

Krissy frowned. "But it might be the girls."

He thought it over. "We'll call them back."

She worried over her lower lip, and Blaine knew he had to answer it and put her mind at ease. Ignoring the pangs of disappointment, he lifted the portable phone from the bedside table and pushed the TALK button. "Hello, Robinsons'."

"Yes, may I speak with Kristin?" the male voice at the other end asked.

"Who's calling?"

"Matt Sawyer. I'm the principal of Wellsprings Academy."

"Oh, right. Sure. Hang on a sec." Covering the mouthpiece, he held the phone out to his wife. "For you."

"Who is it?" she asked, sitting back on her haunches on top of the bed.

"Your new principal."

Blaine watched as Krissy paled in one second and blushed in the next. In fact, she turned scarlet right down to her collarbone. He narrowed his gaze, trying to gauge her odd reaction.

"What does he want?"

"Beats me," Blaine replied. "Should I tell him we're, um, busy?"

Krissy nodded, looking almost afraid to take the call.

Blaine put the phone to his ear. "Sorry, but Krissy's unavailable. Can I give her a message?"

"Yes, please. Ask her if she'd mind bringing a pan of brownies to the picnic tomorrow. My caterer's mother got sick, so I'm trying to put together an impromptu potluck."

Blaine pursed his lips and looked at Krissy who was staring back at him curiously. "Sure, I'll ask her."

"If there's a problem, tell her to give me a call. She's got my number."

She does? Blaine swallowed a tart reply. There was just something in this guy's tone he didn't appreciate. "Okay, I'll relay the message."

"Great. Thanks."

Blaine pushed in the OFF button with his thumb. "Who's this Matt Sawyer anyway?"

Krissy felt as though there was a hot blade piercing her insides. Inadvertently, she placed her hand over her stomach, but then she told herself she'd done nothing to feel ashamed about. "Matt's the principal of Wellsprings Academy," she answered honestly.

"Yeah, that's what he said. And he wants you to make a pan of brownies for tomorrow's picnic. Did I know about this picnic?"

"No, because I wasn't planning to go."

"Hmm. . .well, you'd better call the guy back and tell him. He said you've got his phone number."

Krissy frowned. "I have his number. . . ?" Then she realized what Matt meant. "Oh!" she said with a good dose of relief. "We all have it. It's in the staff directory."

"So, why do you look so guilty, Kris?"

"I don't know. Do I look guilty? I shouldn't. I haven't done anything wrong."

Blaine sat on the edge of the bed. "Is this guy hitting on you or something?"

Krissy shook her head and glanced at the printed spread. The last thing she wanted to do was discuss Matt Sawyer with her husband.

"He's not the one threatening you and making you feel like quitting your job, is he?"

"Matt isn't making threats against me, no," Krissy said. How could she possibly describe the kind of threat the man posed? Matt walked into her classroom and she suddenly felt sixteen again, all weak-kneed and nervous. When he sought out her company, she felt flattered, honored. They shared many common interests, and Krissy sensed the mutual attraction. Still, he knew she was married. . .so what was he thinking? The same thing she'd been thinking? That in another place, another time, they might have pursued a romantic relationship? But the fact remained: she was married. Very married. . .and Krissy planned to stay that way, despite her wayward emotions.

Blaine cupped her chin, bringing her gaze up to his. "Everything okay?"

"Yes," she replied, unsure if it were the truth or a lie. She felt so troubled in her heart, so stressed. Hadn't she gotten all this settled during the worship service?

"All right. If you tell me things are okay, then I believe you."

Krissy forced a little smile before Blaine leaned over and touched his lips to hers. It was like salve on a painful red welt, and she closed her eyes at its sweet familiarity.

But then all too soon, he ended the kiss. "You never answered my question," he said, wearing a silly smirk. "What do you want to do this afternoon?"

Krissy grinned as her hand clutched the corner of a pillow and before he could duck, she whacked him upside the head.

Chapter 8

Krissy leafed through the staff directory, found Matt's phone number, then picked up the telephone and began to punch in the digits. Before she could finish, however, Blaine came up behind her and stole the phone out of her hand.

"Hey, I've been thinking. . .why don't we go to this picnic tomorrow?"

Krissy dropped her jaw. "You? Want to go to a picnic? With a bunch of teachers and their spouses?" She held her hand over her heart, feigning cardiac arrest.

He shook his head. "You'd starve to death if you went into acting."

She shrugged.

"But I'm serious. Maybe we should go. I mean, it's your new school and you're debating whether God wants you there. . .perhaps He'll show you at tomorrow's picnic."

Nice try, Krissy wanted to say. She wasn't that dumb. She knew the reason behind Blaine's interest in attending. He was curious about Matt. She likened it to the times she and the girls would return from an afternoon of shopping and Blaine would ask, "How much money did you spend?" to which Krissy replied, "Not much." Then Blaine would say, "Lemme see the checkbook." It wasn't that he didn't believe her or didn't trust her. He'd made that much clear over the years. And he never once berated her for overspending. Simply, he liked to see the facts for himself. In all probability, the same held true now with the principal of Wellsprings Academy. Obviously Krissy hadn't adequately hidden her feelings when Matt phoned earlier, so now Blaine wanted to appraise the situation for himself. Unfortunately, it made Krissy feel terribly uncomfortable.

"Blaine, I don't want to attend this picnic."

"Free food. You don't have to cook. . .except for a pan of brownies."

"I'll make you your own personal pan," she promised. "And I'll make your favorite cream cheese brownies, but only if we can stay home."

"Sorry, Babe, I'm on a diet." He patted his tummy for emphasis. "Besides, you accused me of not enjoying the same things you do, so here's our chance to do something together. Something you enjoy."

Krissy inhaled deeply, then let out a slow breath.

Blaine tipped his chestnut-brown head. "Want to tell me why you're so dead set against going to this little shindig?"

She considered the request. It would be nice to clear the air. But at the same time, she didn't want to hurt Blaine by admitting her attraction to another man. Would he ever trust her again?

"Don't you think I'll understand?" he asked, his expression soft, earnest.

"No, I don't think you will."

"Well, why don't you try me and see?"

"Because I don't want to take the chance. Besides, whatever I'm going through is something very personal. It's between God and me."

Blaine folded his arms. "I feel kinda left out."

She tried to ignore the pained look on his face. "Want to go to the zoo this afternoon?" she asked, purposely changing the subject.

"Not particularly."

"I thought maybe we could even ask Jill if we could take her kids. You know, get them out of the house for awhile so she and Ryan can have some time alone."

Blaine grimaced. "I'd rather go to fifty school picnics than take a bunch of whining kids to the zoo."

"Oh, come on, Blaine, it'll be fun."

He puffed out an exasperated sigh. "How'd you manage to come up with this harebrained scheme?"

"Harebrained? Thanks a lot."

"The idea, not you, Krissy."

She folded her arms, trying to stifle her irritation. "For your information, I heard Jill and Ryan arguing at one o'clock this morning. They were in their kitchen with the window open and they woke me up. I couldn't fall back asleep, and I started thinking about how we could help them. We can't enroll them in Christian marital counseling or a Bible study because they're opposed to anything religious. But then, during the worship service, I came up with. . .with this *harebrained scheme* of taking their kids to the zoo. It's a way to reach out to our neighbors."

"The zoo, huh?"

Krissy nodded.

Blaine rubbed his stubbly jaw in consideration, then finally agreed. "Okay, I'll go to the zoo this afternoon, but only if we can go to the picnic tomorrow."

"I'll think about it. I mean, I can always phone Matt later with our regrets."

Blaine shook his head. "No picnic. No zoo. I drive a hard bargain."

Krissy stared hard at him, and Blaine stared right back. She could see the spark of determination in his dusky eyes. Against her better judgment, she relented. "Oh, all right. We'll go to the picnic. But I don't want to hear one complaint about being bored."

He grinned wryly. "Got it."

"And you don't have to tell every stupid joke you know and embarrass me."

"Me? Tell stupid jokes? C'mon, Hon, my jokes are always hilarious."

"Yeah, right." Spinning on her heel, she marched toward the front door. "I'll go ask Jill if we can take the kids."

"Sure. And I'll be here on my knees praying she says no."

❧

Krissy felt pleased that Jill agreed to allow her four children to go on the outing. In addition, Jill promised to spend some quality time with Ryan.

"I'm sorry we disturbed you last night," she muttered, looking embarrassed.

Krissy gave the woman a warm smile. "I wasn't so much disturbed as concerned, and I hope you don't think I'm a nosy neighbor trying to butt into your business."

"Are you kidding? You're a godsend. With the kids out of the way this afternoon, I might even accomplish a thing or two around the house and that'll make Ryan happy. He's forever complaining about the messes. But I just don't have any time to clean."

Krissy thought Ryan had better lighten up. But then she reminded herself that there are two sides to every situation, and she didn't know the other half of this one.

Sitting on a step in the back hall, she helped baby Haden on with his shoes. Then she lifted him into her arms, thinking he was about the cutest thing she'd ever seen, with his blond curls and deep brown eyes.

"Wanna go to the zoo?" she asked the eighteen month old.

"Zoo. . .Mama. . ." He pointed at Jill and Krissy wondered if he was going to cry when she took him home.

"Don't worry," Jill said as if divining her thoughts, "Haden will go anywhere with anyone—especially if his brothers and sister are along."

"Okay, then, let's go." Krissy carried the youngest on one hip while the three other kids followed her back to her house.

"I guess I wasn't praying hard enough," Blaine mumbled when she entered.

"Hi, Mr. Robinson," the oldest said cheerily. At eight years old, he was a red-haired, freckle-face kid with a smile that displayed a future need for orthodontics. "You coming to the zoo with us?"

"Yep. Mrs. Robinson is making me."

"She is?" The boy looked at her curiously.

"He's teasing you, Grant." Krissy gave Blaine a stony look.

He grinned back at her in reply.

"I like the aminals at the zoo," four-year-old Chelsea announced. Her coloring was similar to little Haden's. "I 'specially like the bears."

"I like the snakes," Royce interjected. The second-oldest, his features were a mix of his siblings'. He had reddish-brown hair and brown eyes but only a smattering of freckles.

"I like the snakes, too." Blaine grinned and pulled out his car keys. "Mrs. Robinson hates snakes, so we'll have to make her stay in that part of the zoo the longest."

"Yeah!" the two older boys agreed.

"Oh, fine," Krissy retorted, "but then I'll make you all go to the gift shop where I'll stay for hours!"

"Yeah! We like the gift shop, too!" Royce said.

Blaine laughed and headed out of the house. Krissy and the children trailed behind him. When they reached the van, the kids piled in and Krissy converted one of the back passenger benches to a child's harnessed seat into which she strapped Haden. With the task completed, she made sure the others were belted in safely before she took her place up front.

Blaine gave her a sidelong glance from where he sat behind the wheel. "You sure you want to do this?"

"Too late now."

With a sigh of resignation, he started the engine and backed out of the driveway.

They arrived at the Milwaukee County Zoo, parked, and Blaine paid the admission fee, grumbling under his breath about the cost of four children and something about highway robbery. Krissy ignored the remarks, knowing that he was only half serious anyway, and entered the gates with the children. The welcome sign proclaimed that this particular zoo was considered one of the finest in the country, and it housed approximately twenty-five hundred different animals. Krissy remembered from bringing her third-grade class here on field trips that it was virtually impossible to see everything in a span of a couple hours.

"Okay, what animals should we look at first?" she asked.

"Can we go on the train first?" Royce replied, and in the next moment the calliope-like blare from the down-sized steam locomotive heralded its arrival at the midget station.

The children were all in agreement; the train ride which circled the zoo had to come first. Blaine murmured a little louder this time as he bought the six tickets, but he seemed to enjoy the ride on this sunny September afternoon.

Krissy enjoyed it, too. Moreover, she relished holding

a little one on her lap again. Her once-a-month nursery duty at church never seemed to completely satisfy the longing she'd harbored for years to have another child. Well, it obviously wasn't in God's plan. She would have to wait for grandchildren.

After the train ride, they visited the polar bears and sea lions. Then it was on to see the snakes and sundry other reptiles, all of which made Krissy's skin crawl. Next the alligators, and they finally moved on to the monkey house.

"Now you boys'll feel right at home," Blaine said as they entered the area where the chimps were swinging from tree limbs, jumping around, and picking at each other. "This reminds me of you guys playing on your gym set."

"Uh-uh," Grant said, an indignant frown furrowing his auburn brows. "We're not monkeys."

"It's a joke," Krissy assured the boy. "Mr. Robinson is always making bad jokes."

"Uh-uh," Blaine mimicked juvenilely.

"You're more trouble than these kids," she whispered, giving him an elbow in the ribs.

"Oh, yeah?" He caught her arm in fun and drew her tightly to his side. "Well, just for that little comment, you get to buy us all popcorn and soft drinks."

She shrugged, figuring it was the least she could do. Overall, Blaine was being a good sport.

A half hour later, they sat on a park bench, munching on popcorn and watching the children who were preoccupied with the elephants.

"You know, that little guy is awfully cute," Blaine remarked.

"Haden? Yes, he sure is."

"I used to often wish I had a son. . .not that I ever felt displeased about our twin daughters. But I prayed hard and long for a boy. Guess God answered that prayer with a 'no.' "

Krissy whipped her gaze around and stared at him. She would have never guessed Blaine harbored such a desire all these years. He had never said a thing. "We could have adopted. We still could, I suppose."

"Naw, I don't have the energy or the patience for kids anymore."

"That's just because you're out of practice."

"Yeah, maybe."

A rueful smile tugged at the corners of her lips while she studied Blaine's profile. Did he have any other regrets? The very question seemed like evidence enough that she really didn't know this man the way she ought to.

Two sides to every situation, she thought, recalling her speck of wisdom concerning her neighbors. And in that moment, Krissy realized how one-sided, how self-focused she'd been. Blaine was hardly some amoeba, like the kind scaling the aquariums here at the zoo. He was a man with emotions, ideas, feelings, and. . .disappointments.

"I'm sorry I never gave you a son," Krissy said. "I would have loved one, too."

He glanced at her, and with his sunglasses hiding

his eyes, she couldn't quite make out his expression. But if she had to guess, she'd define it as surprise. "It's not your fault." He turned his line of vision back to the kids. "Just wasn't meant to be. I accepted that a long, long time ago."

Acceptance.

Oddly, the word seemed to cling to Krissy's heart for the remainder of the afternoon.

Chapter 9

Blaine groaned and then stretched out on the sofa and placed his head in Krissy's lap. "I think I outdid myself at the zoo today. My back is killing me."

"Oh, I'm sorry," Krissy replied, feeling guilty for insisting they go. "Sometimes I forget you're recuperating."

"Sometimes I do, too, and therein lies the problem."

Smiling at the retort, she ran her fingertips through Blaine's chestnut-colored hair. It felt thick and coarse, and although he kept it cropped short for the most part, he really had quite a lot of it around the sides and on top of his head.

"Say, Blaine, can I ask you something?"

"Sure you can." He peered up at her expectantly.

"I've been thinking ever since you said you wished we'd had a son. . .well, do you have any. . .regrets?" she asked on a note of hesitancy.

"Regrets about what? Our relationship or life in general?"

"Life in general."

"Sure I do. Who doesn't?"

Krissy grew more curious. "What do you regret?"

"Not becoming a Christian sooner in life for one thing. The girls were, what, in third grade or something when we accepted the Lord?"

She nodded, recalling how the twins had gone to vacation Bible school one summer and how at the closing program she and Blaine had heard the gospel preached for the first time. Neither had any trouble accepting the Word of God as truth. Each had been raised to revere the Bible and God; however, they had both trusted in something other than Jesus Christ for their salvation.

"On occasion I think that if we'd known then what we know now. . ." He chuckled. "What's that old cliché? Hindsight is twenty-twenty vision?"

Krissy had to agree. "What about our relationship, Blaine? Any regrets there?"

"None whatsoever. And you?"

"No. . ." She hedged slightly.

"That didn't sound very convincing, Kris."

Contrition filled her being. "Sorry. It's that I'm a different person today with different interests, likes, and dislikes. I'm not the same woman you married."

"Tell me one person who stays the same over twenty years' time." Blaine frowned.

"But that's what I mean. . .if we had to do it all again, would we?"

"That makes no sense," Blaine said on a note of exasperation. "The fact is, we can't do it all again, so why even bother speculating?"

"You're right."

"You know as well as I do that we can't change what's happened in the past. We can only go forward."

"True."

Krissy continued to caress his scalp, running a finger down the side of his face and around his ear. It obviously felt good because Blaine closed his eyes, looking like he might fall asleep. She wondered if he were right that perhaps she had begun to dwell on things beyond her control. . .and imagine things she had no right thinking about, such as Matt Sawyer. Try as she might to rid her thoughts of the tall, broad-shouldered man with a sparkling blue gaze, it seemed impossible. Was she obsessed, or was this something that happened to people at one time or another during their marriage?

"Can I ask one more thing?"

"Shoot."

"In all the years we've been married, were you. . . well, did you ever find yourself attracted to another woman?"

Blaine cocked one eye open. "Nope."

"Oh, come on, you're a red-blooded man and you're not blind."

"Sure, but I don't allow myself any appreciative glances. It's like Pastor once said from the pulpit. The first look is accidental, the second look is sin." Blaine grinned. "On my life, Kris, I never needed to take a second look. I've got it too good at home."

His words should have comforted her, but instead they caused Krissy to feel even more guilt-ridden.

Blaine pushed himself into a half-sitting position and searched her face. "Are you feeling insecure about us? I mean, you don't think I'm doing something I shouldn't. . .do you? Was it because Jill came over that day I was grilling? Honestly, I wouldn't dream of—"

She placed her fingers over his lips. "The thought never even entered my mind. I trust you. Completely. The truth is, I trust you more than I trust myself."

Confusion swept across him. "What's that s'posed to mean?"

"I. . .well. . .I. . .I guess I don't know how to explain it."

"Try." He narrowed his gaze speculatively. "Does it have something to do with your not wanting to go to this picnic tomorrow?"

"Yes."

A glacier of fear suddenly began to slide from his forehead, down his face, neck, chest, and spread to his limbs. What was Krissy getting at? Was she trying to tell him that she'd been unfaithful?

Tamping down his anxiety, he knew he had to stay calm. If Krissy sensed his upset, she'd shy away and wouldn't confide in him.

"Tell me, Krissy," he whispered.

Tears filled her eyes. "I want to tell you, Blaine, because after today I realize that I. . .I need your help."

"Okay." He felt willing to help her any way he could.

She swallowed hard. "But I'm afraid you'll hate me if I tell you. I hate myself."

Blaine thought this might be as bad as he feared. Swinging his legs off the sofa, he stood and walked to the large picture window on the far wall of their living room. He stared out across the lawn, noticing that the leaves on the trees were starting to change colors.

Change. It was frightening, and Blaine felt like he had an icy death grip around his neck. Prayer seemed impossible. But after several long moments, he took a deep breath and turned back around. "Honey, I could never hate you," he said sounding more composed than he actually felt. "You're the love of my life."

Rising, Krissy strolled slowly toward him, wiping a tear off her cheek. "You know I've been in this funk since the girls went away to college."

Blaine nodded.

"Well, then I began teaching at the academy where I met. . .the principal, Matt Sawyer. Almost immediately we discovered that we had common interests. What's more, Matt listened to me and validated my feelings, and he wasn't so macho that he couldn't share his. . .and he did."

Blaine bit his bottom lip, struggling to keep his temper in check. He suddenly felt like hopping in his truck, driving to the guy's house, and knocking his block off. "So how far did it go?" he heard himself ask.

"How far did what go?"

"The affair."

A look of horror crossed Krissy's features, and

Blaine felt mildly relieved.

"You didn't have a fling with this guy? That's not what you're trying to tell me?"

"No, Matt's never touched me."

"You gave me heart failure for nothing?"

"It's not 'nothing.' " Krissy threw her hands in the air. "See, that's what you do. You make light of everything important to me. I'm torn in two over this. Doesn't that matter?"

"Of course it does. I'm not taking any of this in stride. I'm merely trying to understand."

After an audible sigh, Krissy sniffed back the remainder of her tears. "I'm attracted to Matt. I know it isn't right and our friendship is inappropriate at best, but there's this part of me that enjoys his company. . . and I know he enjoys mine. That's why I don't want to attend the picnic tomorrow. I don't want to see him and be reminded of all these crazy things I feel—and I certainly don't want them to develop. You're my husband, Blaine, and I'm committed to our marriage no matter what. It's just that. . ."

"It's just that your heart isn't in it anymore," he finished for her.

Looking ashamed, she bobbed her head in silent affirmation, and Blaine felt tears prick his own eyes. The admission wounded him; however, it wasn't nearly the travesty he'd first imagined. For that he felt grateful. But even if it were, he would have fought for his marriage, and with God on his side, he would have won, too.

Tell her that.

The inner prompting was so strong, Blaine didn't dare ignore it.

"Come here, Sweetheart," he said, although he didn't give Krissy a choice in the matter as he pulled her into his arms.

"You must be so angry with me."

"No, not angry. . ."

"I'm sorry, Blaine. I didn't want to t–tell you because I didn't w–want to h–hurt you."

"It's all right," he said, kissing the top of her head while she sobbed into his sweatshirt. "I'm glad you told me. I love you and I want you to be happy." He pushed her back slightly and gazed down into her tear-streaked face. "But I want your heart, Krissy. It belongs to me and I want it back." With his thumb, he gently brushed away the sadness marring her lovely countenance.

"I want you to have my heart, too, Blaine."

"Okay, well, your willingness is half the battle, I guess. . ."

He pulled Krissy close to him, feeling like an apprehensive soldier. The war was on. . .

But could he win?

Chapter 10

The sound of children laughing outside her bedroom window awoke Krissy from a sound sleep. It took a moment, but then she realized the kids next door were playing in their yard.

With a yawn, Krissy rolled over and glanced at the alarm clock on the bedside table. Surprised, she lifted her head from the pillow and stared hard at the glowing numerals. Could it really be 10:30 in the morning? She looked at the vacant place beside her and the obvious registered; Blaine had gotten up already.

Climbing out from under the bedcovers, she strolled to her closet and pulled on her robe for warmth. The house felt chilly, but since it was only September, Blaine wouldn't want to turn the heat on yet. However, it wouldn't be long. Winter was rapidly approaching.

She stopped in the bathroom, freshened up, and brushed out her hair. Then she made her way to the kitchen where she found Blaine, standing in front of the sink, holding a cup of coffee in his hands, and gazing out the window.

"G'morning."

He turned around and gave her a tiny smile. "It's about time you woke up, Lazybones."

Krissy scrunched her countenance in a sassy reply and walked toward him. "Any more coffee?"

"Uh-huh." He handed her a mug from the cupboard.

"Blaine," she began, as she poured the fragrant dark brew from the carafe, "you haven't said a whole lot since our discussion yesterday evening. Does that mean you're upset?" Taking a sip of coffee, she turned to view his expression. It was thoughtful, serious.

"What guy wouldn't be upset?"

Krissy grimaced. "I know. . ."

"But I'm glad you told me. And I've given the matter a lot of thought. I didn't sleep much, and with every lap I swam this morning, I asked the Lord what I should do about the situation."

"And?"

"Well, first let me tell you what I *wanted* to do. I wanted to phone Sawyer and tell him that not only are we unable to attend his picnic today, but that you aren't returning to work tomorrow. . .or ever." He sighed. "It took every ounce of strength I had not to give in to the urge. But the Lord showed me that I really need to trust you and let you decide how to handle this situation."

Krissy's heart warmed to his words. "I've got good news for you. I'm not going back to the academy. I've already decided that much. I'll call Matt today and let him know, and I can clean out my desk tomorrow morning before school starts." She paused, encouraged to see a look of relief on Blaine's face. "But I want you to know that I could probably face anything now, knowing that you're praying me through it." She took a step closer. "With you and God on my side, I can do anything."

Again just a hint of a smile. "I'm glad you're feeling better, Hon."

"But you're angry, aren't you? I can sense it."

"Yeah, I'm angry. . .at him! The jerk." A muscle worked in Blaine's jaw. "He knew you were married all along. He should have kept his distance."

"I'm not exactly innocent. I should have kept my distance, too."

"True, but I've got a hunch that guy wouldn't have minded busting up our marriage."

Krissy didn't agree. She rather thought Matt fell into the situation just as she had. It wasn't a premeditated thing. The attraction, the chemistry between them, had been apparent from the beginning.

"Listen, I'm a man, so I know how men think. The thrill of a conquest and all that. But as a Christian, Sawyer shouldn't have ever befriended you. I mean, if I sensed a woman was attracted to me, I wouldn't go out of my way to discover all the great things she and I had in common."

Mulling it over, Krissy had to admit he had a point. She took another sip of coffee and recalled the many times Matt had sought out her company. She'd rationalized it away, feeling badly for him because of what he'd gone through with his wife. She thought he merely wanted someone to talk to—a comrade; however, she'd mistakenly opened her heart to him when her heart belonged to Blaine.

Krissy shut her eyes and anguished over this whole mess. "I'm so sorry." Sudden tears threatened to choke her. "Can you ever forgive me? Can you ever trust me again?"

"I can, yes, on both accounts."

She peered forlornly into her black coffee. "But it'll take time, won't it?" When Blaine didn't answer, she looked up at him.

"It's going to take more than time, Kris," he said, his dusky eyes darkening in earnest. "It's going to take patience, communication on both our parts, commitment to our relationship, and. . .last but hardly least, it's going to take a lot of love."

Krissy felt oddly impressed by his answer. It sound rehearsed, but that only meant he'd really been giving the matter his utmost attention. Finally, he was taking her thoughts and feelings—he was taking her!—seriously!

"I'm willing," she said, setting down her mug on the counter. She slipped her arms around Blaine's midsection and smiled despite her misty eyes. "I do love you. And I think you're pretty terrific to put up with me."

He set his forearms on her shoulders, coffee cup still in hand. "And I think you're pretty. . .period."

She tipped her head, feeling both flattered and surprised. "You really think I'm still pretty?"

"No, actually I think our girls are pretty. You're. . . beautiful."

Her smile grew. "It's been a long time since you told me that."

"I tell you all the time."

"No, you don't."

"Well, I *think* it all the time."

Krissy shook her head. "Too bad I can't read your mind."

Blaine looked properly chagrined. "Okay, so I should say what I'm thinking more often. I'll try."

"And that's all I can ask for."

He nodded. The pact was sealed. Then, as Blaine regarded her, a tender expression wafted across his features and deepened the hue of his eyes. Slowly, he lowered his mouth to hers. On contact, she closed her eyes, deciding this was most pleasurable kiss he'd given her in a long while. Gentle, undemanding, yet heartfelt and sincere.

After several long moments, Blaine lifted his chin and kissed the tip of her nose, then her forehead.

"You smell like chlorine," Krissy blurted.

"From the pool."

"Kind of a different smell for you." At his questioning frown, she added, "I'm used to you smelling like smoke."

"Those days are gone."

"And I'm glad. No more fretting over you fighting fires."

A wry grin curved the corners of Blaine's lips. "So now that we're both unemployed, what do you want to do with all the time we're going to have together?"

"The rest of our lives," she murmured. Funny how the thought didn't seem so oppressing anymore. She grinned up at him. "Blaine, I'm sure we'll think of some way to amuse ourselves."

That evening, Krissy watched Blaine stack kindling in the fireplace and light it. Then she glanced across the dimly lit room at their neighbors who sat together on the love seat, sipping hot cocoa, and she marveled at the turn of events this afternoon. While Blaine had manned his post at the grill, slopping thick barbeque sauce on fat spare ribs, Ryan had sauntered over and began complaining about wives, kids, and marriage in general. After a lengthy discussion, Blaine had invited Ryan and Jill and their brood over for supper.

That was the first thing to blow Krissy's mind. Blaine had always acted more irritated by the Nebhardts than concerned for them and their marriage.

The second thing that sent her reeling was when Blaine suggested the younger couple get a sitter and come over after their children were settled. Surely, he would have much preferred to plant himself in front of the television tonight rather than entertain Jill and Ryan.

But when Blaine sat down at the piano and began to play for their guests, Krissy's head really began to spin. She hadn't heard him play in years.

"I wrote this piece just after I left for college," he'd announced. "I hated leaving Krissy behind. So I composed this sonata. I called it 'September Sonata.'" He grinned over his shoulder at his audience. "It was the very piece that made her say, 'I do.' "

His fingertips danced across the ivory keys of the baby grand in the corner of their living room and Krissy's face flamed with self-consciousness. The stirring melody evoked a host of memories that she didn't feel like reliving in front of her neighbors. That sonata—an instrumental musical composition consisting of three or four movements—how like their relationship it seemed. From falling in love to their perfect wedding day, to becoming parents and watching their daughters mature into lovely young women, their song of life had now begun to play a tune of rediscovery.

Suddenly their future together looked more than promising. It seemed downright exciting.

Krissy felt proud of Blaine, and the Nebhardts seemed impressed with his talent and applauded when he finished playing. Suddenly embarrassed, he announced he'd make a fire.

Brushing the wood dust from his hands now, Blaine walked over and claimed his place beside Krissy on the couch. It may have been her imagination, but she thought his blue jeans fit a little better and instead of wearing one of his usual, worn-out sweatshirts, he wore a dark gray pullover which he had neatly tucked into his pants. Making himself comfy, he stretched his arm out around her shoulders.

"You guys are so cute together," Jill remarked. "Like newlyweds or something."

"Well, we are. . .kinda," Blaine said, giving Krissy a meaningful wink.

"So you survived raising kids, huh?" Ryan asked.

"Just barely," he replied. "And if I've learned anything, I've learned I need to cherish my wife." Looking at her, he added, "If I ever lost her, I'd have nothing. I'd be nothing. I only wish I would have realized it years ago. I wish I would have made time for her. . .for us. . .in spite of our hectic schedules."

There beside him, Krissy felt like her wanderlust heart had come home. Blaine wasn't a man to make public professions, especially when they pertained to his personal life. He had sincerely meant every word he'd just spoken.

She glanced up at him in a measure of awe, and for the first time in years, she felt unmistakably loved—and, yes, even cherished.

Epilogue

I cy fear gripped Blaine Robinson's heart as he raced down the hospital corridor. He'd been conducting a routine insurance inspection for the company at which he'd been employed for the past year when he'd gotten Krissy's page. He had left right away, but was he too late?

A nurse in lime-green scrubs and a matching cap stepped into his path. "Can I help you, Sir?"

"My wife," he panted, "her name is Krissy Robinson."

"Right this way."

Blaine followed the woman through a set of doors and down another hallway.

"If you want to go in with her, you'll have to put a gown over your clothes."

"Fine." Blaine didn't care what he had to do; all he wanted was to be with Krissy.

The woman handed him a blue printed gown and he immediately pulled it on and tied it at the back of his neck.

"Okay, you ready?" The nurse smiled.

"Ready as I'll ever be, I suppose."

"Aw, come on now," she said with a teasing smile, "you've got the easy job."

"Yeah, so I've been told."

She laughed and escorted him into the birthing room where Krissy reclined in a specialized delivery bed.

Blaine rushed to her side. "I got here as soon as I could." He noticed the beads of perspiration on her brow as he bent to kiss her forehead.

Krissy held out her hand, and he took it. "The contractions came on so fast."

"No kidding. You were fine this morning."

"I know. . ."

Her body suddenly compelled her to bear down hard, and she was helpless to do otherwise. A moment later, she collapsed against the back of the bed, letting go of the hand grips.

"Okay, this is the big one," Dr. Herman announced, her soft voice carrying a note of excitement to Blaine's ears. Despite Krissy's routine ultrasound exams, they had decided against learning the sex of their unborn child. "Another push. That's it."

But this was the part he hated, those agonizing last few minutes. Standing by Krissy's side, he knew his "job" was to encourage her, except it was hard to get past the feeling of utter helplessness.

Krissy squeezed his hand and cried out in final travail before falling back against the bed again. Blaine brushed the hair from her face and then the newborn's squall filled the room. Exhausted, Krissy went limp.

"I'm too old for this."

Blaine grinned, then looked at the doctor with anticipation coursing through his veins. "Is it a he or another she?"

The woman's round face split into a smile. "It's definitely a he!"

"Are you sure?" After he'd spoken those words, Blaine felt like an idiot. The doctor's incredulous glare only confirmed it.

"Of course I'm sure!"

"Don't mind him, Dr. Herman," Krissy said. "I think my husband is just overwhelmed."

"To say the least," Blaine admitted. He had to take several quick swallows in order to keep his emotions in check. He and Krissy had prayed for a son ever since they discovered she was expecting. Now that God had answered that fervent request, Blaine could scarcely believe it. He never thought this day would come and over the past seven months, he had found himself praying like the man in the Gospel of Mark: "Lord, I believe; help thou mine unbelief."

One of the nurses placed the baby on Krissy's abdomen. She clamped the cord in two places, then offered the scissors to Blaine. He took it and cut the umbilical cord, feeling glad that the hospital staff allowed men to take such an active role in the birth of their children. He'd read everything he could find on the Internet pertaining to pregnancy and childbirth, he'd monitored Krissy's diet, and he had even attended the birthing classes with her. But now he felt cheated because he'd arrived so late. He had looked forward to assisting with the delivery.

However, his disappointment paled beside the joy he felt at having a son. Putting an arm around Krissy, he watched as she cradled him. Blaine reached out and touched the infant's tiny hand, marveling at God's phenomenal creation of life.

"Let's call him Luke," Blaine said.

"Sounds good to me."

Leaning forward, he gave Krissy a kiss. "I love you," he whispered in her ear.

"I love you, too." She placed one hand against Blaine's face. He kissed her palm. "This is one of the happiest moments of my life."

"Ditto."

Krissy smiled. "We have our little boy at last."

Blaine's eyes grew misty.

"And you know what else?"

"Hmm. . . ?"

"You're my very best friend, and I couldn't stand the thought of bringing our baby into the world without you by my side. I tried my best to hold back the labor, but I couldn't fight the inevitable for long."

"You did just great, and God saw fit to get me here in the nick of time." He gave her shoulder an affectionate squeeze. "And for the record, Kris, you're my best friend, too. Want to know something else?"

"What?"

"It's going to stay that way, despite diapers, bottles, and frenzied schedules. Neither your day care center nor my part-time job. . .nor our precious children will come between us as long as I'm alive and have something to say about it."

Krissy smiled and glanced down at their latest little blessing who had fallen asleep. Looking back at Blaine, she said, "That's a promise I'm going to hold you to."

"Good."

Several moments passed before Krissy spoke again. "This marks a whole new season of life for us. We've got a baby again."

"You're just realizing that now?" he teased, although he knew what she meant. God was still composing their life's sonata. . . .

And this was simply the next interlude.

ANDREA BOESHAAR

Andrea was born and raised in Milwaukee, Wisconsin. Married for almost twenty-five years, she and her husband, Daniel, have three grown sons. Andrea has been writing practically all her life, but writing exclusively for the Christian market since 1994. To date, she has authored eleven **Heartsong Presents** titles of inspirational romance.

As far as her writing success is concerned, Andrea gives the glory to the Lord Jesus Christ. Her writing, she feels, is a gift from God in that He has provided an outlet for her imagination and her desire to share biblical truth, whether it's presented in an evangelical light or subtly implied. In either case, Andrea ultimately wants her stories to fill her readers' hearts with hope and happiness.

Visit her web page at: www.andreaboeshaar.com.

October Waltz

Waltz

by DiAnn Mills

Dedication

This story is dedicated to Debbie,
my sister and my friend.

LORD, you establish peace for us;
all that we have accomplished you have done for us.
ISAIAH 26:12

Chapter 1

"Oh, great. Ron Bassinger is here early, and I don't have the figures ready for his accountant." Abby Martin smacked her coffee cup onto her desk and spilled a dribble on the papers before her. From her loft office she could see every square foot of Martin's Western Wear, but her gaze fixed on the striking figure heading her direction. "Well, he came alone. Maybe I can stall him."

Ron glanced up and gave her a smile, the same smile that must have captivated his mother's heart—along with a string of other women since then.

Candy, her part-time secretary sighed. "I sure wish I could be on the receiving end of his irresistible charm."

"If you were the owner, he'd want you to think you're special, too," Abby said, slapping papers together to make her cluttered desk a bit more presentable.

"Hmm, white hair, white teeth, tanned skin," Candy replied, batting her eyes faster than a hummingbird's wings. "And he's incredibly rich."

"Oh, please. He's older than your dad," Abby said, reaching to the floor to pick up a pen.

"Doesn't matter, he's awesome. Watch how he walks."

"Like the Pink Panther," Abby replied, not once glancing up from the haphazard assortment of papers before her.

"What's the matter with you? Have you gone blind?" Candy asked. "He's drop-dead gorgeous."

Abby attempted to give the dark-haired beauty a disgusted glance but laughed instead. Knowing Ron's reputation with younger women, she decided to give a word of caution instead. "Better watch yourself, Lady-bug. He's a pro."

Candy snatched up three half full cups of cold coffee and headed to the back room. She tossed a grin over her shoulder. "No danger of me getting a second look. When he comes in here, he has dollar signs stamped across his eyeballs and words of honey dripping from his mouth for you." The cups clinked on the sink and the spray of water hissed against the stainless steel.

"I don't think so," Abby whispered. "I'm not his type."

"What do you mean? I wish my mom looked half as good as you."

"Are you talking me into a raise?" Abby asked, searching for the file marked Bassinger Enterprises.

"Maybe."

Triumphantly, Abby seized the missing folder. "Honey, I couldn't sit in church beside your parents if I didn't warn you about him. I care too much for you to stand by and do nothing while you slip under his spell. He's a city slicker from Houston, and we're a wee bitty burg on the outskirts."

Candy turned off the water. "Me? Why Miss Abby, I intend to be only friendly with my potential boss. Besides, my parents would ground me for life." She giggled. "I'll head downstairs and see if they need a hand. I'm sure Mr. Bassinger would prefer to talk with you alone."

The stairs below them creaked with the heavy foot-steps announcing Ron's arrival.

"Bye," Candy mouthed and disappeared.

"Hi, Abby," Ron called. The deep timbre of his voice rose as he neared the landing.

She shuddered with the memories of how the sound of him calling her name used to make her feel. *No wonder he has so many women following him around.* She questioned the sanity of the countless other women she'd read about in the papers who graced the arms of Ron Bassinger—the playboy tycoon of Houston. Her notions about him ended when she married Kevin Martin thirty-two years ago.

By this time, Ron faced her, filling too much of her small loft office with his presence, his cologne, and his expensive clothes.

"Hi, Ron, you're early," Abby said and rose to shake his hand.

He grasped it firmly. "Oh, your hands are much too cold." When she didn't respond, he chuckled. "Usually I'm fashionably late, but I wanted to see those figures."

She took a deep breath and withdrew her hand before replying. "Oh, really? I counted on you arriving a little later." She wrung her hands. "Sorry, but I don't have them ready."

"I'm not pressuring you," he claimed. "I only requested them this morning."

"But I'm the seller here." His presence unnerved her after all these years. "Excuse me, won't you sit down?" She waited until he eased onto one of the wooden chairs facing her desk. "If you like, I can work on them and get back to you tonight."

He shook his head. "No, I'll wait. A pretty lady like you doesn't need to work so hard."

Now she wanted to gag. Pretty was for those under thirty-five, not fifty-two and a half. She forced a smile. "No problem. I'd like to have your decision as soon as possible. May I phone you at home, or would you rather I fax or e-mail?"

Ron wet his lips. "Since I won't be around tonight, you can fax them to my office. . .unless you'd like to join me for dinner with friends?"

"No, thank you. I'd prefer we keep our relationship purely business," Abby said, the possibility of a run-in with the gossip column of the local *Texan Press* wreaking havoc with her mind. "I'm appreciative that you are interested in purchasing the store, but nothing more."

"Guess my reputation speaks for me," he replied with a sheepish grin. She remembered when he used to lean against her locker in school and offer the same look.

She felt his steely gaze attempting to capture hers, but she refused to fall prey to his infamous charms. How well she remembered them. Her gaze traveled to a picture on her desk of Kevin on the slopes at Breckenridge. How happy they'd been on their last vacation together.

"Abby?" Ron asked.

His voice pulled her back to the present, and she lifted a curious brow.

"How long has Kevin been gone?"

She took a sharp breath. His question tormented her, as though he'd been reading her thoughts. "Four years next month."

"I see the loneliness in your eyes," he said. His voice sounded gentle, but she didn't trust him for a minute.

"I'm perfectly fine, and I'm not lonely," she whipped back, then bravely forged a smile. Lowering her voice she continued. "I simply want to sell the store and go on to the next phase of my life without complications."

"Which is?"

She leaned back in her chair and hoped she gave the façade of a relaxed business executive. "I'm tired of the fast-paced life. I've seen enough boots, hats, jeans, shirts, and riding gear to last a lifetime. Martin's Western Wear did well for Kevin and me. The boys are through college and neither of them wants the store. I simply want to relax on my little place in the Hill Country."

"And do nothing? I don't think you'd be happy without a career."

"Oh, I have plans." She purposely chose not to reveal her dreams. Those had been Kevin's dreams, too.

Her silence must have bothered him. "Personal?"

"Yes, Ron." She took a breath. "God's been good to me, and I feel it's time to slow down." He shifted in the chair and she added, "I don't mean to run you off, but I do need to get some things done here."

"I understand."

"Do you? Well, good, I'm glad." She cringed at her own curt reply. "I'm sorry, that was rude."

He stood and ducked to keep from hitting his head on the sloped ceiling. He offered his hand and she took it, but he seemed to hold it a mite longer than she liked.

"Do you want me to have my accountant take care of arranging the purchase?" he asked.

"Yes, I do," Abby replied. Odd, as she watched his back descend the stairs, she didn't feel the relief she expected.

❧

Ron loved a conquest, even if the satisfaction came in a woman's silent response. Abby's refusal for dinner shook him to the core—not because he couldn't handle a rejection, but because this little woman had once been his best friend. For old times' sake, she could accompany him to dinner.

As he ambled through the store, Ron radiated his most charming smile in the direction of a raven-haired beauty he'd come to know as Candy. No matter that she looked young enough to be his daughter, if he'd ever gotten married to have had a daughter.

He glanced about the western store that soon would be his. Nothing on those shelves, boxes, and hangers appealed to him, except for the profit statements the thirty-year-old business provided.

His wealth continued to mount, and the higher the figures in his portfolio, the better he felt about himself. Or so he once thought. He invested in different ventures as a hobby, often choosing his next purchase with a roll of the dice. He pursued women the same way. Except now, as he neared his fifty-fourth birthday, he struggled for something else. What purpose had all of this gotten him? Granted, he possessed more material things than most people deemed proper, but inside he felt empty.

Getting old frightened him sometimes. What would he do without the old Bassinger charm? He had enough money to spend his golden years in luxury, but the idea of spending it alone—wrinkled and probably afflicted with cancer or Alzheimer's—rankled him.

Years ago, his granddad had talked to him about leaving this world, except Granddad wasn't afraid. He said God had a mansion in heaven with his name carved on the door. Sounded like Abby believed in the same kind of nonsense.

Alone.

Odd, he'd questioned Abby about being lonely when the term best fit him. Abby Martin. . .she still attracted him as much as she did in high school. He remembered kissing the tip of her turned-up nose and counting her peach-colored freckles. Some things never leave you; they just get sweeter through the years.

But she wouldn't have dinner with him, and he couldn't blame her.

"Mr. Bassinger."

Ron whirled around to where a thin, young man wearing a Stetson stood at the register. "Yes?"

"Miss Abby just called from her office. She asked if you would please wait a moment."

Chapter 2

A smile forced the depressing thoughts from Ron's mind. The familiar exhilaration bounded up his spine. Abby couldn't resist him. He slowly pivoted to watch her walk the length of the store. Over thirty-two years had passed, and she hadn't lost her gracefulness. Must have been all those ballet lessons her parents bought.

He wondered if Kevin had appreciated her. He shook his head. Of course the man did. Abby never looked prettier than when he saw her linked arm in arm with her husband.

"Ron, I forgot to tell you something," she said, running her fingers through short, strawberry-blond curls. "Can I walk you to your car?"

Ah, now she wants privacy, no doubt to accept my dinner invitation. "Sure," he replied. He opened the store's front door and she stepped through.

"A new car?" she asked, as he strolled toward his BMW.

"No, I've had it a few months."

"I thought you drove a truck the last time you were here."

"I probably did; depends on my mood."

She glanced away and brushed a fleck of dirt from her shoulder. "Ron, I apologize for being rude."

"You already did."

She swallowed and wet her lips. "I mean, I said some nasty things during our conversation. You're doing me a great favor by taking the store off my hands. Plus you're willing to pay a fair price. I owe you gratitude, not what I offered a few minutes ago. Surely you understand how I prefer my privacy."

Her forehead creased, and he sensed her sincerity. Abby had never been one to act facetiously.

"Does this mean you're willing to reconsider having dinner with me at another time?"

Tilting her head, she paused before answering. "Not really. Seriously, I don't want a social relationship."

"Are you seeing someone else?"

She shook her head and clasped her hands. "No, I'm not."

"Then, what's the problem?" He spoke gently, and it surprised him. "Abby, a long time ago we were close."

She blushed and cast her attention to a noisy pickup advertising its speaker system.

"Too close," she finally said, peering into his eyes.

"But you're single now—time to move on with your life—like you said before."

"My life is God's," she said, and her gaze bore into his.

He shivered. Abby seemed to radiate with the mention of deity. She'd always done this to him, frustrating him with her faith.

"Wouldn't God want you to be happy and fulfilled?"

"I am," she said with a faint smile, "and I wish the same for you, too."

"It's not my style."

"I remember when it was."

He wiped the perspiration from his brow. Hadn't he just felt cold? This conversation had swerved far from where he intended. "So, if I want to see you, then I have to go to church?"

"I'd rather you attend church because of your need for God."

He blew out an exasperated breath. "This sounds like the discussions we had when we were kids."

She laughed. "Some things are timeless."

He couldn't help but chuckle. "We did argue a lot about your beliefs, didn't we?"

She nodded and continued to smile. "Think about it, Ron. At one time, you agreed with me."

He glanced at his watch. "I'm going to be late for my next appointment."

"Of course," she replied. "I wouldn't want to make you late. Oh, it's Pinewood Community Church, 10:30 on Sunday morning."

He hurried around to the driver's side of his sleek, black car. "This is only Tuesday. Who knows what I'll be doing by then? Besides, I think I've already made plans to play golf."

"I'll remind you on your voice mail." With those words, she turned and walked back into her store.

Ron could not help but appreciate her slender figure encased in a denim skirt. Why did she have to make him remember? How could she make him feel so good about himself in one instant, then furious in the next?

❧

Trembling like an insecure schoolgirl, Abby managed to walk back through the store and up the stairs to her office. All the while, she vigorously massaged her arms in an effort to dispel the chills. She didn't know whether her quivering came from facing Ron without his accountant or from speaking to him about her faith. That issue had been a source of arguments many years ago. . .along with a list of other things. Truthfully, simply being around him brought back a flood of memories and a wheelbarrow load of shame.

She knew shame didn't come from God, but it had a habit of cropping up whenever her thoughts drifted back to before she and Kevin were married.

Nibbling at her lip, she wished she could forget those young impetuous years, but her conscience refused such admonitions. Unfortunately, people didn't have the option of selective memory. Maybe those days lingered in her mind to keep her humble and prevent her from repeating the same mistakes.

Regardless of her weariness in dealing with Ron, he needed the Lord. During the summer of his junior year in high school, his grandpa led him to salvation. Up until the day he left for college, Ron had seemed sincere in his faith.

Then school started, and she entered her senior year of high school while he headed off to college and immersed himself with new friends who practiced a different set of standards. In the course of one semester, the world and what it had to offer meant more to Ron than his relationship with Jesus Christ. His education promised a job with a future, and he intended to make his fortune. When Abby protested, he called her a prude and attempted to change her focus. For awhile it worked.

The phone rang, propelling Abby abruptly back to the present. Snatching up the receiver before the second ring, she heard the comforting sound of her older sister's voice.

"Hi, Debbie. So glad you called."

"How did the meeting go with Ron and his accountant?" Debbie asked, her soft voice disguising her age.

Abby laughed and brushed off the dust on a small exposed portion of her desk. "The accountant didn't come, just Ron."

"Ouch."

"Oh, the meeting went fine, despite my bad case of jitters. You would have been proud of me, Sis. Other than a few curt remarks, I thought I handled my apprehension around him pretty well," Abby said, propping her elbow on the desk.

"Good for you. And what about Ron? How did he act?"

"Charming as usual."

"I can't imagine anything less," Debbie said. "Be honest with me. Did either of you say anything about the past?"

"A little." Abby hesitated. "Thankfully, precious little. He asked me to dinner."

"And?"

"Naturally I refused and informed him I wanted only a business relationship. I never dreamed when I put the store up for sale that he would be the one to answer the ad."

"And how did he react?"

"As I expected—insistent. He asked as many questions as you do."

"Well, you don't ever offer an ounce of information, so I have to resort to prying. What else did you talk about—other than buying the store?" Debbie asked.

Abby rubbed the back of her neck, rigid with tension. "Similar to the same conversations we had as kids. I urged him to attend church, and he gave me excuses not to go."

"How ever did you get on that topic?" Debbie asked. "I mean his lifestyle doesn't exactly support Christian ethics."

"Hmm, let's see. I think it was when he said I looked lonely. I denied it, and one thing led to another."

"I see. I don't suppose it occurred to you to talk about what happened back then and come to a closure."

"Sis, I don't want to talk about it."

Debbie expelled a heavy sigh. "If God forgave you, then why can't you forgive Ron?"

Indignation pulsed through Abby's veins. "I have, a long time ago. But forgiveness doesn't mean I want to talk about something that happened thirty years ago."

"So you're going to spend the rest of your life denying you once loved the man? Ashamed you ever knew him? Now that's real Christ-like."

"Debbie!"

"Honey, it's the truth. Face Ron squarely, deal with your problems, and get over the whole mess."

"You sound like our mother."

"I'm the oldest; I have a right to parent you."

"At our age—you are *grand*parenting me."

They both laughed.

Abby knew her sister spoke the truth, but she'd never be able to tell Ron what happened. "I can't talk to him about the past," she finally said.

"You don't have to do it alone," Debbie replied, her tender chiding reminding Abby of their elderly mother.

"Think about telling him the truth, or rather pray what God would have you do."

Abby saw her other phone line light up. "Some things are best left alone," she said. "Hey, my business line needs my attention."

"All right, but take the advice from your dear, old sis. You forgave the man years ago, and today God may have given you the opportunity to nudge Ron back to Him. Talking about what happened years ago could be a healer for both of you."

"I'll pray about it—I promise," Abby replied. "Talk to you later." She shivered and hung up. Forcing a smile, she dived into the call, momentarily pushing Ron Bassinger back to the dark recesses of yesteryear.

Long after the store closed, Abby strode down the aisles, her fashionable boots clicking against the wooden floor. She fingered the fabric of the wearing apparel, rearranged the lopsided boots, admired straw and felt hats, and stooped to examine silver and gold belt buckles through a glass display case. Martin's Western Wear held more sentiment than she cared to consider. The store represented a lifetime of work and dreams for her and Kevin.

She remembered when Zack and Zane were toddlers and the endless job of keeping them occupied and out of the "cowboy" clothes. As the boys—only fourteen months apart—grew older, they took on more responsibility until both of them could run every facet of the store by themselves. Kevin had burst with pride, hoping one day his sons would take over the business. Cancer ended his life much too soon to realize his heartfelt aspirations. He never knew the boys held dreams of their own.

Both of his sons wanted careers aside from their parents' western store—Zack as a veterinarian and Zane as an English professor at the University of Texas.

She walked to the far side of the store leading to the tack area, added ten years ago. Every saddle, bridle, halter, blanket, and piece of equipment was available for the horse lover. How many worn saddles had they taken in trade so a family could purchase a new one? Abby smiled. So many beautiful moments right here in this very store. Hopefully, Ron planned to maintain the Martin name.

"Oh, Kevin," she whispered. "How I miss you. I know selling the business is the right thing, but I feel like I'm betraying what you worked hard to build. If only I knew Ron would care for the customers and the quality of merchandise like we did."

She shrugged. Whoever Ron hired to manage the store would determine the level of commitment. Bassinger Enterprises cared about profit and loss—not necessarily what she considered important.

She closed her eyes and remembered the strength of Kevin's embrace. Inhaling deeply, she could almost smell the woodsy scent of his aftershave and the way it lingered on his skin all day long. For a moment, she allowed the delicious remembrances of him to flow over her, washing away the pang of loneliness—the feelings she'd denied earlier. Lonely, yes. Alone, no. She had God every step of the way.

If boldness laced her skin, she'd share her feelings with him about the store. Ron might never care for what it all meant to her and Kevin, but she should tell him.

Should. Now that word had a powerful effect on some people. For her, it designated where the coward stepped in and bravery jumped on the fastest horse out of town.

Suddenly realization hit her squarely. She had to move on to the next phase of God's plan for her life. Granted, she felt a bit hesitant about the farm—boarding horses and running an antique glassware business—

but the easy life intrigued her.

The boys were excited for her. They thought it high time their mother stopped working six days a week. Abby smiled. She'd *always* be the type who enjoyed working. Idleness invited depression in the spirit and pounds on the thighs. In no time at all, her legs would look like truck tires.

With a laugh, she headed back to her office. She'd left the computer running and hadn't sent Ron the fax he requested.

A pounding on the front door grabbed her attention. Dressed in a black tux and carrying a dozen red roses stood the last man on earth she wanted to see.

R on peered through the door into the darkened store. Abby must be inside; her car sat in the parking lot. He cupped one hand on the glass in an effort to find her, although nothing moved. What a waste of time and money.

When the impulse had hit him to surprise her with roses, he thought she stayed open on Tuesday nights. His plan sounded like a great idea at the time. He'd sweep her off her feet, and she wouldn't dare refuse him dinner. Fat chance. The store didn't even have a light on.

Something stirred, and he saw Abby leaning against a display near the front register with her arms crossed. He wished he could see her face. Her expression had to be priceless. A moment later she spun around and moved toward the back of the store.

"Abby," he called and pounded on the door. When she didn't respond, he banged again. "Abby, I'm going to beat on this door until you answer it."

She stopped and slowly turned with her arms still

crossed. Shaking her head, she motioned for him to leave.

Leave. He had driven from Houston to Podunk, Texas, to be turned down by an old high-school flame? A lot of women would be bringing *him* flowers. Ron swallowed hard. Who was he fooling? Abby knew him better than all the women he'd spent time with in the past umpteen years. The others had been interested in Ron Bassinger, business tycoon, entrepreneur. None wanted to invest in a relationship. Of course, those women hadn't appealed to him either.

Not since Abby broke it off with him and married Kevin Martin had he seriously been interested in another woman.

He knocked again, not hard, just enough to show his persistence. She stared at him, and even though he couldn't see those apple green eyes, he envisioned the smoldering fire. From what he could see, he doubted if she ever got over that flaring temper.

Ron continued to stare at the little woman on the other side of the glass. She stepped forward and unlocked the door, not once glancing up at him.

"Yes," she said, pushing it open far enough to speak. "We're closed."

"I didn't plan to buy anything," he said. "I brought you flowers."

"I see; they're lovely," she said, smiling appreciatively.

"Are you going to let me give them to you?" Exasperation edged his words.

"Why are you bringing me roses?" she asked, reaching through the crack in the door to touch a petal.

Why had he brought them? With Abby standing in front of him, he felt foolish.

"Did you think I'd accept your dinner invitation if you showed up here dressed like a dandy and carrying flowers?"

"I hoped so." He issued his best smile like a banker with new bills.

"And you drove all the way from Houston to Cypress with that assumption?" She pressed her lips firmly together.

"Ah, yes, I thought the flowers and my charm would sweep you off your feet."

"It didn't work." She started to pull the door shut.

"Abby, please, for old times' sake." What was wrong with her? Didn't she see who stood outside her door?

"Which is exactly why I won't go anywhere with you."

"Can't we talk about this like the mature adults we are?"

She seemed to consider his question, for in the next moment she slipped outside onto the sidewalk. "Now talk," she said.

A car horn diverted their attention, and an elderly woman waved. Abby smiled and returned the gesture.

"Wonderful," she said through clenched teeth. "Maudie will have us on the front page of the *Texan Press*."

Ron glanced at the car slowly driving away then back to Abby. "Why is that?"

"Because she writes the gossip column," she said while still smiling at Maudie. "It's a wonder she didn't snap a picture with her infamous Polaroid."

"It wouldn't be the first time I've been linked with a beautiful woman on a gossip page."

"Please, Ron, this is me. I don't need to be impressed."

Silence. That last barb cut just a little too deep.

"I only wanted you to accompany me to this dinner tonight," he said expelling a labored breath.

"You haven't a date?" she asked and immediately her hand flew to her mouth. "I'm sorry. That was not called for."

"Apology accepted. And no, I'm meeting friends."

"I thought you wanted to talk to me. . .about other things," Abby said, wringing her hands.

"Don't know where to begin and time is racing away." For the third time today, Abby Martin had succeeded in frustrating him to the hilt.

She glanced away and wrinkled her nose, as she used to do when contemplating something. "We could talk over lunch after church on Sunday."

"I can't do that, Abby," he replied, masking his irritation.

"Then I guess you don't want to talk to me very badly." With those words, she stepped back inside and locked the door.

A mixture of anger and confusion washed over Ron as he glanced around to see if anyone had overheard his and Abby's conversation. He'd pay big bucks to keep that kind of information from leaking out to the papers. Satisfied the conversation remained private, he dropped the roses outside the door and hurried to his car.

The years hadn't changed her much—stubborn, unpredictable woman. Her whole life centered around the God-thing, and she used her faith to justify everything she did. He doubted if she got out of bed in the morning without first praying about it.

A trickling of perspiration traced a path down the side of his face, and his hands felt clammy. A long time ago, he'd marched the same roads as Abby. They'd been active in the youth group, gone on mission trips, volunteered in nursing homes, and taught a second-grade Sunday school class. But then he headed off to college and discovered he'd wanted more in this life than a promise of a hereafter. His new friends convinced him to seize all he could from this world—money, power, fast cars, and a reputation among women. And he grabbed it all.

None of those creature comforts eased the ache in his heart. None of those things comforted him in the dark of night when he felt God tugging at him, urging him to come home. The older he got, the more callused his resolve not to listen to God's voice. He searched for other ways to cure the fear of getting old—and dying alone.

Ron hated the thought of being abandoned like an unwanted dog on the side of the road, just as he hated attending this dinner without a woman on his arm. What he needed to do was call a lady who wanted her name coupled with his. But he wanted Abby there. The years didn't matter, nor the fact he never understood why she married Kevin. She'd been his best friend, and he desperately needed a semblance of younger days again.

Speeding down Highway 290, he took the 610 loop and raced to the Galleria area. *Why am I in such a hurry,* he wondered, *to get to a party that I'll despise the entire night?* He could already hear the sound of ice chinking against the sides of the glasses, the murmur of voices, and the obnoxious laughter of drunken people.

He craved a purpose, beyond the business deals, the executive meetings, the European vacations, and the cutthroat tactics of those who hungered for his success.

Reluctantly, Ron faced the truth. Peace seldom touched him in the never-ending struggle to keep what he didn't really want.

Abby exited the front door and viewed the roses decorating the sidewalk. A white satin ribbon tied them together with a neat little bow. In fact, the flowers looked as though Ron had meticulously laid them there. . .and maybe he had, but she doubted it. The man she remembered had a temper to equal hers. The roses most likely fell where he'd dropped them.

After locking the store, she bent to pick up the discarded bouquet. Their sweet fragrance and exquisite design enticed her to pick through each one, searching for the best. She didn't want the flowers, but neither did she want to leave them on the sidewalk for the area dogs to water. A thought passed through her mind, and it brought a smile to her lips. The roses would be a special treat for Debbie. She'd run them by before going home.

A cascade of stars lit up the night sky as Abby climbed the steps to her sister's porch. Debbie and Les lived on a sizeable cattle ranch fifteen miles north of Cypress. Their kids were gone with children of their own, leaving the couple time to relax and enjoy their home.

Abby's stomach growled, and she hoped her sister had leftovers from dinner. Naturally, she expected interrogation in its finest form.

"Hi, Abby. So glad you stopped by," Debbie said when she opened the door. "Les just left for a meeting." She noticed the flowers. "Those are breathtaking. Did you rob a florist?" Her brown eyes sparkled as she lightly caressed the petals.

"Not exactly. These are for you," Abby said, handing them to her sister.

"Why?"

"Because they were given to me and I couldn't care less," Abby said. She toyed with the leather strap on her shoulder purse while keeping her gaze level with her sister's.

She ushered Abby inside, still studying the roses. "Ron gave these to you?" she asked with a grin.

"Well, he tried," Abby replied and told her the story.

Debbie laughed until the tears rolled down her cheeks.

"So you think I did the right thing?"

"Who knows?" Debbie asked. "I can just hear Maudie now." They made their way through her sister's perfectly kept house to the kitchen where the smell of chicken and apple pie wafted through the air. She laid the flowers on the sink after inhaling their sweet fragrance. "Hungry?"

"Starved. I can't believe you cook like this for just you and Les."

"It's a habit," Debbie said and proceeded to pull food from the refrigerator.

"One I'm glad you keep," Abby replied, reaching for a glass and plate from a cabinet. "Any tea in there?"

Debbie handed her the pitcher. "I made it this evening."

Abby filled the plate with baked chicken, green beans, and potatoes. She placed a paper towel over the top and set it in the microwave. "I smell pie," she said and lifted the plastic container containing the dessert.

Debbie sighed, but a grin lifted at the corners of her mouth. She placed the roses in a vase and stepped back to admire them. "And to think you could have had an elegant dinner with Ron."

"Right. From the stories I've heard, it would have been like having dinner with an octopus."

They both shared a laugh.

A few moments later Abby eased onto a stool at Debbie's counter and buttered a warm roll. "Thanks, this is great," she said between mouthfuls. "I'm ready now."

"For what?"

"The questions and sisterly advice."

Debbie rubbed the palms of her hands together, reminding Abby of a pitcher preparing to launch the killer ball. "Okay, so were you flattered?"

Abby thought a moment. With her sister, pretense

was not an option. "A little, when I first saw him. You know, the tux and the roses. He hasn't lost the ability to charm the fins off a fish either." She hesitated. "For one small span of time, we were sixteen again."

"Then?" Debbie leaned across the counter.

Abby stabbed her fork into a piece of potato. "Then I realized I would be an ornament on his arm. The idea of sliding into an egg basket with a bunch of other chicks sent me back to the henhouse."

Abby's remark sent Debbie into another fit of laughter. "Where do you come up with these lines?"

Abby shrugged and chuckled. "I have no idea; they just pop out of my mouth when I least expect it."

A moment later, Debbie tapped the tip of her finger on the table. "Another question: did you feel a spark of anything?"

"Yes," Abby said. "Pity. Somewhere in the years, he lost his enthusiasm for life—I suppose when he finally turned his back on God." Remembering his distant look, she added. "He looked. . .well, sad."

"But you did invite him to church?"

"Yeah. We'll see if he shows up. Frankly, I have my doubts. From what I've read on occasion about his lifestyle, it doesn't look good."

Debbie nodded and became uncommonly quiet.

"What are you thinking?" Abby asked.

"Oh, it's odd he has entered your life after all these years."

"I've been busy being married and raising boys," Abby replied, reaching for the saucer of pie.

"Right, but since God is in control of our lives, Ron's appearance has to be for a reason."

"I'm not interested in Ron's money, name, or social status."

Debbie reached across the table and patted Abby's hand. "You never were."

Chapter 4

Ron left the party early—bored, perturbed with Abby, and his mind filled with remembrances of his granddad. Years had come and gone since he'd allowed himself to think about the dear man who had raised him.

Charles Bassinger took Ron in the same day his parents died in an automobile accident. He remembered sitting in fourth grade science when his granddad came to the door with the principal. Ron thought he'd gotten into some kind of terrible trouble, especially when the teacher stepped from the room to speak with them. Granddad said little when the principal called him from his seat, but his face looked strange—vague. He put his arm around Ron's shoulders and squeezed hard.

"I'll have him back in school in a few days," Granddad said, reaching out to shake the principal's hand. "Let's go, Son. We've got some talking to do."

As they trekked down the long hall to the front door of the school, Ron tried to remember what he could have done so awful that the school phoned his granddad instead of his parents.

Granddad cleared his throat. "Ronnie, I've got some bad news for you, Son. This is going to be hard on you, 'cause it's already hard for me."

"What's wrong?" Ron asked, peering up into the man's face. "Have I done something real bad that Mom and Daddy sent you to get me?"

Granddad took his hand, the calluses rubbing the side of Ron's small fingers. "No, you're not in trouble, not at all."

He said nothing more until they were inside the old Dodge pickup. He pulled Ron close beside him. The smell of leather mixed with Prince Albert pipe tobacco wrapped comfort around Ron and he snuggled close. Suddenly he felt afraid.

"God's called your mom and dad home," Granddad said, his voice breaking with the news. He wiped a tear from his weather-hardened cheek. "I reckon I don't understand why, but He must have a powerful job for them to do in heaven. I imagine your grandma and your parents are rejoicing right now because they are all together."

"Gone?" Ron asked, attempting to imagine life without his mom and dad. Terror choked him, and he pushed against the old man to free himself from the pain. He reached for the door, to run as far as he could from the awful news, but his granddad stopped him and pulled him tighter.

"Don't worry, Son. I'll take care of you. From now on, it's you and me and the good Lord."

Granddad became his dad, his mom, and his friend. They never quarreled, and always Ron listened to the older man's words. His granddad lived his faith in God and saw His hand in everything around them—from the birthing of an animal on the farm to the first shoots of corn springing up through the soil. Every day became a lesson, and every night they recounted the Lord's blessings.

He couldn't remember his granddad ever being sick, but one night he died in his sleep while Ron was away at college. He'd been a senior at Baylor and became alarmed when Granddad didn't answer the phone. A neighbor found him, said he'd gone home with a smile on his face.

Since then, Ron had barred the door on his faith—not that he blamed God for taking his granddad—he simply gave up trying. Granddad probably didn't feel a lot of pride for the way Ron's years had pulled him farther away from his youthful teachings. He listened to others laugh at Christianity, but he'd never been able to deny Jesus. He merely shoved Him away, like he'd done to his granddad the day his parents died. Granddad hadn't allowed him to run, but God had done nothing to stop him.

In the wee hours of the morning, Ron allowed himself to reminisce about some of the cherished times he shared with his granddad. A tear rolled down his cheek, and he brushed it away with the swipe of a smooth fingertip—not like the rough hands of a man who had worked hard all his days.

His thoughts drifted to Abby. They'd grown up together, struggled through adolescence and the tender feelings of first love. He'd never wanted anyone but his little red-haired Abby, and he thought she felt the same. Oh, he knew he changed when he went off to college, but he thought she'd agree to his new beliefs once she matured. The world held a grand array of exciting adventures, and he wanted to capture them all beyond the small town of Cypress and share them with her. He wanted to travel and lavish her with special gifts, then marry her and build her the biggest house in Houston. Had it all been so wrong? Granddad told him those things weren't what God cared about. Then Abby married Kevin Martin, a country boy full of love for the Lord and obviously love for her.

Tonight Abby reminded him of the girl he fell in love with, real and genuine. He liked their sparring; it revitalized him, and he wanted more. But church? Dare he risk a confrontation with God over how he'd spent his years?

Pushing the thoughts about God, his granddad, and Abby from his mind, Ron rose from the bed and swallowed a couple of aspirin to relax him. He'd never been one to take medicine. For that matter, he didn't smoke or drink. His abstinence justified all the other things God frowned upon.

Setting the glass back on the bathroom counter, he wondered if he should attend church on Sunday. At least he could finally get the answers as to why Abby suddenly turned to Kevin Martin so long ago.

Saturday morning, Abby left a message on his voice mail reminding him about church. The soft country sound of her voice thrilled him and filled him with apprehension at the same time.

Saturday afternoon, he confirmed his golf game with an old friend.

Saturday night, he canceled the golf game, stayed home, and set his alarm for early enough Sunday morning to head to Cypress for church. All night he dreamed of boyhood days.

Sunday morning he couldn't climb out of bed. Depression weighed on him heavier than Houston's humidity. Instead he rolled over and went back to sleep.

❧

Abby waited with Debbie outside of church while Les spoke with the pastor inside. Her sister had riddled her with one question after another as to why Ron hadn't shown up. Abby tapped her foot on the sidewalk, attempting to concentrate but ready for Les to break away from his conversation and escort his wife home.

"Aren't you listening to me?" Debbie asked, smoothing the skirt of her pale blue suit. "Why don't you think Ron showed up this morning?"

Abby shook her head and glanced away. "I don't know. He must have had other plans. Obviously talking to me or seeking God didn't rank very high."

"Are you going to call him?"

Abby startled. "Heavens no."

"Why not?" Debbie punctuated her question with a nod.

"Because how he spends his time is none of my business."

"But you have a responsibility as a Christian to lead him toward the Lord."

Abby stared at her sister; the questioning had gone as far as she could handle. "Ron talked about playing golf this morning. Maybe he went to a late party last night. Who knows? Maybe he had a sleepover."

Debbie's wide-eyed gaze matched her gaping mouth. "Abby Martin, I don't believe you said that—and standing right here on the church steps, too." She touched the back of her hair and peered about at the diminishing crowd.

"God knows what he's doing." Abby stifled a sigh. "Besides, read the papers. Everyone knows Ron has an active social life."

"Right, but aren't you a bit judgmental?"

"Me?" Now, Abby glanced around her. "Of course not. I'm merely stating a fact."

"Gossip best describes it. I think seeing Ron affected you more than you care to admit."

"That's ridiculous," Abby replied, feeling her heart pound just a bit harder than usual. "This is strictly business."

"Face it, Sis. You had a beautiful marriage with Kevin. God may want you to have another beautiful relationship with Ron."

"Ludicrous," Abby said as she twisted a curl behind her ear.

"Oh, I'm right," Debbie continued. "You're just too

stubborn to admit it."

Abby nearly raised up in her heels, which by now had begun to hurt her feet. "Deb, you know the history—his, mine, and what happened before Kevin and I married. Ron and I have nothing in common anymore, and furthermore, he and Kevin are not remotely the same type of men."

"Who says they have to be?" Debbie demanded but promptly quieted as a young couple walked by with their children.

Mentally exhausted, Abby formed her words. "If I were to seriously contemplate another man—which I'm not—my choice would not be Ron Bassinger. He'd be at the far end of the food chain rummaging through the bones."

Debbie laughed and forced Abby to giggle. "Someday I'm going to write a book, *The Things My Sister Said.*"

"Better hurry. You're not getting any younger."

Debbie gave her a less than enthusiastic smile. "You're not far behind me."

They both smiled at friends who waved before heading to their cars.

"Think about it," Debbie continued. "If Ron was anyone else you invited to church and didn't show, wouldn't you call and find out why? Confirm another Sunday?"

Abby felt defeat tickle the soles of her feet. "Yes, you win, Sis. I'll make the call. He is a man who needs the Lord."

"Thank you. Now when are you going to call him?"

"Don't you ever give up? Where's Les, anyway?"

"He's still inside with the pastor—something about a couple who needs marriage counseling—and you didn't answer my question."

Abby wet her lips. Why did her sister always have to mother her at their age? "I'll call tomorrow morning."

"Thank you," Debbie replied with a lift of her prim chin. "Why don't you have lunch with Les and me? We're heading into Houston then to visit the kids."

The thought of seeing Debbie's daughter and son along with their four precious children tempted her. "Only if you promise not to ask one single question."

Debbie grinned. "Why? And ruin the fun I've had for all these years?" She glanced behind Abby. "There's Les."

"As much as I hate being the recipient of your endless questions, I do enjoy your company. As long as Les doesn't mind, I'll tag along with you."

⌘

Monday morning, Ron's secretary told him Abby had phoned, but he refused to return the call. After all, their business could be handled through his accountant. She'd chosen to part company with him years ago, and she'd made it clear last week that nothing had changed. Besides, he'd heard enough of her ramblings about religion. Let his accountant handle the purchase of her store. He had more important things to do.

The remainder of the day and through Wednesday he spent in business negotiations for a large parcel of land inside the loop—a prime spot for office buildings.

On Friday, Mac, one of his golfing buddies called him. "Hey Ron, a couple of us are planning a Sunday morning game at the club. Want to join us?"

Without taking a breath he replied. "Sure, Mac. This week's been horrible. I need a break."

"Tee off at ten?"

"I'll be there. Sorry about last week," Ron said, signing the set of contracts on the desk before him.

"Everything going all right? Business as usual?"

Ron loosened his collar. He'd been edgy all week, and now this clown wanted information. For two cents he'd back out of Sunday morning, but he knew his golfing buds well enough to understand they'd be spreading trash by Monday morning if he didn't show again. "Oh, yeah, just busy closing deals and making money. You know how it is."

Mac chuckled, and Ron knew he forced it. "Here I thought you might have women troubles."

The sound of his voice grated against Ron's nerves. "Not me. Someday I'll tell you my secret."

The conversation ended a short while later. Ron wished he had a few good friends he could trust, and not those who'd stab him in the back at the first opportunity. Lately it seemed as if every man or woman he encountered wanted something from him. He should be used to their philosophy, but the older he got, the more he wished for sincerity.

Must be the last birthday I had, he told himself, checking the time on his Rolex. His accountant had a ten o'clock appointment and hadn't arrived. Five minutes later his secretary informed him of the man's arrival.

When Jim Caldwell entered, Ron stood and shook his hand. The man lived and breathed numbers and remembered facts and figures from twenty years ago. Contrary to many reports, Ron ran a scrupulous business, and he knew he could count on Jim for whatever needed doing.

"I have the figures ready for the Martin purchase," Jim said without a hint of a smile.

"You're late," Ron stated, ready to verbally pounce on him.

"Traffic; my apologies," he said and immediately opened the manila envelope. Removing a spreadsheet, he handed it to Ron. "I don't have a definite figure for the manager's salary. Is Mrs. Martin going to continue in that capacity?"

Ron raised a brow. He hadn't taken care of hiring anyone. "I need to discuss the matter with her," he replied. "I don't recall if she has an employee with management qualifications."

Jim sat stiffly like a parakeet perched in a cage, waiting as always for direction. "It really doesn't have a bearing on whether or not you're purchasing the store, but I wanted to bring it to your attention."

Ron averted his gaze. "Handle it for me, will you, Jim?" He glanced through the salaries on the spreadsheet. "Doesn't look like any of her employees could take over a management position. Pay her whatever she wants until we find someone suitable."

"All right," Jim agreed. He lifted another folder from his briefcase and proceeded to review the next order of business.

Ron half listened to Jim's report. He doubted Abby would want to be under his employ, unless she thought she could evangelize him.

"I changed my mind," Ron interrupted. "I'll replace Mrs. Martin with someone else."

Chapter 5

O n Friday morning, Abby sat at her desk in the loft of Martin's Western Wear and stared at the phone. Her fingers drummed against the laminated wood, as she mustered the courage to call Ron and invite him to church again. He hadn't returned her messages left at his office, and her conscience refused to let the matter rest. Granted, she felt uncomfortable in Ron's presence, especially when the past jarred her senseless, but that didn't mean she'd left him for gloating demons. This had become a spiritual battle, and God never tasted defeat.

She realized the situation had become a challenge. . . one of stubbornness and determination. Ron must have known what she wanted, because business dealings were to be handled through his accountant. As long as he avoided her, he wouldn't have to invent an excuse to not attend church.

Persistence, she told herself. Ron had been an active part of God's family before and had probably felt His gentle urging for years. Her invitation to join her for worship only triggered his resolve to trek through life his way.

He, of all people, should remember God didn't give up on people and neither did Abby. She felt confident he hadn't shut the door completely but kept it open wide enough for God to continue chasing him.

Too bad the best person to help Ron was his grand-dad, except he'd been gone for years. Abby had put the matter to prayer and accepted her role as the one who must pray for Ron's relationship with Jesus Christ.

"Okay, Lord," she whispered, "I need intestinal fortitude and the right words."

Picking up the phone, she rang the front register downstairs. "Hi, Candy, would you hold my calls and make sure I'm not disturbed for a few moments? I'll let you know when I'm finished."

The young girl confirmed the request, and Abby went back to tapping her desk with her fingertips. With a deep sigh, she picked up his business card where he'd written his home number. Grasping the receiver, she punched in Ron's home number.

One ring, two rings, three rings, four rings. The answering machine clicked in. "This is Ron Bassinger here. I'm not available to take your call. Leave a message and I'll get back to you as soon as possible."

She wet her lips and resolved to sound cheery. "Hi, Ron, this is Abby Martin. I wanted to invite you to church Sunday morning, and I'd also like to talk to you about the store's management since you have agreed to purchase it. Please give me a ring at the store or on my cell phone. Here are the numbers. . ."

Sitting alone in her office with only the muted sounds of voices rising from below, she wondered if mentioning the store would trigger him to phone, or if he'd have the accountant take care of it on Monday.

Ron Bassinger, you always were a pickle to figure out.

Abby rose from her chair and peered through the glass to the people below. A number of customers meandered through the store, most of whom she knew by their first name. All of her clerks looked busy and could use help.

The blare of the phone broke into her thoughts, and she whirled around to see the light on her private line flicker. *Probably Debbie,* she mused, *pestering me about Ron.*

"Hello, this is Abby," she said.

"And this is Ron. I'm returning your call, actually all of them."

He sounded friendly, and she braved ahead. "I missed you at church last Sunday."

"I had plans."

"You mentioned that, golfing I think. What about this Sunday; are you free?" Her heart thumped like a puppy's tail. Good thing she didn't fall prey to the other matters triggered by a puppy's excitement.

"No, can't this Sunday. I've scheduled a golf game." He paused. "You wanted to discuss the store?"

"I guess I didn't make myself clear with my message," Abby replied. "I have a concern for the customers, keeping them happy and catering to their needs."

He cleared his throat. "My goal has always been to

maintain the current profit status," he replied. "And to continue making money, whoever manages your store must naturally be a people person."

"I know, but I wanted *you* to understand what this store means to me. It started as a small dream and grew as Kevin and I established our integrity within the community." Suddenly she felt like her ramblings weren't conveying at all what she meant. "I'm sorry, Ron, I'm not stating what I intended to say."

"Abby, slow down. Take a deep breath and let the words come."

She felt a shiver wind up her spine, and she nearly dropped the phone. His words were an echo from the past, when she couldn't communicate what her feelings dictated.

"Thank you," she said and managed to regain her composure. "My heart is here. Every inch of this place is precious to me. Although I understand the new management will be qualified, will that person be committed to the employees and to the people of this community?"

"I can't assure you those things will happen," Ron said gently. "I own several businesses, and my people's decisions are based on whether money is being made or not. Are you sure you really want to sell? Because it sounds like you're having reservations."

Abby combed her fingers through her hair and snagged a tangle. "Yes, I'm certain I've made the right decision. I simply wanted you to know how I feel about the employees and the customers—they're more like family."

"You know things will change. No two people ever run a business the same way," he said, then his tone softened. "But I promise to do my best to hire a person who will respect what you've done."

"I can't ask for anything more," she said, her emotions spiraling down with the reality of unhappy employees and customers swept along by the waves of change. Selfishness nudged at her heart. Lately, she'd been more worried about her own loss than those around her. "How long will you give me to work with the new manager?"

"Two weeks sufficient?" he asked.

"Yes. . .yes that's fine." Embarrassment coursed through her body, and she sensed her face likened to the color of her hair.

"Well," Ron said lightheartedly, "we could continue this discussion over dinner."

She smiled. "You know my criteria for that."

"Stubborn, aren't we?"

"Yes, we are," she replied, lacing her words with professionalism. "Thanks for listening, and if your game is rained out, I'll save you a seat."

He chuckled. "Stalemate. I think we need an arbitrator."

"We have one," she said, punctuating her words. "Bye, Ron. I'm praying for you." Abby replaced the receiver and wrapped her arms around her shoulders.

Am I shivering from the cold? Or have old feelings for Ron surfaced? She swallowed hard and glanced at Kevin's picture on her desk. *Oh, Kevin, I don't want to betray your memory.*

Ron clasped his hands behind his head and propped his feet on the heavy mahogany desk. Melancholia swept over him. Why must Abby always stand on that pious rock of hers? They could enjoy each other's company and talk nostalgia without his making an appearance in church. Next she'd be insisting he make some foolhardy rededication to Christianity.

But in the deep recesses of his heart, he knew it all mattered—Abby, the past, and God.

Unlike most Friday nights, Ron chose not to stop by the club for dinner and mingle with the familiar crowd. For certain, he did not feel sociable. Instead he drove home to an empty house. After changing into sweatpants and a T-shirt, he found himself hungry for, of all things, bacon and eggs. As a kid, he and Granddad had fixed breakfast for dinner when they were too tired to cook. Tonight it suited him fine.

He ate and rummaged through his new DVD movies until he selected one about espionage. He slipped in the disk and attempted to concentrate, but his mind continued to reminisce. Odd, his thoughts of Granddad and Abby blended together; he couldn't think of one without the other—picnics in the spring, school dances, learning to hunt, berry picking.

Shortly after ten o'clock he headed to bed. The next morning held a crucial meeting with an investor, and he needed to be rested to swing the deal. Maybe he'd arrange a date for tomorrow night to rid his mind of Abby and everything she represented. Slowly he felt himself drift toward the haven of sleep.

"Ronnie, Ronnie, you awake, Son?" Granddad asked from the doorway.

He squinted to see the shadowy figure blocking any semblance of light from the hall. "Yeah, I'm awake. Is it time?"

"Sure is. We want to catch them fish while they're biting."

Ronnie threw back the old quilt his grandma had made for him as a baby, his fingers catching in a worn spot. "I'll be dressed in a minute."

"Good, I've packed us breakfast and lunch. We can eat in the boat."

Ronnie stepped into his jeans and, remembering the October chill from the previous night, pulled on a sweatshirt. Soon, he scrambled down the stairs and out the door, giving Old Jake a pat on the head as he dashed by. He climbed into the truck with his granddad and scooted onto the ripped seat recently repaired with duct tape. Ronnie couldn't think of anything better than Saturday morning fishing with his granddad. Didn't matter to him if the fish refused to bite; he just plain enjoyed the quiet of predawn, the rhythmic sound of water lapping against the rowboat, and the presence of the dear man he loved.

As soon as they had rowed out to the middle of the lake, fog set in so thick Ronnie couldn't see in front of him. He reached for his granddad, but he couldn't find him. He wanted to cry, but panic paralyzed his throat. Unfathomable fear gripped him.

"Ronnie," Granddad said, his deep voice calm and reassuring. "We're by the shore, Son. Stretch out your hand and I'll lead you from the boat."

As much as he wanted to obey, he couldn't speak or move.

"I can't help you if you don't take my hand," Granddad said.

The urging prompted Ronnie to try even harder, but his body stayed fixed to the boat.

"I'm here, Ronnie," Granddad said. "I won't leave you. Let me lead you home."

Ron woke with a start. Perspiration streamed down his face and chest. His breathing came in heavy spurts. He opened his eyes in the darkness, but the reality of the dream thundered about him.

"Oh, God," he moaned in the silence. "Where have I been all these years?"

I'm here, Ron. Let me lead you back home where you belong—where you won't ever be alone again.

His legs felt like iron, and he realized the God of his youth wrestled with the demons of today. His chest ached, not with the threat of a heart attack, but with the ache to have Jesus back in his life.

"Help me, Lord," he whispered through tears. If he could get to his knees and repent of all those years, he'd know true peace.

The effort to slide from his bed to his knees took every ounce of strength left in his body. Once to the floor, he lay prostrate, crying, praying, and later worshiping the God who had never abandoned him.

Chapter 6

Early Sunday morning, before Abby's clock radio broke the tranquility of her sleep, the doorbell rang. Trembling with the interruption and fearing the worst for a family member or friend, she reached for her robe and rushed down the hall.

She glanced out a window. Had she lost her mind, or was Ron's BMW parked in front of her house? First rubbing her face, then wading her fingers through her hair, she opened the door.

Ron stood dressed in a pinstripe gray suit, grinning from one cheek dimple to the other. "Morning, Sunshine," he said and promptly looked chastised. "Oops, got you out of bed, didn't I? I'm sorry; guess my timing is bad."

"Uh, no, you're fine," she said, fully aware she stumbled through her words. "It's okay, really." He hadn't called her sunshine since they were kids. "I thought you had a golf game this morning."

"I cancelled it. Is the invitation to church still open, or did you give my seat to someone else?" The grin returned.

She met his gaze, and her pulse quickened with what she saw, or rather what she hoped she saw.

"Oh, it's open," she said slowly, wondering what had transpired between Friday and Sunday morning to change his mind.

"I've been up since five and I'm starved," Ron said. "Is there anywhere we can get breakfast before church?"

Completely bewildered, Abby didn't know what to say. "The only place open is Abby's kitchen or the donut shop."

"The donut shop will do," he replied. "Do you mind if I go get us a dozen?"

"No, of course not. I need a few minutes to shower and get ready—well, actually a little more like thirty or forty."

He waved his hand in front of his face. "I'll take my time. Raspberry filled still your favorite?"

She couldn't resist the smile tugging at her lips. "You bet, and the donut shop is the same Whippy Cream, only Mr. Anderson's daughter now runs it." She hesitated. "I could scramble some eggs and bacon in no time at all."

"Actually I'm in the mood for donuts and. . .by any chance do you remember how to make coffee with hot chocolate like Granddad used to fix for us?"

Her eyes widened. "Yes. I make it pretty often." She jammed her hands into her robe pockets and stared at him. "Ron, are you all right?"

"I'm wonderful," he said and teetered back on his heels. "I'm a miracle man."

"A what?" Suddenly she remembered her manners. "I'm so rude. Won't you come in?"

"No, this is fine. I'll just go after the donuts and you can get ready, that is, as long as you don't mind."

She shook her head. "Guess I'm just baffled. What did you mean by 'a miracle man'?"

Then she knew what happened—the look of contentment in his eyes, the easy smile that never made it past his freshmen year in college.

"The Lord and I have been talking. I'm tired of my way, Abby. I've come home."

She stepped through the door and threw her arms around his neck. Who cared what the neighbors saw? Who cared about her raggedy bathrobe with the coffee stains? Who cared that she didn't have on a trace of makeup or that her hair stuck straight up? Ron had found the Lord, and she felt the same joy from over thirty years ago when he told her his granddad had led him to glory.

"I'm so happy for you," she managed through her emotions.

His arms encircled her waist, and she became acutely aware of his touch. Only Zack and Zane hugged her with such vigor.

"I haven't felt this good in years, too many years in fact." He released her, and she scrambled to pull her tattered robe over her pajamas. Her cheeks flamed.

"Only, I should have called first about it, instead of surprising you like this. I've embarrassed you," he said, taking a step back.

She tilted her head. "Maybe just a little, but I'm tickled with the news."

He nodded and the plastered grin continued. "Thought you'd be. Started to call you yesterday." He stopped as though pondering his words. "This happened late Friday night, and I needed yesterday to consider what God wanted of me."

"I bet the angels are turning cartwheels," she said, "and singing the same flower-child songs we did in the sixties."

Ron chuckled. "I see you haven't lost your way with words."

"My sense of humor keeps me sane." She laughed. "Seriously, can we talk later? I want to hear all about this miracle man change, if it's okay."

"You bet. I was hoping you didn't have plans so we could spend the afternoon together."

Logic told her to think about his request, but she tossed aside her reservations. "Sounds good. Now, I really need to get cleaned up."

Ron waved good-bye, and she shut the door. Abby jumped up and down and attempted a feat she hadn't done in years—a cartwheel. And she made it, landing only inches from an antique coffee table.

"Thank You, Lord," she sang while the water grew hot in the shower. She bet old Granddad was singing with the angels over this exceptional, wonderful, positively exhilarating news.

❧

Ron laughed all the way to the donut shop. His Abby

hadn't changed a bit. The way she wrinkled her nose and held an impish sparkle in her eyes reminded him of the girl he fell in love with on the back of Jud Howard's hay wagon. If he admitted the truth, those same old feelings had washed over him when he wrapped his arms around her waist just moments before.

With a satisfied sigh, he wondered how long had it been since he observed a woman blush. To Ron, it meant a woman of high morals and inner purity. A rarity in his sordid world. He knew other business people were Christian, but they didn't run in his circles.

Lord, is Abby a part of the plan? Is this where You're leading me?

He glanced about the quiet streets of his hometown. It looked much the same, and the memories drew him back in time. Some buildings had received a facelift, and a few others had been replaced, but the cozy country atmosphere warmed him all the way through.

At the Whippy Cream, he elected to drink a cup coffee and leaf through the paper to give Abby a chance to shower.

"Don't you want a donut or kolache to go with your coffee?" the woman asked. She studied him closely. "Aren't you Ron Bassinger?"

He glanced up. "Sure am, and I will take a dozen donuts as soon as I finish your fine coffee."

She beamed. "Coming right up. Glazed or mixed?"

"Mixed, but make sure you have two raspberry filled and two chocolate cream." He smiled broadly. "You're Kathy Anderson, aren't you?"

"Uh-huh, well, Kathy Walker now. What brings you here so early on a Sunday morning?"

"Church," he replied taking a big sip of the hot liquid. "I'm going to church this morning with Abby Martin."

"Hey, what did you say?" squeaked a woman from a corner table.

"Oh, Maudie, your newspaper column doesn't need any of this," Kathy said and rolled her eyes at the matronly woman.

"Of course it does. The world thrives on timely reported news." She turned her attention back to him. "Mr. Bassinger, what church are you attending?" She scribbled on a pad of paper positioned beside her half-eaten glazed donut. "Hmm, didn't I see you standing outside Abby's store a week or so ago dressed real nice in a tux and carrying roses?"

Ron folded his paper and gulped the rest of his coffee. "I can't remember exactly what happened then."

"Sure looked like you." Her words were edged with sugar, and she rose from her chair to move closer to him.

"I'll take those donuts now," he said and gave Maudie his best charming smile. "I'd love to sit and chat, but I've got to get going."

He paid for his and Abby's breakfast with a fifty and told Kathy to keep the change. He'd pay any amount to escape the Whippy Cream before Maudie pounced on him.

Understanding he needed to kill a few more minutes, Ron drove by the church. The building still looked the same, save for a fresh coat of white paint and a huge two-story brick addition to the side. He remembered back when he was a bit of a kid, some older boys discovered the preacher had taken a walk to the outhouse, and they decided to rock it. Ron never thought the boys intended to turn it over, but it happened. Funniest thing he'd ever seen. Unfortunately, the incident took place during a church picnic to kick off a countywide revival. Everybody and anybody witnessed the preacher's predicament. Ron laughed out loud remembering the rather large preacher and his red face.

A look at his watch told him, Abby would be waiting. . . .

"Maudie was there? At the Whippy Cream?" Abby asked, her eyes growing bigger by the moment. "And she heard you mention going to church with me this morning?"

"I'm afraid so," Ron replied, amused at the trapped look in her eyes. He smelled the chocolate in his coffee, took a drink, and let the hot liquid slide down his throat. "Wonderful. Wonderful."

She shook her head and began to laugh. "Ron, she will have a field day with this one."

He pushed the donut box her way. "Have another. There's two raspberry, and I saw Kathy stick in a lemon filled."

Abby appeared to examine each delicious delicacy.

"By the way, you look lovely this morning," he said, dipping half a chocolate cream into his coffee. "You always did have a way with green."

"Thanks," she replied between mouthfuls.

"There's more," he finally said.

She lifted a questioning brow, and he brushed a sugar crumb from her lip. The touch did more to him than he cared to admit.

"More of what?" she asked, reaching for the glass carafe holding their coffee.

He hesitated to reveal the rest of Maudie's words.

Abby paled. "It's Maudie isn't it?"

"Yes, Ma'am. She remembered seeing me the evening I stopped by your store with the roses."

"Oh, no," Abby moaned. "We will be tried, convicted, and hung by Wednesday's edition."

"Be glad she wasn't driving through your neighborhood at six this morning." Ron couldn't resist the urge to tease. How strangely nice he could joke with Abby as though the years had somehow melted away.

Abby wagged a finger. "You're right. She'd have been happier than a Pulitzer prize winner with that information."

"God's good," he said.

She smiled. "Yes, He is, and I'm very thankful this morning."

He leaned closer and fought the urge to take her hand. "Can we take a drive this afternoon and talk until we run out of words?"

Her gaze swept across the table, and she encircled the mug with her fingers. "Yes." Her words came soft, reminding him of a light breeze on a summer day. "I'd. . . I'd like to hear what brought you back to the Lord, and

I suppose you should hear about—"

"Yesteryear," he completed with a half smile, but she avoided him. "Abby, I know you had a wonderful life with Kevin, and I want to hear all about it—your sons, everything. And yes, I have questions about us and Kevin when you're ready."

"Thanks," she whispered. "Goodness, Ron, look what time it is. Church starts in fifteen minutes."

Shortly thereafter, he felt proud to escort Abby Martin to Cypress Community Bible Church on a spring morning in beautiful, quaint Cypress, Texas.

As he climbed the steps of the old church and Abby greeted those around them, a peculiar sensation lifted the hairs on the back of his neck. He shrugged. Must be a storm coming.

Ron graciously accepted the introductions of strangers and renewed the status of friends gone by the wayside, but the strange feeling remained, and as hard as he tried, it would not leave him. *Why?* he asked. *Why now?*

The sermon, the music, and the people were all he hoped for and more. The pastor took the time to welcome him, and one high school couple asked him and Abby to join them for lunch. Abby and Ron appreciated the invitation but declined, stating they'd made plans.

But the odd prompting, as though God wanted his undivided attention, held him captive. As the two laughed with Debbie and Les, Ron agreed to the inner voice. He'd spend the afternoon with Abby then he'd embark upon an important journey, one which might never lead him back to Texas or Abby.

Chapter 7

R on glanced around The Blue Denim Restaurant packed full of churchgoers and those who simply wanted good, country cooking. After eating all those donuts earlier, he'd ordered the lunch size portion of chicken fried steak, thinking it would be smaller. But his plate overflowed with the tender, breaded meat and mashed potatoes and gravy. He could hear his personal trainer's complaints now. No matter, the taste took him back decades, certainly not like the restaurants he frequented in Houston.

He stole a look at Abby, only for a second, because Maudie sat across the room, her pen and paper attached to her body like an appendage. At least he'd have Abby all to himself this afternoon. As much as he wanted to know the truth, he wouldn't prod her. She'd have to initiate the topic.

He thought back over the church service. The pastor had chosen a sermon on renewal of faith. Ron chuckled. The man must have a direct line to God. How many years had gone by since he'd heard real

Bible preaching? How good it felt to be home.

"Would you care for dessert?" the teenage waitress asked, revealing a mouthful of braces.

Ron had seen the glass display case of piled high meringue pies and triple-decker cakes when he came in.

"Not me," Abby said. "I can't eat another bite."

Ron peeked around the waitress to the desserts. "Why don't we take two and eat them this afternoon?"

She cringed. "Why not one, and we'll split it? Look at the size of those things, Ron."

"I concede," he said, and they settled on a German chocolate cake with a half-inch thick layer of coconut and pecan topping.

Shortly thereafter, he drove Abby home where she could change from her dress and heels, although he did like the shade of green she'd worn. He waited in her living room, feeling very much out of place and wishing he'd thought to bring extra clothes. Her furnishings were homey, not the latest in fashion and design, but comfortable and practical. Of course that described Abby.

Although Kevin was gone, reminders were everywhere. Pictures of him and Abby rested on the fireplace along with family shots of their sons and a few shots of Martin's Western Wear. The gallery had a haunting effect. Ron suspected Kevin or one of their sons would walk into the room at any given minute and demand to know why he'd invaded Abby's life again.

Truth be known, this business with Abby had him in a tailspin. Not only had he been given a second chance with God, but he'd been given another opportunity to prove his love for her. Yesterday's reflections had definitely put Abby in the forefront, or maybe he simply needed to learn from the past. Thinking of her scared him to death—not like his usual assortment of shallow women. He certainly didn't want to make the same mistakes as before. He was young and cocky back then, and he'd pressured her to do things she didn't really want.

Standing from the cream-colored sofa, he strode across the room to view a clearer picture of her sons. They looked alike with Abby's strawberry-blond hair and Kevin's rugged build. Guess that's how kids should be—pieces of both their parents. Later, he'd have to ask their names.

"Bored out of your mind?" Abby asked from the doorway.

He turned to see her dressed in jeans for the afternoon. "No, but after all I've eaten, a nap sounds great."

"That's no problem. I mean if you want to head back to Houston, we can talk another day." She smiled sweetly and he knew she meant every word.

"Absolutely not. We're taking a drive to the country."

Abby laughed. "We *are* in the country."

How he loved the musical lilt of her voice. "I mean way out in the boonies. What about your land in the Hill Country?"

She clasped her hands together in that special, little girl way he remembered so well. "I'd love to show it to you, but it's a good two-and-a-half-hour drive from here."

He jiggled his keys in his pants pocket. "Suits me fine."

The matter settled, they headed west toward San Antonio.

❦

Abby felt strange riding beside Ron in his fancy car. She saw enough bells and whistles to fly a plane. Besides that, Ron meticulously showed her how to control her own air-conditioning unit for the passenger side and the various positions of her cushiony, black leather seat. *Like riding first class,* she thought.

Trepidation nudged at her about Ron's obvious interest in her, or did he treat all his lady friends with such enthusiasm? She didn't know what to think, especially when so many young, beautiful women were available. Dare she give him the benefit of doubt with his rededication to the Lord?

"What are your sons' names?" Ron asked, steering with his left hand and leaning her direction.

"Zack and Zane," she said. "They look a lot alike but act like they came from different planets." She laughed and shook her head.

"And you're extremely proud of them," he added. "Where do they live?"

"Zack just began work as a veterinarian in Austin, and Zane is an English professor at the University of Texas."

"What a mix. Are they married?"

"Yes, and I'm expecting my first grandbaby in the fall."

Abby watched the lines on Ron's face tighten to sadness.

"You are a very lucky lady," he said. "Shows the

world what happens when you follow God and not your own selfish desires."

Guilt crept over her for her earlier deliberations about his sincerity, but she did her best to mask them. "Ron, you've done a lot of good for people," she replied, wanting to touch his arm but not certain of his reaction. "Tell me about your work. It sounds fascinating."

He started to speak then appeared to contemplate her request. "Nothing great about it. I wheel and deal in the age-old commodity called land. Sometimes I build on it and sometimes I just let it sit until I can sell it for the right price. One minute I'm everybody's favorite fair-haired boy, and the next minute they hate my guts. It's business, cutthroat and stressful."

"Do you enjoy it?" she asked, thankful her job had always been a delight and the rewards a blessing.

"Used to, but not anymore. The pressure is unbelievable—making an old man out of me and more enemies every day."

"I'm sorry."

"Don't be. It's my chosen profession."

She pointed to a road sign. "Take the next right, turn left, and go down about fifteen miles."

"I'm anxious to see where you intend to live," he said, peering in the direction of her property.

"Oh, it's bare land right now. When I sell the store and my house, then I can build."

Once they reached the hilly terrain, complete with live oaks and sparsely grassed land dotted with junipers, she pointed out the various landmarks known only to her and the boys. They left the car far behind them and paraded along a narrow tractor path leading to a dilapidated barn.

"I plan to replace this," she said, pointing to the old structure, "before building my house." She faced a hill to the west of them. "Over there is where I want to put it."

Ron smiled in an appreciative fashion. "I bet you're excited, and it's beautiful."

"Hmm. All I have to do is make friends with the scorpions and the rattlers," she said. "The coyotes and prairie dogs already know me by name."

He laughed, and she relished the deep sound of his voice. Ron was a handsome man, always had been, and like Candy had noted, his white hair and white teeth gave him a definite distinction.

"Remember all the fun we use to have on Granddad's place?" he asked, seeming to drink in the expanse of the land. "I really miss that old man."

"Me, too. He held more truth in his little finger than most men do in a lifetime."

Ron nodded. "I dreamed about him Friday night. In fact, the reality of how he lived his life is what brought me back to the Lord."

She tilted her head, eager to hear his words. Once he finished relaying the dream, her eyes pooled and a tear flowed down her cheek.

"God uses all kinds of things to capture our attention," she said, blinking back the wetness.

"Well, I'm glad He didn't decide on a bolt of lightning," he added, and they both laughed.

She'd done a lot of laughing with Ron today, like old times. Perhaps the time had come. "Ron?"

"Yes." His eyes had never looked so incredibly blue, nor had the color so closely matched the cloudless sky overhead.

She trembled and hesitated to go on. Too many years of guilt had built a wall around this portion of her heart. "I want to tell you what happened. . .back then, but first I need to ask your forgiveness for not being honest with you when I should have been."

"You don't have to tell me a thing," he replied, and she knew he meant it. "I hurt you over and over again, long before you left me for Kevin."

They walked ahead slowly while she silently prayed for guidance in poking at the ashes of the past.

"I didn't break it off because of Kevin, not altogether," she said, wringing her hands. "He and I were just friends. Even when we first married, our relationship was based purely on friendship. The love came later."

Ron stopped and expelled a heavy breath. A curious, yet questioning look spread over his face. "You weren't seeing him while I attended college?"

"Oh, no," she said softly. "I didn't want anyone else."

"Then what happened?"

Abby swallowed hard. Only Kevin and Debbie had heard this story. "Ron, you and I were too close," she began. "The intimacy made me feel dirty, ugly, and certainly not one of God's children. I tried to justify it by saying we were merely expressing our love for each other and someday we'd be married, but it didn't work."

He nodded and stared out over the land. "I played a big part in that, too."

"I could have said no and stuck by my convictions," Abby said. "I acted immature, thinking only of myself and fearing the possibility of losing you."

She glanced down at the ground and stepped away from an ant bed. "One Sunday night after you left to go back to school, I drove to church in hopes of talking to the youth pastor. I knew I needed to break it off with you, but I couldn't bring myself to go through with it. This particular evening, the services had been canceled, so I sat on a front pew all by myself and cried about the mess I'd got myself into. Well, Kevin drove by on the way home from a friend's house, saw my car, and stopped in to find me in tears. I broke down and told him what we'd been doing and how I hated myself. Then. . ."

"What Abby?"

"I told him what I hadn't been able to tell you, or anyone else, that I was pregnant. Every time I thought I had the nerve to tell you about it, I couldn't find the right words—not when you looked forward to your future. Well, Kevin comforted me. He put his arms around me and told me he'd marry me the next day. He said he'd loved me for a long time but didn't want to say anything because of you. I had no idea, but the notion of him taking care of me filled me with hope. I thought about his proposal and realized there were a whole lot of things worse than marrying a good friend." She heard Ron sigh but couldn't bear to look at his face.

"What about the baby?" he asked through a ragged breath.

She turned away from his poignant stare. "I miscarried on our honeymoon."

He said nothing, and when she gathered the courage to look into his face, his set jaw and narrowed eyes told it all.

"I'm sorry, Ron. I couldn't tell you about the baby, although Kevin begged me to. Finally we stopped arguing about it and let it be."

They walked on and she waited and prayed.

"Abby, that was my baby. I had a right to know the truth."

What was she thinking to tell him this after so many years? "You're right," she said slowly, "but I didn't want to see or talk to you. I simply wanted to forget. I'm. . .I'm sorry."

The nightmarish event swirled around her, vivid as the present. She remembered the desperation—the utter hopelessness of carrying an illegitimate child and the ridicule certain to come. She couldn't tell her parents, not even Debbie until it was over. Kevin had been an answer to prayer. She remembered the night of torment following the wedding ceremony and the terrifying reality of losing the life within her. They'd both grieved the loss of the child.

Silence. Deafening silence with only the sound of a crow call to break the quiet.

"I'm trying to put myself in your shoes," Ron said, his angry gaze piercing her heart. "Would you have ever told me?" he demanded.

"I don't know," she said, her mouth quivering. "I've asked myself that question a million times. Marrying Kevin was a way to fix the moment—not the years ahead."

On they walked, farther from Ron's expensive vehicle and the safety of her world today. Miserable, she wished she'd never uttered a word.

"You two stayed married," Ron said at last.

She nodded. "I learned to love him; we had the boys and built a good life for ourselves."

He stopped at the rim of a hill and shielded his eyes from the western sun. He must loathe her, and she couldn't blame him.

"I'm sorry," she repeated.

He sighed and looked beyond the horizon line. "I can't let you carry all the load," he said. "Truthfully, who knows how I would have reacted? My life was focused on my grandiose plans for the future, and I believed I had all the answers, but it didn't change the fact that I loved you. The hurt of your marriage tore me apart, so I chose my goals over my feelings, over Granddad, and most certainly over God. As I look back over my life, I realize I would have made a lousy husband and father."

He turned to face her. "The hero here is Kevin. I hated him for years, and now I'd like to shake his hand."

A tear slipped from her watery eyes. "Precious Kevin. He gave so much of himself to everyone he met."

Ron took her hand into his. "I need to work

through all of this and get a grip on what happened, but I do thank you for telling me about the baby."

She nodded, for to speak meant an ocean of tears.

"Should we start back?" he asked a moment later.

They began the walk to the car, hand in hand—a loose hold, but still touching.

During the ride home, they talked of easy things from the weather to the latest hometown news. Yet, she felt the wedge between them, and she'd slapped as many bricks against the wall as Ron.

Later at her doorstep, he seemed to linger, grappling for words to convey his feelings. "Abby, I thoroughly enjoyed today, despite what we needed to discuss."

"Thank you for listening and not judging me," she managed. "I'd like to pray about forgiving and forgetting the past."

He nodded. "But I don't want to lose sight of the good times." He stared up at the sky then back to her face. "Abby, there's something you should know."

She raised her gaze to meet his. The warmth radiating from his eyes surprised her.

"I'm heading to Montana in the morning after a meeting with my board, and I don't know when or if I'll be back."

Chapter 8

Abby walked through the empty store anticipating the arrival of employees and the new manager. Ron's secretary had informed her that a young man would be arriving this morning who would need to work with her a couple of weeks to learn the store's procedures. Abby felt a twinge of doubt when she heard the word "young," wondering if he'd be open to her sentiments about what all Martin's Western Wear meant to her.

Three weeks had passed since Ron left for his ranch in Montana, and she found herself missing him more every day. At first she denied it, but Debbie had forced her to see where her heart lay. Before his departure, he phoned and asked if he could e-mail and call on occasion.

"What a splendid idea," Abby had replied. She wanted to say more but felt like a teen again. They'd spent one day together, but it unearthed years of memories. "I'd like to keep in touch."

"Me, too. Abby, you should have seen the looks on

the board's faces when I announced my rededication to the Lord. Their chins dropped to their chests. I'm sure they think I've gone crazy." He laughed low and she pictured him seated at a massive desk in a conference room lined with business executives.

"Are any of them going with you to Montana?" she asked.

"Oh, no. My trip is personal, which also alarmed them. Now, I'll be labeled a recluse, but I've got a good man here to run things. They'll do just fine, probably better, and can contact me at the ranch if necessary. I have my laptop—don't want to cut off all means of communication."

"But you said you might not be back?" Abby asked. "Are you ill?"

He chuckled. "Spiritually, but not physically. I feel God pulling at me to spend some time alone at the ranch. Whatever He has in mind must require peace and quiet. Who knows? I may collect my social security there." She could tell he was nervous.

"I'll be praying."

"Thanks," he said. "I know this sounds strange, but after one day, I'm going to miss you."

Abby smiled in remembering their parting words. She liked the idea of being missed as much as finally revealing the truth about their younger days. Since that Monday morning, he'd e-mailed every other day and phoned three times. And her heart inched closer to the love of a certain business entrepreneur.

With fifteen minutes remaining before the store

opened, she decided to check her computer for new E-mail. Zack and Zane were better at keeping in touch through cyberspace than picking up the phone, and she was anxious to read Ron's latest.

Scrolling through her messages and responding to those from the boys, she saw one entitled "Montana Sunset."

Hi Abby,

You should have seen the sunset last night. With the mountains for background, God blazed the colors of orange and yellow right across the sky. I'd been out riding at the time and had to stop and drink in all that color. All of a sudden I wished you were here with me.

I love it on the ranch. I've never known such peace and beauty—not since Granddad and I used to watch sunrises and sunsets on his farm. Don't miss Houston at all. Strange, don't you think?

Ron

She reread the post, noting how every message from him grew a little more personal. Clicking reply, she typed back:

Ron,

I'm sitting here in my office, eyes closed, and imagining your solitude, and I'm as jealous as an army of ants overlooking a picnic. And yes, I'd like to see the sunset with you, too.

You'd mentioned a ranch foreman and a few hired hands who take care of your horses and their training. What kind of operation do you have there?

The new manager reports today. Do you suppose I'll have enough patience with him? Pray for me!

Abby

She heard the bell jingle above the front door and saw Candy carry in a box of Whippy Cream donuts. The sight reminded Abby of Maudie's newspaper column after Ron had attended church. The town's columnist had suggested a variety of reasons for him to be visiting his hometown, most of which centered around Abby, although she did squeeze out a rumor about the business tycoon purchasing Martin's Western Wear. If Abby had not felt so good-natured, she'd have given Maudie a piece of her mind about linking the two romantically.

"Let the matter go," Debbie had insisted. "Who believes Maudie anyway? Everyone knows her gossip column is worthless."

Abby nodded. "She writes an ounce of truth and a pound of fabrication."

"But for sure Ron had eyes for only you that Sunday," Debbie continued. "Anything you want to tell me?"

"I've already told you all he and I discussed," Abby replied, feeling Debbie's questioning creep forward.

"But how do *you* feel? Are you two going to pick

up the pieces? Did he kiss you? When will you see him again?"

Abby shielded her face with her hands. "Help, I'm being attacked by an old lady who fires questions like shotgun shells, and this isn't hunting season."

Candy shouted up the stairs interrupting Abby's musings.

"I've got raspberry filled, and there's a gentleman here to see you."

Back to reality, she told herself, but thinking about Ron kept her warm and tingly. Maybe he'd call again tonight.

Ron leaned against a huge rock and opened his Bible. His fingers slipped between the pages until he found Matthew 25:40, the Scripture plaguing him for two weeks: "I tell you the truth, whatever you did for one of the least of these brothers of mine, you did for me."

Ron took a deep breath and lifted his gaze to view the hundreds of breathtaking acres surrounding him—the land God saw fit to give him when he deserved it the least.

The least.

All right, Lord, I'm listening. What do You want me to do? I'm here waiting, trying to be patient when I've never been a patient man. You're the CEO and I'm taking notes.

Some time later he mounted his Appaloosa and picked his way back down the mountainside to the house. Traveling on horseback rather than utilizing one of his expensive vehicles was a humbling experience. His muscles could testify to that.

Once he took care of business in Houston, he phoned Abby. He wanted to see how she handled her first week at home, plus he had a rehearsed speech prepared for the lady.

The phone rang several times, and when he'd given up hope of talking to her, she picked it up.

"Good morning, Sunshine. How's the lady of leisure doing?"

Abby laughed lightly. "She's pulling weeds before it gets too hot."

"I see. Everything's okay then?"

"If you mean my early retirement, I'm fine—a little antsy perhaps but not ready to slip on down to the store and check on things. By the way, the new fellow is capable and personable, and I thank you."

"Good," he breathed and trudged forward. "Have you listed your house, yet?"

"As a matter of fact, no. I wanted to do a little painting and fixin' up first. Why?"

Ron sensed his heart taking leave of his body. Big business was nothing compared to this. "Would you hold off a little while until we have a chance to talk face-to-face? In fact," he said, hoping she couldn't detect his labored breathing. "I'd like to fly in to see you the end of next week, if you don't mind."

"Wonderful. I'd love to see you. The boys and their wives will be here for the weekend, too, and this way you could meet all of them."

He smiled. He should acquaint himself with Abby's sons. "I'll call you when I get into town on Friday afternoon."

As he replaced the phone and powered up his laptop for a few hours of online research, a stab of apprehension seized him. God had outlined a huge project and given Ron the blueprints.

Less than two weeks later, Ron drove to Abby's. He glanced back at the stack of files, pictures, and recommendations from professionals all over the country. He could only pray Abby would fall in love with his plans. . . and the new Ron Bassinger.

His corporate board meeting had exploded in tension when he announced his decision to step down from Bassinger Enterprises, but he didn't care. They'd continue to make their money under the careful supervision of qualified personnel.

When he stopped in front of Abby's brick home and flipped off the ignition, uneasiness wound around his nerves. Odd, he held the reputation as one of the most ruthless businessmen in the country, and he feared one little red-haired woman.

Gathering up his paraphernalia, he armed his SUV and braved the steps to Abby's door. Her sons were visiting friends—fortunate for him that he had her attention.

Abby grinned in the doorway, a denim sundress hugging her petite curves. He couldn't wait to collect his long overdue hug, and it didn't help that her perfume drove him to distraction or the fact he held a bundle of papers in his arms.

She ushered him into the kitchen where he set his load on the table and held her close. Abby fit right next to his heart, where she'd always been.

"Montana life suits you," she said and shuddered just a little.

"Thanks. And so do you."

She reddened, and he braved forward, feeling more confident. "If you have the time, I'd like to show you what God's been up to in the north."

She nodded at the mound of papers on her table and laughed. "And this is part of it?"

"The beginnings," he replied. "But I'm excited."

They chatted while he positioned files, stats, and a huge drawing of his ranch. He asked her to take a chair.

"For the presentation?" she asked, folding her hands neatly in her lap.

"Humor me, Lady." He chuckled. "This is serious stuff."

Rubbing the palms of his hands together, an old habit for good luck, he began. "First of all thank you for answering all my E-mails and listening to me ramble on the phone. It meant a lot. You had asked me about my ranch in Montana. It operates solely to breed quarter horses. The foreman is a great horseman, and the place works efficiently without me. It's the perfect spot for a retreat, which is exactly what God has called me to do."

He paced across her kitchen and for the first time detected the scent of paint. Obviously, she was preparing her house to sell. "During the first six weeks there, I spent my time in Bible study and prayer—getting reacquainted with the Lord in an attempt to make up for lost time. I sensed He had plans for me, but I had no clue what. So I waited and waited until He revealed to me the most astounding idea." He shook his head. "Certainly nothing like my ventures in the past. This," he said, pointing to the paperwork, "is the beginning of a youth camp."

"A youth camp?" she asked and leaned forward to peer at his drawings.

"Yes, a place for underprivileged teens to visit for a summer and find God. They can learn to ride and properly care for horses, hike, fish, practice wilderness skills, and work as a team on a variety of ranch type projects, but most importantly, they will learn who God is and what He wants for their lives."

"Oh, Ron," she managed, as emotion appeared to overcome her. "This gives me chills. And you're going to fund this project?"

"I'm going to live there," he said proudly. "I'm turning over my control of Bassinger Enterprises to one of my top men and living out the rest of my days serving the Lord at Trinity Ranch. You know, to be a part of changing young people's lives is, as the kids say, awesome."

"I don't know what to say," she said, standing to study his drawings. "Except congratulations."

Ron pointed out the various buildings already there and the bunkhouses and lodge he envisioned. "I don't know why I had to bring in all this data. Didn't have to sell you on a thing."

"Of course not," she said, the sparkle in her eyes dancing. "I'm envious."

"Oh, you don't need to be," he said, praying for the right words to continue. He placed both arms on her shoulders. "I had a selfish reason for asking you not to sell your home just yet." He swallowed hard. "Abby, I can't do this thing alone; I don't want to do it alone. And I know an E-mail courtship is not a substitute for the real thing, but I'd like for us to pray about spending the rest of our lives together. I love you, Abby; I've never stopped loving you."

"Ron." Her eyes widened.

"Don't tell me no right now. I'm willing to fly here every weekend until you're ready to say yes." He smiled. "This time I want to court you God's way. And I'll build you any house you want, give you anything you want—"

She covered his mouth with her hand. "I never wanted those things before, and I certainly don't need them now. What I want is your heart. And I see yours is with the Lord. How could I ask for more?"

"But this means leaving Texas, starting your life over with me far away from your family and friends."

"I've lived right here in this little community all my life. It's time I moved on to a real adventure."

"Are you sure, Abby? Really sure? I don't want you to have any regrets."

"I've done a lot of thinking while you were gone,

and I believe God put us together again for a reason. For some reason, I couldn't picture myself living on my land—no matter how hard I tried, plus I've discovered I need to be around people." She glanced at the papers. "Looks like I could be around a lot of people."

He gathered her up in his arms and pulled her to his chest. "I haven't kissed you in over thirty years," he whispered.

"Have you forgotten how?" she asked sweetly, brushing the side of his face with her fingertips.

"I don't think so, but I'll need a lot of practice—enough to last a lifetime."

DIANN MILLS

DiAnn lives in Houston, Texas, with her husband Dean. They have four adult sons. She wrote from the time she could hold a pencil, but not seriously until God made it clear that she should write for Him. After three years of serious writing, her first book, *Rehoboth*, won favorite **Heartsong Presents** historical for 1998. Other publishing credits include magazine articles and short stories, devotionals, poetry, and internal writing for her church. She also conducts writing workshops and speaks to various groups. She is an active church choir member, leads a ladies' Bible study, and is a church librarian. She is also an active board member with the American Christian Romance Writers organization.

November Nocturne

by Dianna Crawford

Chapter 1

Jill Lawrence wasn't usually the impatient sort, but this was ridiculous. Glancing at her watch, she rose from one of the many blue vinyl chairs lining a cavernous waiting section of the Dallas airport. Ten past five.

At that moment yet another flash of lightning streaked down from dark roiling clouds. Quite a spectacular one, really, she conceded, as she watched through floor to ceiling windows overlooking the tarmac.

But the lightning was unappreciated by her and the crowds of other grounded passengers. A collective groan echoed along the long corridor, competing with the roll of thunder outside. Her plane's takeoff had already been delayed an hour, and other flights had been waiting even longer. Airliners were parked at every port.

All because they were not allowed to fuel during an electric storm.

The powers that be had no problem scaring her half to death on the flight from Virginia when the 727 started bucking like a wild bronc as it pierced the thick thunderclouds above Arkansas. No one seemed the least worried about an airliner flying through streaks of lightning at thirty thousand feet loaded with highly flammable fuel. No, they just wouldn't fuel one sitting safely on the ground.

She looked at her watch again. She had a twelve-hour shift at the hospital tomorrow morning, and every hour she was delayed from continuing on to Los Angeles meant one less she'd have for sleep tonight.

"Jack Van Fleet," blared over the loudspeakers. "Please report to Delta Flight 268 Check-in Desk."

Another irrelevant announcement in a long, irritating string. Only one announcement would interest Jill. . . the one that stated she could board the plane languishing outside.

"Jack Van Fleet," the loudspeakers repeated.

Jack Van Fleet? The name broke through her frustration. Could it be?

Jill swung away from the plate glass to take a look at whoever approached the counter. She hadn't seen her childhood friend since they were fourteen years old. Almost thirty years ago. Even if it was her Jack, would she recognize him?

A tall, rather thin man in a business suit approached the boarding counter. Graying at the temples and with a slight slouch to his shoulders, he did look to be somewhere in his forties, but the last time she'd seen Jack, he'd been nowhere near this one's six-foot-plus height. She'd been a good two inches taller than Jack when, as high school freshmen, they'd said their last wrenching good-bye.

Jill turned back to the windows. In a couple of months it would be thirty years, but suddenly, every memory of him was as clear as if he'd left only yesterday.

Jack and Jill, their mothers had named them when the two neighbors had given birth within thirty-six hours of each other. It had been merely good-natured humor among friends. But for the children, growing up next door to one another had created a bond they thought could never be broken. They'd played and fought and dreamed all their dreams together. And plans. . .they'd made and changed so many plans those growing up years. But one, in particular, they'd never changed. He would become a doctor, she his nurse, and they'd spend the rest of their lives helping the sick and injured.

Jill couldn't count the times she'd wondered if he'd actually gone on to medical school as she had nursing. She shouldn't have stopped writing to him. So what if his father had been transferred to the oil fields of Ethiopia, then took his family even farther away to Saudi Arabia. Surely Jack, if not the others, would have returned someday. But to an impatient teenager even that first year had seemed like an eternity. Their letters to each other became less and less frequent until, by the end of the second year, she gave up corresponding and moved on with her so-called life. Her girlfriends kept reminding her, *You're in high school only once. Don't waste this time on someone who may never return.*

But looking back from this much wiser age, she

knew her youthful impatience had cost her so much more than just her teen years.

She prayed her son's youthful decision to join the navy right out of high school wouldn't end up haunting his future as her own foolish decisions had hers.

Wishing the tall man at the counter had actually been Jack Van Fleet, Jill took a second look.

He must've said something humorous. The young uniformed woman behind the counter spurted into laughter.

He turned away smiling.

And Jill's heart literally lurched. He had Jack's unmistakable deep dimples—the ones he'd inherited from his Kewpie doll mother. He must've shot up like a weed after Jill last saw him. Of course. . .the way her son, Steven, had after he turned sixteen.

She headed straight for her oldest friend.

🐃

Jack got a kick out of the fact that he'd managed to wipe the defensive gloom from the airline employee's face. She'd been taking the brunt of the Los Angeles-bound passengers' impatience since he'd first reached this crowded waiting area. Turning away, he smiled. The young woman's infectious giggle helped make up for him getting stuck on a milk run from D.C. instead of drawing a nonstop flight.

He shrugged off his ingratitude. After all, the government was picking up the tab. Besides, unlike most of these Americans, he was used to waiting.

An attractive woman with straight blond hair came

toward the desk. He hoped she wouldn't wipe the smile from the worker's lips. From the questioning expression in the blond's clear blue eyes, he couldn't be sure what she had in mind.

She stopped short of the counter, directly in front of him, blocking the path back to his seat. "Jack Van Fleet? That is your name, isn't it?"

"Yes. . . ." There was something familiar about her, but for the life of him, he couldn't place her. Had she been at the conference? In that trim black pantsuit and white-cuffed pinstriped shirt, she certainly looked as prosperous as all the rest of the American doctors he'd encountered.

"From Bakersfield, California?" she added urgently.

Jack frowned. "How would you know that?"

"It really *is* you!" An amazing smile lit up her face, and she clutched onto his arms. "I'm Jill. Jill Lawrence—Jill Preston, back then. We lived next door for a long time. Remember? Jack and Jill ran up the hill to fetch a pail of water?"

Jack couldn't believe his ears. Or his eyes. Before him stood a really fine looking woman who appeared no older than her early thirties, yet she claimed to be his Jill. If she was, she had to be his age. Forty-four.

Squeezing his arms, she frowned. "Surely you have not forgotten the first fourteen years of your life."

It was her! *"Jill."* Overwhelmed with emotion, he hauled her to him, hugging her, patting her back, hugging her tighter.

By the time he pulled away enough to look into her

face, he couldn't see past his blur of tears.

She was laughing and crying, too, as she let go long enough to wipe at her own stream. Abruptly, she glanced around, self-conscious. "The way we're acting, people will think we haven't seen each other since the beginning of time."

"Well, we haven't," he reminded, his voice a hoarse whisper.

"You're right." She grabbed hold again, her moist blue eyes searching his face. "We really are long-lost friends, aren't we?"

"Too long lost. Much too long." He pulled her close again, reluctant to ever let go. He couldn't believe he'd found her after all these years and in this most unlikely of places—a waiting room halfway between Washington and LA. Jill, his Jill, with the silky blond hair. He breathed deeply of its faintly perfumed freshness.

Before Jack was quite ready, Jill eased away and stepped back, her hands still gripping his coat sleeves. Her ring finger was bare—something he noted before returning his gaze to a face that was still as evenly tanned as ever. The lucky girl, he remembered, had never burned no matter how long they'd stayed out in the sun.

"You've grown," she remarked as she looked up at him.

"And you've *grown up*. Quite beautifully, too."

"Why, thank you," she said with an uncharacteristically shy smile. "The credit really goes to my daughters. They refused to let me fly to my son's graduation looking like an old frump."

Daughters? A son? Of course. Despite the lack of a wedding ring, she had used another last name when she'd first spoken. Jack tried not to show his disappointment. "I seriously doubt you could ever look like a frump," he said as lightly as he could manage.

She chuckled, that uniquely throaty laugh he hadn't heard since. . .forever. "You've yet to see me after I've come off three twelve-hour shifts in a row. I did go into nursing, by the way. What about you?"

"Just call me Doc," he said, pleased, though still wondering about her bare finger.

A thrilled smile spread to her eyes. "You did it, too. You went into medicine. What's your specialty? Where do you practice?"

Her enthusiasm was contagious. Still, he didn't want to answer just yet, not until he knew more about her. "I take it you're waiting for the flight to LA, too. Let's see if we can get seats together. Then we'll have plenty of time to catch up on each other's lives."

"You do the asking. I'm sure you and your dimples are still just as good at charming the ladies into giving you anything you want."

Not always, he thought, fully aware of all the years the two of them had lost. Not always.

Chapter 2

Jill contemplated pinching herself to make sure she was awake as she waited several steps behind, watching Jack speak to the airline attendant about seating them together. She couldn't be more pleased that he'd retained some of the youthful exuberance that, as a girl, she'd thought a touch immature.

The counter clerk appeared no less affected by his charm, as the young woman gave him a smile and her rapt attention. Jill had no doubt he would come away with new seating assignments.

Then Jill's better sense took hold. It had been decades since she'd known anything about him for sure. And as the worker handed him new boarding passes, he was proving before Jill's very eyes just how persuasive he could be. To what ends did he now use that ability?

But when the tall, lanky man turned back toward her with such a disarmingly open grin, she decided not to ruin this happiest of reunions with unfounded suspicions. Besides, to look at him, it was clear that his boyish charm hadn't even managed to get him enough food to fill out his frame. Noticing he wasn't wearing a wedding band, she figured he was probably in need of a steady dose of good home-cooked meals.

Or was she just letting her foolish heart run away with her head? She needed to know more about him—much more.

As he handed her one of the new boarding passes, she took the lead toward a scarce pair of empty seats. "Since you're on your way to LA, is that where your practice is?" Only a mere hundred miles from Bakersfield, she wanted to add.

"No. Actually, I'm on my way to Bakersfield. Believe it or not, my folks have just moved back there to retire."

"Really? When? They haven't contacted any of us. Mom would've told me."

Jack caught her hand. "Then, you all still live there." He looked honestly pleased.

"Yes. Compared to your family, I suppose we're just a bunch of ol' sticks-in-the-mud."

"This is great, just great!" Reaching the empty seats, he sat in one, pulling her down beside him before he let go of her hand. "We'll have more chances to see one another while I'm visiting. I can't tell you what this means to me. Tell me, you mentioned some children, I'd like to meet them, too. And your husband, of course."

My husband. . . . So quickly Jack would learn about her biggest mistake, her worst failure. "You'll be able to meet my girls while you're in town, Rochelle and Melissa, but my youngest, Steven, has joined the navy. Fact is, I'm returning from seeing him at Norfolk Naval Base in Virginia. This will be his first Thanksgiving away from home." She paused long enough to brush a strand of hair away from her face while taking what she hoped was an unnoticed calming breath. "As for a husband, well, I'm afraid I don't have one. He left us when the kids were small and a few years later, he died of hypothermia while working up on the Alaskan pipeline."

"Froze to death, hmm. . . ." Jack's voice conveyed his compassion.

She wondered what his reaction would have been if she'd included the fact that Randy had passed out from too much booze on his way home from a bar. He'd lain unnoticed a few feet from his front door in fifteen below weather until the following morning.

Jack tilted his head, as he always used to do when he was puzzled. "I find it hard to believe anyone would ever willingly leave you."

"You'd be surprised," she replied across a harsh laugh. "No, really, it just came down to we wanted different things. I wanted a husband who put his family first. You know, one who came straight home from work, one who would—if not be the spiritual head of the house—at least be willing to go to church with us on Sunday. But he was more interested in having a good time with his drinking buddies. He just never seemed to get past that."

Jack laced lean fingers through hers as his expressive hazel eyes searched her own. "That's too bad."

She gave his hand a squeeze and pulled away. "Not

so terribly bad." She didn't want him to think of her as some pitiful creature. "I've been blessed with three really superb kids. And, I don't mean to sound over-religious, but the Lord has really been there for us. He's always seen us through."

"Hey, be as religious as you want. I love it when people brag on what God has done in their lives."

Was he putting her on, or was he for real? She couldn't be sure. "I've been doing all the 'fessing up so far. It's your turn. What about you? Are you married? Children? Where've you been for the last thirty years?"

Jack sat back in his chair. "I have two sons." He grinned. "They're a couple of real characters."

He had a family. Of course. What else should I expect?

"I wish I could've brought them with me." Jack reached inside his jacket and pulled out a small manila envelope. "I've got pictures. Lots of 'em to show Mom and Dad."

Taking the container, Jill opened the end flap and pulled out at least two dozen snapshots, more interested in seeing the woman he'd married than his children.

In what looked like a tropical background, the first photo had a dark-skinned boy of twelve or thirteen with large, almost black eyes and a flashing grin. The only thing about the shorts-clad youth that even remotely resembled Jack were his long legs and arms. Beside him stood a smaller boy whose skin looked all the browner because at least half of his limbs and head were wrapped in white bandages.

"Oh, was that picture on top?" Jack rasped a chuckle.

"Poor Manny," he said, pointing to the bandaged one. "It's the price he pays for being Tipu's younger brother. Tipu plans to be a doctor like his old man, so he's honing his bandaging skills. And Manuel is his guinea pig—like how you were mine. Remember?"

Jill flashed a smile of recollection, then started shuffling through the other photos, hunting again for his wife. But his wife wasn't there. Jill glanced up at Jack. "Didn't you bring a picture of their mother?"

He placed a hand over hers, thwarting any further search. "They don't have the same mother. . .or father, for that matter. I adopted Tipu in India when I was working at a mission hospital there. And I adopted Manny in the Philippines. When I came to the States for this medical conference, they wanted to come, but they would've missed too much school."

Still no mention of a Mrs. Van Fleet. "In the care of your wife, I trust," she further prodded.

His grin turned maddeningly smug. "To answer your question, Jill, no, I am not married. Never have been. You see, not too many women think mosquitoes, bed pans, and jungle rot are really all that romantic."

As Jack brought Jill up to date on his years in India and the Philippines, Jill couldn't help the deep sense of loss that overtook her. And disappointment in herself. He'd remained true to his dream and his convictions. Not only had he become a doctor but a missionary. He hadn't let himself be swayed from what he'd felt was his calling, despite the fact he'd moved from place to place as a teen. He hadn't sacrificed his dream just because it seemed too difficult or because he was lonely as she had been. Nor had he taken it upon himself to marry as a quick fix.

Feeling rather noble at the time, Jill had married Randy Lawrence after an accident had forced her dad into early retirement. Not only was she attracted to the football hero, she'd wanted to relieve her parents of the financial burden of her nurse's training. Too her it had seemed the perfect solution, even though she knew Randy wasn't a committed Christian. And, fool that she was, she'd convinced herself he'd change for her.

What a costly error in judgment. "Wait on the Lord" had long since become her motto. Wait for God's leading.

And she had done just that to the best of her ability these past sixteen years since Randy walked out. But now, sitting here beside her was the living, breathing reminder of what her fear and impatience had cost her. And of what might have been.

"Since we always have more patients than we can handle," he was saying, "and being so far from America, we're always running out of something. So we've gotten pretty good at improvising. But with AIDS spreading so rapidly. . ." He sighed. "That's why I'm here. I've been to an international conference on the disease. But enough about that," he said, his boyish dimples back. "Tell me about you. Do you have any pictures of your kids?"

"Actually, I'm more of a proud grandmother these days." Jill reached for her shoulder bag.

"*Grandmother? You?* That's impossible."

"That's very flattering," she answered lightly while digging for her wallet, "but if you do the numbers, it's really quite possible. Here, here it is." Withdrawing a small print of a studio portrait, she handed the latest picture of her towheaded darlings to Jack. "The oldest, Matthew is two and a half and such a serious little man. The questions never stop. And this is Mark," she said, pointing to the baby. "He's nine months and already walking. Into everything. And there's a glint in his eye that says, 'Look out, I'm going to take a whole lot of watching.'"

"They really are cute. And blond like their grandmother." His dark gaze brushed across her hair before returning to the picture. "I suppose, being a nurse, you don't get to see them as often as you'd like."

"Actually, I sometimes think I see them too much. My daughter and I trade off taking care of them. Rochelle is an obstetrics nurse, like me, and we each work three twelve-hour shifts a week. We schedule our days off opposite each other so the babies never have to be taken to a sitter—that was my biggest regret when I was raising my own children, leaving them with strangers."

"I see." There was a tinge of disappointment in his voice as he returned the picture. "But I'll bet it sure keeps you busy."

"Hey," she said, turning more directly toward him. "Not too busy that I can't squeeze in some time for my oldest friend while he's in town. In fact, why don't you and your parents join us for Thanksgiving dinner?

Mom and Dad would be thrilled, too. Do say you'll come. You can meet my brood. Rochelle has switched days, so even she'll be there."

"Sounds great, but I don't know. I'll have to ask the folks."

"Delta Flight 268 ready to board," came over the loudspeaker.

The waiting area erupted into clapping and shouts of joy as everyone rushed to grab their carry-ons and get in line. . .everyone except Jill. As far as she was concerned, the longer it took to reach Los Angeles, the better.

~

"Hope you don't mind that I requested seats at an emergency exit instead of by a window," Jack said as they settled in aboard the jumbo jet. He stretched out his long legs. "I need the extra room."

"No, this is wonderful." Turning toward him, she leaned against the bulkhead and curled one leg up beneath her. "With all the clouds there wouldn't be anything to see anyway."

All the better for him to concentrate on every graceful aspect of this elegantly beautiful woman he couldn't quite believe his friend had become. Realizing he was staring, he started to ask her about the hospital where she worked, but her attention shifted to a young woman walking past holding a baby bundled in pink.

"I hope the pressure changes don't hurt the little one's ears," Jill remarked.

"You and the rest of us." A crying babe could make

the trip miserable for everyone within hearing distance. "Speaking of baby girls, we've had one at the hospital for several months, now. And I've really grown attached to her. Her mother wasn't married, and when we told her Lucena needed heart surgery, she said she couldn't be responsible for her any longer. She took off, and she's never come back for her daughter. Lucena has had her surgery and is doing fine now. She could go home, but we can't locate her mother."

"You can't just keep the baby at the hospital indefinitely, can you?"

"No. But at the same time, I don't want to give my little Lucy up to strangers either. She's had such a hard time of it, and there's just something about her. . . . If you could see those dark round eyes light up every time I drop by to see her. . .her cute gap-toothed grin. She's such a sweetheart."

"If you feel that way, why don't you adopt her, like you did the boys?"

"I've given that a lot of thought. But I really don't think I should try to raise a girl by myself. You know, there's all that female stuff they need to learn about."

"*Female stuff.* You're a doctor. Surely, you could handle a few female questions."

"I may be a doctor at the hospital, but at home I'm just your average bumbling male. I really feel I should get married before I adopt her. Lucy deserves to have a mother."

Jill shot him a disturbingly unreadable look.

"I'm not saying this right. There's a woman who

teaches at the American school who I'm pretty sure would say yes if I asked her to marry me. She's in her thirties, and we seem to gravitate to one another whenever I find time to attend the American colony get-togethers. She's a great gal and all. And she's dropped a few hints. But I don't know."

"Are you saying you don't find her attractive?" Jill probed.

"No, that's not the problem. It's, well, she comes to church fairly regularly, but I get the feeling it's more of a social thing than anything else for her. I could be wrong. But, so far, I just don't sense she's God's choice for me. No matter how much I'd like to adopt Lucy."

Jill leaned forward. "Then don't do it." She sounded sure, almost adamant. "I married because at the time it seemed like the sensible thing to do. I should have prayed about it, asked for the Lord's leading. But I just assumed it was the right thing. And don't forget, if it doesn't work out, it's not just you and your lady friend. You have two boys to consider." She leaned back again. "By the way, who's taking care of your children while you're away?"

"I have a Filipino housekeeper. She's really good to them. But she's older and isn't at all receptive to the idea of taking on a baby."

"Babies are a lot of work, but it sounds like you and your Lucy are meant for each other. Maybe you could hire someone else to help your housekeeper." Then Jill absently caught her lower lip in her thumb and finger and gave him a sidelong glance—the same as she used to do when she was a kid. "If you're sure, that is, that the schoolteacher isn't God's will for you. Being a bachelor so long, you may just be having a case of cold feet."

Leave it to Jill to go straight for the jugular. Jack shifted into a more comfortable position. "I don't know about having cold feet. But one thing I do know. You and I didn't meet again just by accident. There's got to be much more to it than that."

Chapter 3

What did Jack mean by that? *You and I didn't meet again just by accident.*

Jack burst out laughing. "Relax, I haven't been stalking you. What I'm saying is, I think God wants me to take another look at my *benchmark*. Through the years, I've measured every woman I met by you."

"Me? But we were just kids when you left for Ethiopia."

"Not that young. But since we were raised as close as brother and sister. . ." He shrugged, looking a bit embarrassed. "I never did manage to work up my nerve to come right out and say the words. I always just assumed we'd get married someday."

"No, I didn't know that, but I did, too."

"Really?" He looked pleased, relieved. "Well, anyway, after we were separated, my imagination started working overtime. I dreamed up this super-woman I was sure you'd turn out to be. You know, smart, clever, compassionate. . .beautiful. No one else has ever managed to knock my image of you off that pedestal I built.

Lately, I've been trying to convince myself to get realistic, stop letting my romantic ideal cloud what could be God's true plan for me. But here you are, more gorgeous than even I imagined."

Jill felt the heat coming into her cheeks. "Don't get carried away. What you see is not the real me. I usually pay little attention to my looks. My daughters took me shopping before I left on this trip. Got my hair cut, updated my makeup. The poor dears didn't want their drudge of a mother to embarrass their brother at his graduation from the navy's radar school."

"You could no more be a drudge than. . . In fact, I want to make up for lost time. I want to see pictures of you from the time I left up till now. There's so much to catch up on and so little time."

"When do you fly back to the Philippines?"

"The day after Thanksgiving."

"So soon? That's less than a week."

"I know."

"Your folks must have pictures of you, too. I especially want to see when you grew that extra foot."

"You've got a deal. But for now, I very much need for you to tell me your every fault, your every annoying habit. A mother for my Lucy may very well depend on it."

"Nothing like putting pressure on a girl."

🐃

After spending just this short time with Jill, Jack couldn't imagine anything she might say that would chip off any of her perfection. He was already just as in love with her as he'd ever been. More, considering all the years he'd been deprived of her company. But he couldn't let himself get caught up in some schoolboy fantasy. Three decades of living and eight thousand miles separated them. But there she sat with that same lively light in her deep blue eyes, that same air of expectancy.

"Well," she said, taking on a rather serious look. "If you must know, I guess my latest imperfection was trying to keep Steven under my wing. I argued long and hard to keep him from joining the navy right out of high school. I felt it would be much safer for him to keep living at home and go to college. But, my fears seem to be unfounded. He looked fine, better than fine, and very handsome in his dress uniform."

"That doesn't sound like a fault, just a genuine concern. Surely you can do better than that. Give me one of your annoying habits."

"Annoying habits. Let's see. . . . Oh, yes. I still love to chew ice. The sound still drives everyone crazy."

"That's not even worth mentioning. Try again."

Jill caught her lower lip again, reminding Jack of the statue of *The Thinker*. Only, of course, she was much prettier.

Then the light bulbs in her eyes clicked on again. "Whenever I'm passionately for or against something, I try to make others see things as I do. I write letters to the editor. You know, become obnoxious."

He shrugged. "Hey, as long as they're the same beliefs as mine, I've got no problem with that."

"Yes, but they may not be, and I can be very stubborn when I think I'm right."

"What's new? You always were a bit of a crusader. And as determined as me. You wanted to be a nurse, and you are one. So, let's get back to more of the ice-chewing stuff. But something really annoying this time. Do you—"

"No. It's your turn. I've already given three. It's only fair that you should have to confess one of your quirks for every one of mine."

"No problem. I've got plenty. But, as for yours, I wish I had more ice to chew on in the tropics. With me, it's gum, spearmint. My nurse gets really uptight about my chewing it, especially in the operating room."

"The operating room?"

"Yeah, and she gets that same crimp you've got above your nose right now, every time she catches me. She always makes me spit it out."

"I should hope so."

"My, aren't we being judgmental all of a sudden. By the way, how's your Scrabble game? Do you still cheat?"

Jill stiffened with mock indignation. "Just because I'm not always the best at adding up the score doesn't mean I cheat."

"I've gotten pretty good at the game." He sent her his smuggest smile. "I'll bet I can take you even with your *creative* score-keeping."

❧

Into the darkness the plane flew, and time flew even faster as Jill watched Jack as much as listened while he brought her up to date on his younger brothers, relayed a few anecdotes of happenings at his hospital, talked about the people, the culture, the persecution of Christians on the Muslim-dominated outer islands.

She mentioned it wasn't always that popular to be a Christian in America anymore, either, especially for those who took the Bible at its word. She then caught him up on her own family by conveying the details of the accident that put her dad in a wheelchair, told Jack her own younger brother had followed in her father's footsteps and was working for an oil drilling company. They talked about their children, their churches. . .and before Jill knew it, the plane's wheels were touching down at LAX. This precious interlude with her oldest and dearest friend was coming to an end.

Or maybe not. "Jack," she asked, unbuckling her seat belt, "how were you planning to get to Bakersfield from here?"

"Rent a car."

"I know mission doctors aren't exactly rolling in dough, and it is over a hundred miles, so why don't you save your money. Let me drive you home. I left my car in an overnight parking lot."

"Haven't had a better offer all day—all week, for that matter." His warm, comfortably familiar grin confirmed his words.

After collecting their luggage, they took a shuttle bus, along with a few other passengers, about a mile from the airport to a sprawling and poorly lit parking lot. The bus driver drove down the rows, letting people off. When it reached the section where Jill had parked her car, she hollered for the driver to stop for them.

When the bus departed, Jack, his bags in hand, glanced around. He looked none too happy. "If I hadn't come, you'd be out here all alone."

"My car is right over there," Jill explained as she set down her largest piece of luggage to point toward her white Ford.

"A lone woman shouldn't be out here by herself." He picked up her weekender, adding it to his own pieces. "Or drive all the way to Bakersfield alone. Especially this late at night."

"If the plane had been on time, it wouldn't be quite so late."

"It still would've been dark when you arrived." Jack's voice sounded deadly hard. "Your brother or one of your sons-in-law should have picked you up."

"Oh, I'm sure they would've if I'd asked them to. But that would've been awfully inconvenient. Especially considering our two-and-a-half-hour delay."

"*They should have been here,*" he repeated with angry force.

Jill stopped at the rear of her car and pulled out her keys, glad for the excuse to halt the discordant exchange. He was exposing a new side of himself she didn't care for at all.

In silence, they filled the trunk with their luggage.

Once they'd finished, he asked, "Are the LA freeways still as crazy as ever?" To Jill's relief, his tone had now lost its bite.

"Pretty much," she said, hoping that wouldn't bring on another onslaught of condemnation toward her male relatives. "From here to the mountains it can get *really interesting.*" She started for her car door.

"If you'd like, I could drive. I'm used to Manila's traffic which, shall we say, is even more creative. You might even be able to catch a nap once you've pointed me in the right direction."

An offer she couldn't refuse now that he was his affable self again. Still, as she directed him out of the parking lot and onto the nearby freeway, she couldn't shake her uneasiness at his flare of temper. Which was the real Jack Van Fleet?

Once they were safely in the flow of northbound traffic and several miles up the road, Jack turned to her. "I'm sorry. I know I upset you."

"I—uh—" She didn't know how to respond without blurting the truth. Her knight's shining armor had exposed an ugly chink.

"Last week, just as I arrived at the airport for my flight to the States, a couple of ambulance drivers were tending a young woman who'd been attacked and raped on her way to her car. Her mouth was bloody, her clothes all ripped, and she was hysterical, and—"

Jill stopped him with a hand to his arm. "I understand." And she truly did. "In our profession, we see much more than the average person. It makes us a lot more aware of how fragile life can be."

"And precious." With extra meaning in his voice, Jack glanced at her.

With that, his perfection was fully restored, and more. She knew his burst of anger had been brought on by his desire to protect her. It had been a long time since a man had thought of her in that way.

"I know you said you aren't married." Had Jack read her mind? "But as attractive as you are," he said, changing lanes, "you must have at least one man interested in you. Probably several. Are any of them invited to Thanksgiving dinner?"

Did she hear a touch of uncertainty in his tone? "I'm afraid I'm not the heart-stopper you seem to think I am," she joked. "Seriously, I am asked out now and then, but I haven't felt I had the time to get caught up in a romance. Not with three children to raise in an age of drugs and body-piercing and free sex. I've been kept really busy, between the kids and work. I just thank God we attend a church that's always had a vital youth ministry. I can't tell you what a joy it is to know my oldest daughter is now an RN like me and that Melissa is in her first year of teaching school. And, more important, both are in what I trust are good Christ-led marriages. I've been concerned for Steven, though. You know, I thought he might go off the deep end once he got away from his nag of a mother. But I'm beginning to think he'll be all right, too. When he took me to his church on base, the pastor knew him personally and mentioned that Steven had volunteered to coach a kids' basketball team."

"That's great, Jill. Sounds like you've done a wonderful job and can start relaxing. Speaking of that. . ."

Was he going to make a definite date with her? Jill's heart gave an extra thump.

"The freeway signs are easy to follow. I think I can get us out of here without your help. Why don't you take a nap? You did say you had to be at the hospital by seven in the morning, didn't you?"

She glanced at the clock on the dashboard. Ten forty-five. And she'd been up since 6:30 AM, Eastern time. "Yes, that would be a help," she said, adjusting her seat-back to a lower slant. Still, she was disappointed. She would've preferred a different kind of invitation—one that brought them together tomorrow.

Settling back, Jill knew she was probably reading much more into this chance meeting than she should. A week from now he'd be out of her life again, on his way back to the Philippines. It was best to keep things light, casual.

"Jill, one more thing, and I'll let you sleep."

Expectant despite her better judgment, she glanced up at his profile silhouetted in the lights of oncoming vehicles. "Yes?"

"I just wanted to say again how very much I've enjoyed spending this evening with you and how pleased I am that, though we've been separated by three decades and thousands of miles, we've aged in the very same direction. Jack and Jill, still going up the same hill. . . together." He turned his head her way.

Though she couldn't see his eyes clearly, she felt the warmth that would be in them. . .a warmth that coursed straight through her, all the way to her heart—even if he hadn't asked to see her again before Thanksgiving—three whole days away.

Chapter 4

The aroma of coffee and thoughts of Jill had pulled Jack out of the cozy warmth of his guest room bed. By the time he'd dressed, the tantalizing smell of frying bacon was added to the mix. Stomach growling, he walked into the open living area of his parents' new home and headed straight for the U-shaped kitchen space. Yellow curtains at the window over the sink lent a sunny glow and brightened the fading strawberry of his mother's short feathered hair.

Though his petite mother at sixty-three looked a little older than the last time he'd visited his parents in Houston, she still had her amazing energy as she turned the pork with one hand while checking the oven with the other.

"Morning, Mom."

She swung toward him, her Kewpie doll smile in full display. "You're up! I knew the breakfast smells would bring you out. And so skinny. I'm going to put as many pounds on you as I can before you have to go back. Pour yourself a cup of coffee. And there are some persimmon cookies to hold you till the food's ready." She nodded toward a sunflower-glazed cookie jar.

Mom and her men. He never received a package from her that didn't include baked goods. While he was growing up, the one great purpose of her life had always been to make sure her husband and three boys were well-fed and sleeping in what she called proper beds, no matter what corner of the world she found herself in. And she'd always done this in an immaculate house with her makeup on and her clothes perfectly coordinated. The woman would've put Donna Reed to shame.

Jack leaned down and gave her a peck on the cheek and headed for the coffeepot. "I need to take you back to the Philippines with me. I've got two boys who've never tasted your famous sour cream pie."

"Not even in your dreams. I'm back home, and I'm staying right here for the rest of my life. My own walls to paint and paper again to my heart's content."

Women were born nesters, and his mother had been abundantly blessed with that particular instinct. That realization spurred his curiosity about another aspect of Jill. Was she as tied to her house as she was to her kids? He hoped not.

Just as he was about to mention his chance meeting with Jill, his dad, an older, slightly heavier version of himself, sans the dimples, walked in the front door, newspaper in hand. He smiled at seeing Jack. "Ah, you're up," he said in his congenial, unhurried way. "You got in so late, I thought you'd sleep in."

"No, I couldn't do that. I don't want to waste what little time we have together." Cup and the spicy cookies in hand, Jack took a seat at a cloth-draped round table flanked by corner windows. They overlooked a precisely manicured front yard—a yard that attested to the fact that Mom was keeping Dad busy after his retirement from being a petroleum engineer.

"I know you'll want to see the schools you went to," his dad said, "and our old house. We'll take a drive first thing after breakfast. The town's grown into quite the city. You'll hardly recognize it."

"Speaking of that, you'll never guess who I ran into at the Dallas airport. Jill Preston—Jill Lawrence now."

His mother spun toward him with a dripping spatula. "Bill and Paulette's daughter?"

"The one and only."

"Oh dear. You told her we've moved here, didn't you?"

"We were together for hours, Mom—she gave me a lift here from LAX. Drove me right to the door."

"Then, why on earth didn't you tell me that last night? I could've stayed up, gotten more things done. This place is simply not ready to invite anyone to. Oh dear. Jill was upset we hadn't called, wasn't she? The Prestons aren't hard to find, you know. They're in the phone book. Oh, dear." His mother's gaze darted wildly around the great room.

To Jack, the place looked perfectly fine, even elegant in its starkly contrasting shades of whites and browns, accented with lush tropical plants and highly polished brass and dark woods.

"George, you still haven't finished the shelves on either side of the fireplace. The room won't be complete until I can put out my primitive art collection."

"I've just about got the shelves ready to mount on the wall. With Jack's help," he said giving his son a private man-to-man wink, "we could get them up before we go sightseeing."

"Good." She slapped the spatula in her husband's hand and started for the hall. "The biscuits will be done in one minute. I'll be working on our bedroom if you need anything. I'll have to call Paulette today, for sure. Oh dear. Somehow I've got to get this place 'surface' presentable before I call."

As she disappeared, Jack grinned. "Same ol' Mom."

His dad strolled over to the stove with his own grin. "Yup, same ol' Mom. But tell me, how is Jill? I used to get such a kick out of her. Even when she was a tiny thing, she talked so grown-up."

"Dad, you wouldn't believe how great she's aged. She's still blond and absolutely beautiful, inside and out. And she still has that infectious laugh. She's bright and—would you believe it—she became a nurse, just like she said she would. She's given her children a solid Christian upbringing and—"

"And married, I assume," his dad inserted. "From the way you're carrying on, you sound like one of your brothers when they were in high school, talking up a latest *one and only.*"

Did he really sound like that? Jack slowed down.

"Actually, no, Jill's husband walked out on her and her three kids a long time ago. A few years later he was killed. So, I guess in some ways, she's twice a widow. And because of it, she's grown very strong spiritually. Truly, she's a marvel. Wait 'til you meet her at Thanksgiving, you'll see. Her last child, her son, recently left home to join the navy, so she's alone now, and—"

"She sounds wonderful, Son, but just a quick reminder—chance meetings in distant airports are similar to shipboard romances. During these interludes, people don't have the pressures of life pulling at them, and they always seem more appealing, more attractive."

"Better check the biscuits, Dad," Jack prompted, changing the topic. He wasn't ready to have his bubble burst. Not just yet. "If you don't mind, later this afternoon, I'd like to borrow your car. I want to take a run out to a couple of the hospitals. See if they have any extra supplies they're itching to donate to the mission hospital."

Even with the loss of sleep, Jill practically floated through the birthing center during her shift at Mercy Southwest, her mind taking fanciful flights. . .flights all the way to the Philippines with Jack next to her. . . them working side by side. . .making a home together . . .loving one another with a completeness that merged them into that oneness spoken of in the Bible—a oneness she'd never felt with Randy.

"Take slow breaths," she reminded her labor patient, as the young woman's latest contraction intensified. Jill

214

guessed the woman's labor was moving into the next stage. No more time for daydreaming—the reality of the moment now took precedence.

"Excuse me." Jill addressed two children blocking the fetal heart monitor. She tried not to display any irritation. "I need to get a reading." She didn't think she'd ever get used to entire families crowding into a labor room as if giving birth was the latest excuse for a party, everyone laughing and talking at once, video cameras recording every groan, every bead of sweat.

"Here, have some chocolate, Sis," the patient's brother offered as he thrust a candy bar in the face of a woman who was in the midst of such pain she couldn't even focus her eyes.

"Save it for after the baby is delivered," Jill suggested, then addressed all seven family members. "I need to examine Mrs. Rogers. Would you please wait outside?"

"Couldn't we just turn our backs?" a younger sister asked.

Jill simply said, "I'm sorry, no. I'll only be a few minutes." This bunch had been particularly insensitive, and she yearned to remind them that even with modern technology, a birth could turn into a life or death situation at any second. *And that's why,* she wanted to shout, *the lady's in the hospital instead of at home.*

"Take all the time you need," the expectant mother said to Jill as her family filed out. Mrs. Rogers was more relaxed now that the contraction had subsided. "I could use the intermission, myself. Being the star of my husband's little production is not what it's cracked up to be."

Jill couldn't help grinning. As the woman went into the next contraction, Jill checked internally and knew she'd been correct in her assessment. "Everything is just as it should be," she reassured. "I'm calling in the doctor. That baby of yours has decided it's time to join us."

"Thank God," Mrs. Rogers hollered past her pain. "Thank God."

Once the lady had delivered her baby boy and was comfortably settled with the infant in her arms and her family circled round, Jill's mind returned to musings of Jack. Walking out of the room, she checked at the desk to see if any new patients were being admitted. Finding that there were none, she headed for the break room. In the comfortable lounge containing a couch and a dinette set, she noticed Oprah Winfrey was on TV. It had to be after four. The wall phone beside the couch beckoned as it had on her earlier break. She wished she had the nerve to call Jack's house, but instead she went to the snack counter and made herself a cup of tea. He had her number, too. He should call her.

Maybe he had already.

Maybe there was a message from him on her answering machine at home just blinking away until she could get to it. A happy thought. She checked her watch. *Hmm, four-twenty. Only two hours and forty minutes left of my shift, then I can go home and see.*

Today's topic on *Oprah* dealt with relationships between mothers and daughters. A sobering topic, considering the extent in which her life was intertwined with her daughters'. Not only did she share child care with Rochelle, but she was helping Melissa pay off her college loan. Then there were the family gatherings and her church activities, teaching Sunday school in the Junior Department, serving on several committees, mentoring a couple of high schoolers interested in nursing. And the hospital. . . She had seniority. She'd been there since the doors first opened a few years ago. It was state of the art and turning into a really fine facility. Would she want to give all that up?

But then, who said Jack would ask her to?

That thought was a downer. And so was the TV show. She picked up the remote and turned it off. She much preferred dreaming that he would ask her to go away with him.

Even if all logic told her she'd never just up and walk away from everyone dear to her, a life she'd spent years building.

Wrapping both hands around her teacup, she took a sip, then leaned back. Picturing Jack down on one knee and stumbling through the words, a smile tickled the corners of her lips. The most delicious fun, this was, pretending it would happen. And that she'd be utterly and completely swept away by love.

Too soon Jill's break ended, and she exited the nurses' lounge. . .to literally bump into two men. The chief of staff and *Jack*.

"Just the person we were looking for," Dr. Hanson said. "It seems your friend here not only wants to clean out our storeroom, but he's trying to abscond with my best nurse."

Startled, Jill glanced from Jack to the head doctor who, in his fifties, always wore a bit of a frown. She'd always suspected he took too much responsibility on himself while leaning too seldom on the Lord. "Jack asked what?"

"He's asked me to give you the rest of the day off. With pay, of course."

Her gaze returned to Jack who now sported a hopeful grin. "He has?" The man she'd been dreaming about all day really did want to spend more time with her before Thanksgiving.

"We just checked at admissions," the graying doctor continued, "and it looks like the coast is clear. For now, anyway. No new mothers have called or come in. So, I suppose I'll go ahead and hand you over to Van Fleet."

"Without even asking if I want to go with this upstart?" she teased in as serious a tone as she could manage.

"No need to ask," Dr. Hanson returned. "I saw the look on your face when you saw him."

Needless to say, so had Jack. His grin widened.

Jill felt the heat of embarrassment. Quickly, she pivoted away. "I'll get my purse and clock out. Be right back."

Chapter 5

Yesterday, Jack had been attracted to the perfection of Jill in her stylish clothes, but as they descended in the hospital elevator, he decided she was more attractive, more *his* Jill in her nurse's scrubs. And there was something especially endearing about her hair pulled back into a single, practical braid. . .not to mention the unveiling of her slender neck.

"I suppose your mom and dad drove you all around today," Jill prompted as they left the elevator for the entrance.

Jack grinned. "No, it didn't work out that way. Once Mom knew your mother would be coming to visit, Dad and I were recruited into a morning of 'honey-dos.' Around two, I managed to escape with their car and directions to three of the hospitals. Poor Dad, he wasn't so lucky."

"Poor Dad," she commiserated past her own amusement. "It doesn't sound like you got much sight-seeing done, then." Walking out the automatic doors, she pointed toward one of the parking lots. "Let's take my car. I'll drive—you look. A lot has changed."

"*I noticed.* Last night when we drove in, I thought I was confused by the darkness and my failing memory. But in daylight, I still don't recognize anything. Bakersfield's a big city now."

"A lot of construction can take place in thirty years. You shouldn't have stayed away so long."

They skirted a row of cars in Staff Parking until they reached her Ford. Once settled inside, she turned to him. "Have you seen our old neighborhood yet?"

"Yes. I went by there first. But like you said, thirty years sure makes a difference. The trees were a whole lot bigger, the houses older, and I didn't recognize anyone."

"People don't seem to stay in the same houses for life anymore. Mom and Dad are in a condo now. With Dad's paralysis, he doesn't need to be concerned with any exterior upkeep."

"What about the Johnsons? Jimmy Johnson? Where did he move to when he grew up?"

"Jim and his wife Karen bought a house last year just west of the university."

"That's another thing. A university. When I left all we had was a junior college. And look at all these office buildings," he pointed out as he they started down a thoroughfare of architectural beauties. When I'm out of the country for several years, I forget just how wealthy America is. But, do you know what's so funny? No matter where I am in the world, if I mention I'm from Bakersfield, people sympathize, like it's the worst place I could've come from. They think it's nothing but a run-down hick town with Merle Haggard and Buck Owens our dubious claim to fame."

"I know. Johnny Carson started dissing us back in the seventies, and it's never stopped. And as for Buck, wait 'til you see what he's built."

"You mean his Crystal Palace Dinner Theater?"

"That, too, but mostly, what's right behind it. A state-of-the-art heart hospital. I'll drive you by. And on the way, I'll show you our new, very high-tech cancer center. From what I hear they even have a medical physicist on staff there."

Jack had to ask God to take away the envy that was starting to consume him. "That's great. I guess you'd think our little hospital in the Philippines was pretty primitive."

"I wouldn't get too envious if I were you. This all comes with a price, and I'm not just talking money. More rules and regs. Tons of paperwork. Hospital politics, unions. And the HMOs can be a nightmare. Stress to the max. I'm sure things are a lot simpler where you are."

"You're right. At our hospital, we do all work together toward the same goal. Mostly we just have shortages—shortages of just about everything at one time or another. At the moment, we're short of qualified help." He shifted his attention from the swift but smoothly flowing traffic to Jill. "We could sure use someone with your OB experience. Anytime you want a job, all you have to do is say the word."

Glancing over at him, Jill gave a nervous laugh. "Me? Just up and take off. Like some kid running off to join the circus." She sighed. "What a tempting thought. . . . Look." She pointed toward a large Mediterranean-style building with a spectacular fountain in front. "That's the new cancer center."

After seeing this modern city with all its amenities, this city that also held all Jill's family and friends, how could he think his offer could be anything more than a passing fancy? Still, he wasn't ready to give up on her yet. But maybe he'd better take it a bit slower. . .entice her with descriptions of the Philippines' exotic beauty and tell her more about a darling baby girl named Lucena. "It's getting dark. Let me take you to dinner."

The next morning, Jill woke feeling younger than she had in years. Before running into Jack again, she'd seen her life moving steadily along in a very predictable direction—a good practical life, but lacking the pizzazz and adventure of Jack's offhanded offer of a renewed relationship. And she couldn't ignore the possibility of a little romance, either. Her euphoria didn't begin to deflate until she reentered reality at her oldest daughter's front door on this, the only day the two women had off together. She knocked and walked in.

"Hi, Mom." Rochelle's voice carried over the chatter of her little ones. "We're in the kitchen. I'm just finishing up here with Mark."

From the central entry hall, Jill stepped into the family space, appreciating the fire blazing warmth at the far end of the room. The weather had taken a definite turn toward winter.

Matthew, all three feet of him, ran toward her and crashed into her legs, while Mark, in Rochelle's arms, dodged an attacking washcloth as he stretched out his arms to his grandmother.

Laughing, Jill pulled the nine-month-old imp from her daughter and bent to encompass both her straw-headed grandbabies in a hug. "And how are my little munchkins?" Shifting Mark to one hip, she moved to the coffeemaker at one end of the counter and poured herself a cup, then took her usual place at the country dining set of white-trimmed oak. "Did everything go smoothly while I was away seeing your brother?" she asked her daughter.

"Fine." Rochelle, as always, was a pleasure to watch, with that lithe athletic beauty inherited from her father. Her thick, sun-streaked mane danced across her back as she refilled her own mug in quick, sure moves and dropped into the chair opposite Jill. "But I want to hear about your trip. How's Stevie? Is he really doing all right? I tried to call you last night, but you weren't home. Did you have to work overtime on your first day back?"

"No." Although Jill was amused by the rapid-fire questions of her overly serious oldest, she wasn't quite ready to mention where she'd spent last evening. She shifted her attention to the baby and started bouncing him on her knee. "And, yes, Steven is doing just great—much better than I expected. At the graduation, he looked very handsome and quite grown-up in his dress blues. And what about you? Are you still getting Thanksgiving off?"

"Yes. I'm working a makeup shift next Tuesday when you'll be off to watch the kids."

"Good. I particularly want both you girls and your families at the house for dinner on Thursday. I've invited some people I want you to meet."

Rochelle's tanned good looks were now marred by a frown. "You invited strangers to Thanksgiving?"

"Not strangers, Shell. Old friends. They're neighbors from when I was a kid. It'll be fine." Jill handed each grandson a cracker from off a snack plate, then stood the little one on the floor. "Your grandparents will keep the older Van Fleets fully entertained. They just moved back to town after thirty years. There'll be a lot of catching up to do." She took a sip of coffee, still not quite ready to mention Jack.

"Is that where you were last night? Visiting them?"

"Sort of. Not exactly," Jill corrected. "I went to dinner with their son. He's the one they named Jack to go with my Jill. I'm sure I've told you that story."

"Oh, yes. Those people. They were transferred by one of the oil companies, weren't they? To Africa or Arabia or somewhere like that. And from the smile you're wearing, I'd say you had a really nice time."

Jill felt heat creep up from the neck of her teal jogging suit. Obviously, her happy mood was easier to read than one of the boys' picture books. She wished she'd kept Mark on her lap so she could hide behind the sturdy babe. He'd toddled out of reach, heading for a pile of toys in front of the autumn plaid couch.

"Well?" Rochelle urged.

"You're right, I had a nice time," Jill conceded as casually as she could manage.

"Where did you go? Someplace special?"

"No. I was still in my work clothes. We just went to Woody's on the Truxtun Extension. I think you'll really enjoy meeting him. He's led a very interesting life. He's a doctor on the mission field. He's been stationed in the Philippines for several years now." Jill's heart continued picking up pace as she talked about him. She took a stilling breath. Rochelle was too intuitive for her own good.

"That does sound interesting. You should introduce him to Trevor Luton at the church." By her daughter's casual change of subject, she obviously hadn't picked up on the vibrancy in Jill's voice. "Trevor wants to do volunteer work in the Far East next summer. He's been doing odd jobs after school to save up ever since last spring when the missionary from Thailand came to speak."

"That's a good idea. Jack said they were in need of help at his hospital." Jill braced herself. "In fact, he offered me a job."

"Like you'd ever leave Bakersfield," Rochelle remarked lightly, then took a second, hard look at Jill. "You did say no, didn't you?"

Jill felt as if she—not Rochelle—were the daughter. "I really don't recall exactly what I said. I—well, you have to admit," she defended, "flying off to a tropical island to minister to the sick and needy does sound. . . rather romantic."

"*Mother*. . . ." Rochelle's voice had that impatient,

know-it-all tone. "It's not like you're not doing the same work right here. Every day. Aside from giving spiritual as well as physical comfort to your patients, you inspire all of us at the hospital to do our utmost, too. Everyone says so. And don't forget your Sunday school kids. I've never met one who didn't absolutely adore you. You're a regular kid magnet. Just ask your grandchildren—*who would miss you terribly* if you ever did anything so foolish."

"Oh, I'm sure they—"

"And as for traveling to a tropic isle," Rochelle pressed on, "you can do that in the comfort of your own home—just turn on the Travel Channel. The only thing I can see you're missing is the mosquitoes and tsetse flies. And maybe a cockroach or two. And we all know how you *love* cockroaches."

Every single argument Rochelle made, Jill had already considered. Still, if she were on that island with Jack. . . "Pass the sugar," she said, changing the subject.

Rochelle caught Jill's outstretched hand. "Mother, you don't take sugar in your coffee." She gave it an affectionate squeeze. "You know what I think, Mom? You've got jet lag. You're mind is still up there in the air, flying around. But I have a secret that I know will bring you flying back down to the rest of us." She leaned forward. "I'm not supposed to tell you. Melissa planned to surprise you with it on Thanksgiving, but. . ." With a shrug, Rochelle grinned and displayed her beautiful, orthodontically correct teeth. "Mel's pregnant. She's going to have a baby. Isn't that great?"

The news caught Jill off guard. Melissa had just started her first year of teaching at Laurelglen Elementary. Her husband was also in his first year at Stockdale High. "She and Brandon are both still teaching on a trial basis. For the next three years," she added with emphasis. "I doubt if the administrators will think kindly of her taking a leave of absence to have a baby. Surely, Melissa and Brandon didn't plan this."

"It'll be all right, Mom. She's not due until the end of June, during summer vacation. Then she'll have all of July and most of August to get back on her feet before school starts again. After that, you and I will have a sweet new little one to play with when we trade off baby-sitting. I do hope Mel has a girl. I'm dying to buy some of those ruffly pink dresses."

Rochelle had been right. The flight Jill felt she'd been taking landed hard. Her feet stood on rock-solid ground again. Of course, she would have to remain here with her family. Not only did she have children and grandchildren who needed her, but before too many years passed, her parents would become old and feeble. Her life was set. *Bloom where you're planted,* she reminded herself. Her roots reached deep. . .deeper than she'd ever realized.

But, why, God? Why did You bring Jack back into my life if I was just going to have to give him up again? It's cruel. And not fair. Not fair at all.

"Mom?" Rochelle asked urgently. "Aren't you glad for Melissa? She and Brandon put off starting a family all through college and student teaching. Be happy for them. It's finally their time."

Their time. . . "Of course, I am happy for them."
Forcing a smile, Jill rose from the table. She needed to
leave before Rochelle picked up on her personal pain.
"I really should get going. I have a lot of grocery shopping and baking to do before Thanksgiving."

The meaning of the word, Thanksgiving, followed
her out the door. Thanksgiving—that special day set
aside to give thanks for all things. God's Word instructs
His children to give thanks in all things. But Thursday
would be the last time she'd see Jack before he flew from
her life again. How could she give thanks for that?

Chapter 6

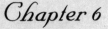

The irritating jangle of the alarm attacked Jill's ear. Dragging her eyelids up, she saw 5:00 illuminated in green.

Too early. She must've set the clock wrong.

Then she remembered. *It's Thanksgiving Day.* She tossed back the downy bedding and clicked on the lamp beside her. The turkey needed to go into the oven right away. And there was still so much to do before Jack came.

Jack. The house would be overrun with people, yet she could think of nothing else?

Springing to her feet, she toed into her waiting terry cloth slippers, then hurried to the kitchen.

Once the turkey was baking and the coffee brewed, she poured a cup and sat at the breakfast table in the bay window, notepad in hand. She needed to check her listing of all she still had to do before Jack and the others arrived.

Then coming fully to her senses, she laid the tablet aside and grabbed her Bible. There was nothing she needed to do more than read from the Word and pray this morning. *Pray.*

She looked past the green and peach floral swags and into the predawn darkness.

"Lord, You know Jack's all I can think about. You know last night I waited, willing him to call me. And when he did, I clung to every word he said, especially those about him and his boys in the Philippines, his little Lucena. And You know I love his humor, his every joke. And more than anything, Lord, I love to hear him laugh. It's been so long since I heard his own unique laughter. And, God, I know he wants me with him, even if he hasn't actually said the words. Not just as a nurse for his hospital, but as his wife and the mother of his children. And You know I want to go. Desperately."

She sighed and took a sip of coffee before continuing. "So You have to help me, Lord. I'm helpless to stop wanting this. No matter how hard I try, I can't get past it. I try to keep my mind on my own family—the precious one You've entrusted to me. And they do need me. And as Rochelle so aptly put it, this is their time. After that, their children's. I had my time years ago, and just because I made a bad choice then, doesn't mean they should have to suffer for it any more than they already have. Yet here I am again, wanting to make my own choice. And do I really know that this marriage would turn out any better than the last? I can't see into the future. Only You can. I must trust You.

"In my mind I know all this. I know I should be filled with joy that Melissa and Brandon are having a baby. And doubly thrilled today, because Mom and Dad are going to be reunited with their dear old friends. But still the gnawing ache won't stop. God, I can't stop wanting Jack. You have to take this feeling, this consuming desire from me. Especially today, Lord. Please give me the strength to say and do the right thing. Let me care again about all I held so dear just four short days ago."

Knowing she was becoming repetitious, Jill picked up her Bible. Maybe if she read a bit she'd find that calm place, those still waters. She turned to the last verses of Galatians 5, those containing the Fruit of the Spirit. She very much needed a fresh infilling—if she would just empty herself and make room.

Love, joy, peace, patience, kindness, goodness, faithfulness, gentleness, and self-control. Self-control. . . She really thought she'd mastered that one, fool that she was.

"Please, Lord, manifest Yourself in me today, especially Your peace and kindness and self-control. Make me happy again with the *very good* life I have right here and now. Take this longing for Jack from me." With her last whispered words, unstoppable emotion welled within her and tears filled her eyes. No matter how much she prayed, losing Jack yet another time seemed unbearable. Such a depth of feeling. . .it was hard to believe their paths crossed again just a mere three and a half days ago.

She threw up her hands. "I'm a helpless mess, Lord. I can do nothing but give it all to You. I have twelve people coming for dinner—I can't sit here blubbering all day."

As the hours ticked away, Jill worked tirelessly in the kitchen and readying her home for the ten adults and two children who would share the holiday meal. She'd just finished setting the big table in the dining alcove and the card table she'd placed in the living room when the grandfather clock above the fireplace gonged twelve times. Only a half hour now, before her parents and the Van Fleets were to arrive. They'd planned to meet here thirty minutes before Jill's girls and their families came to have a little time to get reacquainted.

Jill surveyed her separated tables, wishing she had one of those newer homes with the large open spaces. If she and Jack ended up at different tables, they might not even be able to see each other.

That would never do.

Like a maniac, she moved back the folding chairs and pulled the card table much closer to the entry. The mahogany set she'd inherited from her parents when they moved into their condo, she dragged into the living room, butting the table up against the small square one. "Much better," she rationalized. "We'll all be together. Much more festive."

Quickly, she repositioned her Desert Rose place settings, the ceramic cornucopia with its spill of fruit and the array of candlesticks, then brought up the chairs. Stepping back, she checked to see what Jack would see when he walked in. The tablecloths were different shades of autumn, but that couldn't be helped. All in all, though, it looked colorful and cozy.

Too cozy. The room was much too crowded. In a mad dash, she dragged the striped denim love seat, her cherry wood rocker, and an end table into the alcove and arranged them across from the buffet. Tossing a few floral pillows on them for good measure, she rushed back to the living room and shifted her larger blue denim couch and its accompanying pieces until there was more balance to that space.

Again she surveyed the room. Much better.

But with George Van Fleet being a petroleum engineer and them being world travelers, they would have far better furniture than her unmatched wooden pieces. And these were topped, not with fine art, but mostly the knickknacks her children and friends had either made or purchased for her over the years.

Realizing her thoughts were taking a covetous, "poor me" direction, she quickly reminded herself that she had more comforts than multitudes of others around the globe. *Thank You, Lord, for my many blessings.*

Besides, Jack lived among people far less materially fortunate than she. He would think the room looked just fine.

"There I go again, God. My every train of thought finds its way back to him."

The clock chimed the quarter hour—the grandfather mantel clock, she reminded herself, that her children had presented to her one Christmas after doing odd jobs for almost a year to buy it for her. . . just because she'd happened to mention she'd always wanted one. A true sacrifice of love, and one of her many blessings upon blessings.

She zoned in on the face. Twelve fifteen. Only minutes before the first arrivals would be at her door. She ran for her bedroom, ripping off her sweats as she went. As she replaced them with the clothing she'd selected for the special day, she wondered if she would've worn a dress if Jack weren't coming. She *knew* she wouldn't have bothered with nylons and heels.

Thank goodness, she'd already showered and put on her makeup. She walked into her pink and sea foam bathroom to see if her face or hair needed an added touch. Running a brush through her shoulder-length blond strands, she became aware that there was added significance to the plum-colored jacquard sheath she'd selected. She'd told herself she'd picked it because the color would complement those of the festive table. *But the mandarin collar?* Had she subconsciously chosen an Asian style dress as a signal to Jack? To encourage him to ask her, seriously this time, to come with him to the Philippines?

Jill put her brush down on the pink tile counter. It was wrong to lead him on like that. Reluctantly, she reached for the back zipper.

At that instant the doorbell rang.

Too late to change. She hurried to answer the summons. It could be Jack.

It wasn't. Her parents waited on the porch, her mom, looking trim and stylish in an olive vest over a plaid wrap skirt and high boots.

As Jill helped get her dad's wheelchair through the

door, he sniffed the air. "Everything smells delicious," he volunteered with the zealous love most men have for food. A pumpkin-colored tie set off his wool plaid shirt—a tie Jill knew he wore under protest.

"I didn't see an extra car parked outside," Mom stated. "We can hardly wait to see George and Mitsy again."

Jill quickly searched the street in both directions but saw only her parents' van in front.

"We would've gotten together sooner," her mother continued, "but you know how busy I've been at the store, getting my department ready for the 'Day After Thanksgiving' sale."

"You must be beat." Jill would be very glad when her mother gave in and retired. She'd been working on her feet these past twenty-seven years since Dad was injured. Too long for a woman of sixty-three.

"Keeps me young, Kiddo." Absently, her mom raked back one side of her short, gray cut. "But, still, I think I should've brought at least one dish."

"No. You just sit back and relax. Enjoy your reunion with George and Mitsy. And be warned, if I catch you in the kitchen, I'll run you out. There's some dip and chips on the buffet. Help yourselves."

"Your father will be glad to take you up on that," Mom said as she surveyed the living room. "Good girl. We'll all be able to eat together."

Jill's dad caught her hand. "My, but don't you look gorgeous today. I haven't seen you in a dress in ages. *And heels.*"

Would the rest of her family also make a big deal of her attire? Hoping they wouldn't even notice, Jill bent and gave her dad a hug of thanks.

The arms he wrapped around her were still as strong and muscular as when she was a girl. He'd kept busy since his fall from a drilling rig, wrestling vacuums in his garage as well as the other electrical appliances he repaired for additional income. Jill swelled with an extra measure of love for her aging parents. No matter what came their way, these two kept right on plugging along. . .never giving in to insane impulses.

Knowing the direction her thoughts were taking, Jill lightened the moment by ruffling her dad's thick silver hair.

"Hey!" he protested gruffly, swiping at her hand.

Laughing, she backed out of reach.

The doorbell rang.

This time it had to be Jack. Jill's heart started banging like a bass drum.

Jack stood with his folks before Jill's shiny hardwood door, a fresh-baked pecan pie in hand. While waiting for Jill to answer, he noticed that her neighborhood wasn't as affluent as his parents', but Jill's brick-trimmed house and yard were in neat order. Flower boxes at the windows and a couple of cute birdhouses hanging from the porch eaves added homey touches. It was obvious that she cared a great deal for her home. Even before entering, he knew she shared his mother's nesting instinct. And here in Bakersfield, she had most of her chicks circled about her. His prospect of wooing her away seemed even more remote. *Jesus,* he prayed silently, *aren't You giving her to me? Or is this just my own wishful thinking? I really need to know. Now. Tomorrow, I'll be gone.*

The door swung open, and at the threshold she stood, her cheeks aglow, looking stunningly beautiful. And in an Asian style dress! Did it mean what he hoped?

Chapter 7

J ill, *is that really you?*" Jack's mother, in a burnt orange pantsuit, rushed past him and his dad who juggled not one, but two pies in his hands. The much shorter woman held Jill at arm's length and looked her up and down. "You were always a pretty girl, but my son is right, you've definitely improved with age."

"I'd like to second that," Dad said over Mom's head before stepping inside. "Once I've put these pumpkin pies down somewhere."

"Me, too," Jack added, his gaze locking with Jill's in a private, silent greeting.

Their electrifying exchange lasted no more than a couple of seconds before Jill glanced away as if she'd just forgotten something. "It was really nice of you to bring home-baked pies. Here let me take them from you, Mr. Van Fleet."

"George," he corrected, handing over the desserts. "George and Mitsy. Remember?"

"How could I forget. Mom, Dad—"

"Stop yammering at the door," Jill's father called

from his wheelchair. "Let the poor man in. I want to get a look at him."

Jack couldn't stop grinning as he followed Jill into her dining room still carrying his mother's other contribution to the feast. To see the hugging, hear the crying, the exclamations, and the cooing of the four old friends touched him almost as much as when he first recognized Jill in the Dallas airport.

"Here, Jack," Jill directed while placing the pumpkin pies on the buffet. "Set the pecan one here."

After depositing it between a punch bowl and platters of hors d'oeuvres, Jack moved alongside Jill.

She stood in the archway watching their parents, a tender smile gracing her lips.

His arm just naturally circled her shoulders, and she leaned into his side. And at that instant, all else faded from his mind as he savored the feel of her next to him. . .exactly where he always wanted her to be.

"Get over here, Jack." Jill's mother, Paulette, beckoned with one hand as she clung to Mom's with her other. "Don't think you're escaping these clutches."

Letting go of Jill was the last thing he wanted, but what else could he do? "Coming, you gorgeous hunk of woman."

Several minutes passed while everyone got reacquainted. There was no denying it was enjoyable—like "old home week." Still, Jack couldn't help counting every second that ticked away—time he needed to convince Jill to give up all the overflowing love and comfort surrounding her and come away with him to the hardships of a Third World country. . .to marry him.

At last, Jill disentangled herself from the others. "Now, if you'll excuse me, I need to put the rolls in the oven and reheat the vegetables. There are appetizers and punch in the dining room. Help yourselves."

"I'll come help," his mother offered, starting after Jill.

Jack stopped her. "No, Mom. You stay here and visit. I'll go."

Without the protest he anticipated, she happily returned to talking a mile a minute with Paulette.

Jack didn't waste any time either. He followed Jill through the dining room and into a rather narrow but efficient-looking kitchen. A bay window at the far end overlooked a back patio and yard which was inviting even in the leaf-falling month of November. Food covered the counters and a small table at the window.

Jill picked up a large carving set and with a smug smile, turned back to him. "You really shouldn't have volunteered." She pointed the knife toward a golden-brown turkey sitting on the counter opposite the stove. "You're now elected to carve the turkey."

"My specialty," he lied. "Where do you want me to toss the chunks?"

"I want you to *arrange the slices* on the platter next to the roaster." She relinquished the utensils, then turned her back to him in a flurry of activity, setting the digital dials on the stove, adjusting the level of fire under a pot of carrots and peas. She then started placing rolls on a cookie sheet.

He would've much rather been facing her when he

made his plea, but this might be his only chance without competing with a roomful of people. Stabbing the turkey breast and starting to slice, he glanced over his shoulder at her. "Have I told you how ravishing you look today?"

She rewarded him by looking back at him. "No, I don't believe you did. But then I didn't mention how terrific you look in your matching outfit either."

He grinned, glancing down at the dusty purple sweater and slacks his mother insisted on buying him. "Mom would be real pleased to hear that. The color, she says, is eggplant. Actually, it's almost the same shade as your dress. You'd think we dressed alike on purpose." He heard her suck in a breath and took it for a good sign.

Her sky-blue gaze raked across his. "Jack and Jill," she returned softly, before turning back to the rolls.

He executed a few more turkey slices while steeling himself for his next words. "Aside from the dress looking great on you, what I'm most inspired by is the collar. The Far East definitely becomes you." He noticed a slight stiffness in her back. Had he read her wrong?

In quick movements, she slid the rolls into the oven, then faced him, her expression disturbingly serious.

The doorbell rang.

Jill's attention shifted. "That must be some of my kids."

The greetings and introductions, along with higher-pitched voices of little ones, were loud enough to be heard in the kitchen.

Amid the jumble of overlapping conversations, Jack caught Jill's father saying, "Your mother's in the kitchen."

The patter of approaching footsteps immediately followed.

A towheaded two year old burst into the room, and Jill tossed Jack a dish towel. "Here, wipe the grease off your hands. I want to introduce you to my oldest grandson, Matthew."

Before Jack could reply, the small child was joined by a young couple, each carrying in more food.

"Hi, Mom."

Jill's daughter hadn't inherited her mother's slender blondness but was strikingly pretty nonetheless. And, considering the quilted nylon vest and dark jeans she wore, one might think she was ready for a game of football instead of a dinner. But then, this generation of Californians didn't seem to dress up for much of anything. And, for all he knew, she just might spend the afternoon roughhousing in the backyard.

"Rochelle, Mike," Jill said to the two younger adults. "I want you to meet Jack Van Fleet—a very old and dear friend of mine."

"Oh, yeah." Mike, tall and sturdy with a light brown crew cut, and a slightly crooked nose, extended his hand in a hearty handshake. "Shelly told me about you. Nice to meet you. Do you like football? Vikings are playing Dallas *as we speak.*" He scooted the cranberry salad he carried between two other serving bowls. "Mom? Mind if I turn on the TV to catch the score?" Without waiting for Jill's answer, he wheeled back toward the living room, his pint-sized son at his heels.

"Mom says you're just here until tomorrow," Rochelle remarked in pleasant low tones. "Too bad we won't get a chance to know you better. According to Mom, you were famous friends." She then turned to Jill. "Oh, I forgot to tell you when you came by Tuesday—I called in the reservation for a condo at Huntington Lake. Three nights like we wanted. Split between us, your share comes to a hundred forty-five dollars."

Jill included Jack. "We all go skiing up at Sierra Summit every Presidents' Day weekend."

"Yes," Rochelle added. "And our whole family camps at Yosemite for a week every June, and we spend a few days at the beach each fall. It's tradition, like always having Thanksgiving dinner here at Mom's every year."

By the time Rochelle finished her litany on family togetherness, Jack got the impression she wasn't just making casual conversation but warning him to back off. However, it only served to encourage him since the girl must have been given reason to believe her mother might go away with him.

"We do tend to be a rather outdoorsy bunch," Jill said dismissively, but her expression was a touch apologetic.

Because of her daughter's veiled hostility?

Or was Jill trying to tell him that her daughter had hit the mark, that her life *was* here, solidly grounded, that she couldn't consider going with him to the Philippines?

Jack refused to entertain that possibility. "My boys and I spend most of our free time at the beach," he said, redirecting the conversation to him and his. "But during the dry months we do some hiking and exploring in the mountains. Once in awhile we'll come across a hillside of terraced rice paddies that's so green it almost hurts your eyes. Colors are so much more vibrant in the tropics."

"I've seen pictures," Jill murmured. "I can just imagine."

He wanted to say, *come with me and see it for yourself,* but knew he'd have to wait for another, more private, moment. "It's really nice being here, Rochelle, meeting Jill's kids after all these years. But your mom's got me doing slave labor. I'd better get back to slicing the turkey."

A few minutes later while Jack was bringing a bowl of mashed potatoes to the table, Jill's second daughter and her husband arrived—the first-year teachers. Jack took to Melissa immediately. Especially since she was a duplicate of what her mother must have looked like at twenty-two. And she virtually bubbled with enthusiasm.

"So you're Mom's Jack," she said, all smiles. "I've wanted to meet you since I was five. Mom always said Brandon and I reminded her of you two." She glanced up at her clean-cut, dark-haired husband. "We've been inseparable since nursery school."

Wearing a dark wool sweater and khaki dungarees that were similar to his wife's, Brandon good-naturedly wrapped an arm around her. "Yup, we're joined at the hip. 'Specially now."

Melissa shot him a warning glance, leaving Jack to wonder why.

Jack was then distracted by Jill calling everyone to the dinner table as she slid Rochelle's baby into a high chair at one corner. Jack waited until she took a seat near the other end, then lowered his lanky frame into the chair opposite her.

"Everything's wonderful," he said directly to her. And it was. The table piled with delicious-smelling food, surrounded by loved ones, amiable conversations swirling around him. These were the moments that created memories. He really should've brought his boys. They should have been there, sharing this day with his family and friends. Getting to know Jill.

"Everything and everyone," she beamed back to him. As usual, their thoughts were in sync. She picked up a spoon and tapped it on a crystal water glass. When the conversations hushed, her gaze again found his. "Jack, if you wouldn't mind, we'd really appreciate it if you'd bless this meal, this day."

Mind? He was thrilled she would choose him over either of their fathers. "Sure, my pleasure." He bowed his head and lifted his thoughts heavenward. "Dear Father, God of love and light and mercy, we thank You for Your generous abundance. When I'm away from the States for long periods, I forget how very much You've blessed this nation. I thank those who prepared this delicious meal, and most of all, I thank You for the privilege of coming home to Bakersfield to share this meal with so many of my loved ones. I pray that when I leave tomorrow, I may take the spirit of this day back to my boys in the Philippines. . .that in a small way, they, too, can share in this wonderful reunion. And I pray for my baby, Lucena, that she will be kept happy and laughing until I return. I ask all this in the name of our Lord Jesus. Amen."

"Speaking of babies," Melissa, sitting between her mother and husband, said, "I have an announcement to make—an added blessing to thank God for." Her blue eyes sparkled with life as she caught her husband's hand. "Brandon and I, we're going to have a baby next summer."

After a few seconds of surprised silence, congratulations were passed to the young couple from up and down the table along with bowls of food. Jack offered his own good wishes while wondering if this piece of news would add a further impediment to his own goal.

"And speaking of traditions in our family, Mr. Van Fleet. . ." At the other end, Rochelle's voice rang out above the others. "We also have one concerning babies. Mom was the delivery nurse for both my boys, and she'll be doing the same for Mel. Won't you, Mom?"

Jack prayed the look he saw in Jill's eyes was one of protest.

"And, of course," Rochelle pressed on, "we'll all pitch in to help baby-sit when Mel is teaching. Children are too precious to leave with strangers. Anyway, that's what Mama always says, isn't it?"

Jill's expression dulled into one of resignation. "Yes, Dear, that's what I always said."

Jack's hopes collapsed.

Chapter 8

Jill watched the light in Jack's eyes die, and it took all her willpower not to reach across the table to him. To declare to everyone that she really could fly away with him and not leave behind any gaping holes. But she knew better. Neither could she ask Jack to give up his vital ministry and move here for her. No, they were just a pair of fools for even thinking they could make it work. Their love was nothing but a collection of old clichés rolled into one—star-crossed lovers, Romeo and Juliet, soul mates destined never to be together. . .Jack without his Jill.

Ironic and absurd. Smiling sadly, she gave him a resigned shrug.

Thank goodness the others at the table were in a talkative mood, because she doubted either she or Jack could've carried on much of a conversation after that. She couldn't bring herself to eat much either. Her plate was still half full when her two sons-in-law started calling for dessert.

"I'll go dish up the pie," her mother offered.

"No, Mom." Jill pushed back her chair. "Remember? You're royalty today."

Mitsy Van Fleet then volunteered to help, as well as Melissa.

"No, really. All of you just keep each other company. It'll take only a couple of minutes." Jill wasn't merely being polite. She desperately needed a moment alone—a moment to release some of her pent-up emotions, go outside, maybe, and scream—whatever it took to get through the rest of this meal.

Gathering two of the pies from the buffet, she barely reached the kitchen when a sob welled up from her chest. Quickly she set the pans down and turned on the sink faucet to muffle any sound she couldn't stifle. She grabbed onto the counter. *Not tears.* Tears would streak her mascara and redden her eyes. Everyone would know. She squeezed her eyes shut and held her breath, willing herself to regain control.

Just then, someone walked in, catching her in this stricken state.

Jack, standing there, a stack of dirty dishes in his hands. "Thought you'd want these cleared—" He set them next to the stove and moved quickly, gathering her to him, surrounding her in comfort. "I know, I know. Everything is against us. I had hoped, but. . ." He pulled her closer.

Jill's throat was too tight to speak without croaking. All she could do was bury her face in his shoulder. She wrapped her arms around his waist, not wanting to let go. Tomorrow was only hours away.

"I guess you knew when I walked in today," he said, his breath feathering across the top of her head, "I planned to ask you to marry me."

She could only nod in response.

"I was almost sure it was what you wanted, too. . . and God. I couldn't imagine that He would bring us together like this again unless that was His purpose." Jack filled his lungs and exhaled. "You'd think by now I'd know better than to try to outguess God."

Jill's anger sparked. She pulled back from Jack. "I never thought God was into cruel jokes. Why did He have us meet in the airport, then? He should have just left us be. We were both doing all right. I was okay before." Tears welled in her eyes. "But now? I don't know how I'm going to get past losing you again." She snatched a pot holder from its hook and started dabbing.

Jack caught hold of her shoulders. "Jill, my sweet darling Jill, we're not going to lose each other again, I promise. We'll write and call each other. And there's E-mail now. We won't lose contact like last time. I won't let it happen. And, Jill, there *will* come a day when you're not so needed here, then we—" Jack's words were cut short as he looked over Jill's head.

She swung around and found Rochelle's husband, Mike, standing in the doorway with his hands loaded with dishes. She could read nothing in his expression—neither surprise nor curiosity.

"I brought in the rest of the dinner plates," he said, placing them in the sink. Without another word, the usually talkative man turned and walked out.

How much had he overheard? Enough, at least, not to want to hang around. Would he tell Rochelle? By no means was Jill ready to face any more of her daughter's questions. "Jack, we'd better get this pie served before they start wondering why we're taking so long."

He didn't move, instead he brushed the back of his fingers along her cheek. "Let 'em wonder."

For a second his touch erased all else. Then, recapturing her senses, Jill stepped past him and pulled the pie server from a drawer. "Sure, you can say that," she'd quipped, trying to sound casual. "You're not the one who'll be left here to face everyone after you leave tomorrow." She started cutting slices. "Would you get the dessert plates from the cupboard to the left of the sink? And the whipped cream from the fridge?"

Once they had several desserts placed on a tray and ready to go, Jack picked them up and started out.

"Wait a second." This might be their last moment alone, and Jill couldn't bear the thought. "What time is your flight tomorrow?"

"It leaves at 11:50."

"Let me drive you to LA. I'll find someone to trade shifts with me. It'll give us a little while longer before we have to say good-bye."

A deep sadness filled his eyes. "It'll just make leaving you that much harder."

"I couldn't feel any worse than I do right now."

"But then you'd have to drive all the way home again, alone."

"It'll be fine. I'll take my cell phone in case there's a problem."

"Oh, yes," he sighed, "such a modern world we live in now. Remember back when we were kids watching *The Jetsons* on TV? All the high tech stuff that was supposed to make life easier, simpler. Push a button—problem solved. Didn't quite turn out that way, did it?" With a lifeless smile, he walked out.

When Jill brought in the remaining desserts, her first glance went to Jack taking his seat and her second to Mike sitting at the other end next to Rochelle. She was thankful to see that her son-in-law's attention was wholly on his pie and the pleasure of his first bite.

Just as she put the last remaining slice at her own place, the phone by the couch rang. She went to answer it. "Hello."

"Hi, it's Tipu," came from the other end.

Jack's son?

"Is that you, Grandma Mitsy? Your voice sounds different."

"No, it's a friend of hers. Just a moment, I'll take the phone to her."

"Wait. Is my dad there? It's him I want to talk to. It's important, very important."

"Of course, yes, he's right here." Cordless phone in hand, Jill circled the table toward Jack wondering if there was a problem. "Your son is calling."

Jack looked surprised. "How did he get this number?"

"We have call-forwarding, Dear," Mitsy explained as Jill returned to her seat. "I thought one of your brothers might call, so I punched in this number."

"My mother—one of those Jetsons we talked about, Jill." Taking the phone, his features became somber. "Hello." He looked at his watch. "It's only six AM there. Why are you calling so early? Is something wrong?"

Jill heard the concern in Jack's voice and empathized with him. The Philippines were almost halfway around the globe.

"So basically," Jack said after listening a moment, "what you're saying is that Consuelo wouldn't let you call me last night, so you've sneaked into the kitchen to call before she wakes up this morning. What's so urgent you felt you had to go behind her back?"

Jill watched Jack's face for a clue to his son's words. *Please, Lord, don't let it be too serious.*

"That's good," Jack remarked into the phone. "I'm glad to hear that Pastor Dave invited you boys to share Thanksgiving with them yesterday."

Jill could tell Jack was still waiting for the real purpose of the call. Becoming aware that she was holding her breath, she exhaled.

"That was nice of him. . . . You say he came back by and picked her up later. And Lucy was fine, is fine. . . ?"

The call must have something to do with the baby Jack wanted to adopt. Jill leaned forward.

"*What?* You're kidding." A grin. . .a marvelous, full-dimpled grin lit Jack's face. "I wish I'd been there. This is great, just great."

Jill settled back in her chair, relieved. She heard a

sigh come from Mitsy as well. Everything was okay in Jack's world.

"No," he continued, "you were right to call. The news was too good to wait. But you'd better get off before Consuelo catches you. I should be home in time for church Sunday. We'll go get Lucy again then, okay. . . ? I love you. . . . Tell Manny I love him and miss him, too. Bye."

Jack's grin didn't diminish as he punched off the phone and laid it down beside his coffee cup. He looked across the table at Jill. "The boys were able to bring Lucena home for a few hours yesterday. And it seems she couldn't wait for me to get back to do it." Jack glanced around the table, remembering to include the others in the conversation. "An abandoned baby who had heart surgery at the hospital—little Lucy, who we plan to make part of our family—she pulled herself up on the coffee table yesterday and walked all the way around it. I know that probably doesn't sound like such a big deal for an eight month old. . . ." He glanced at Mark, Jill's robust grandbaby in his high chair blissfully licking the whipped cream off his pie. "But Lucy's had a real hard time of it since she was born."

Jill reached across the table to him.

He caught her fingers and gave them a squeeze.

Retrieving her hand, she turned her attention to her oldest daughter. "Working in obstetrics, Rochelle and I, especially, know how hard a struggle it can be for some of the little ones. Don't we?"

Rochelle's disturbed gaze left Jill's hand, and she

plastered on a polite smile. "Yes. Particularly the drug babies."

"Well, this calls for a toast," Rochelle's gregarious husband, Mike, said cheerily, rising to his feet. He picked up his water glass.

Joining in the merriment, the rest of Jill's guests lifted their own drinks.

"To baby Lucy," Mike saluted. "May her steps be sure and swift and, by the grace of God, may she always be headed in the right direction."

"Hear, hear," Jack's dad called out at the foot of the table as everyone, except for Rochelle's baby, raised their glasses, even little Matthew.

"And while I have your attention," Mike said, still standing, "I have an announcement of my own." Jill's hulking son-in-law looked across to Melissa and Brandon. "I didn't want to steal anything away from your wonderful news, so I've waited until now to give mine." He then took hold of his wife's hand. "Even you don't know this one, Shelly. Yesterday, Warren called me into his office. He's retiring from the oil refinery at the end of the year. And because of my gift of gab, he told me I'm to be his replacement as head of marketing. And. . ." Mike grinned down at Rochelle. "Brace yourself, Girl. With a twenty-five percent raise. Fifteen hundred more a month."

Rochelle's mouth fell open as she stared speechless up at her husband.

"That's right," he laughed, kissing her mouth shut. "You can quit work."

"Oh, Mike." Rochelle sprang up and threw her arms around him. "I can stay home with my babies." She swung toward Jill, her green eyes sparkling with tears. "Did you hear that, Mama?"

"Yes, yes I did. I'm so happy for you."

"And for you, too," Mike said, shifting his attention to Jill. "I'm sure Shelly will want to mother-hen Mel's baby full-time, right along with her own. That'll leave you with a whole lot more time for yourself. And none too soon, I'd say?" Grinning, he nodded knowingly toward Jack. *He had overheard the conversation in the kitchen.*

She swung back to Jack.

A slow grin made its way across Jack's mouth as the significance of Mike's words took hold. Then he sought Jill with a warm, loving, *seeking* gaze. "What do you say?"

She stared back at him. Was he asking her to marry him? Here? Now? In front of their families? Her own gaze went traveling down the table, across Melissa and Brandon and on to her mother and father, Jack's parents, her grandbabies, Mike and Rochelle. Could she really do it? Fly to a place so far from them that Thanksgiving took place yesterday?

Her gaze circled back to Jack. Only a few minutes ago, she'd berated God for sending him to her only to take him away again. But was she really brave enough to leave all that was dear and familiar and actually go live what she'd prayed for?

Then a host of other problems hit her. "Jack," she

said quietly but intently, "I don't have a passport. And I would *have* to give notice at work and—"

Exhaling a pent-up breath, he sat back and chuckled. "Don't sweat the small stuff, my love." He turned to his parents. "Mom, Dad, would you mind taking on my two scamps till after Christmas?"

His dad settled back with a knowing grin, but not his mother. "What do you mean, Son? Are you sending them here to stay with us? Not that we mind, Dear," she qualified, "but why?"

"Because I don't want to be away from them that long. I'll be hanging around here for another month or so. However long it takes."

"You're not leaving tomorrow?"

"No."

Now, Mitsy's doll-like dimples outdid her son's as she looked from him to Jill. "That's wonderful, just wonderful."

Jill felt a blush coming as Jack's father unfolded his long frame from his seat and raised his glass toward his son. "It looks like this is quite the day for congratulations. Jack, I see now that you were right. You and Jill were meant to be. God and His mysterious workings."

"What are you talking about, George?" Jill's father at the head of the table was completely out of the loop. His thick forehead knotted in a frown.

"It would seem," George said, "we're going to be related soon. My son has asked your daughter to marry him."

"Jill?" It was Mom's moment to sound amazed. She

turned to Jill. "Is that true, Dear?"

"I think so." She swung back to Jack, eying him with a tilted smile. "You did ask me, didn't you, Jack?"

His own grin widened. "Yep."

Rochelle's mouth dropped open again, but this time she didn't remain speechless. "And what did you say, Mother?"

"Yep."

Now, Melissa was on her feet, even more surprised than her sister. "But how? When?"

"Sweetheart, I'll explain everything to you and your sister in a few minutes. But first, there are a couple of things I need to discuss with Jack." She rose from the table. "Would you mind coming into the kitchen with me for just a minute?"

Not waiting for him, she left her family behind, walking through the dining room and deep into the kitchen, away from listening ears.

At Jack's approaching footsteps, she turned to face him, her heart swelling with anticipation. . . Jack, her tall lanky, slightly rumpled, and utterly lovable soul mate with whom she intended to spend the rest of her life.

He came straight for her. "Are you having second thoughts? What exactly do you want to discuss?"

"Just this." Jill twined her arms around Jack's neck and pulled him close. . .her best friend, her love.

With his own lopsided grin, he leaned down. "You're right, that definitely needs discussing."

Their lips found each other, searching, melting together in an overwhelmingly splendorous discovery, a oneness she'd never felt before.

Even in the midst of these new feelings, this exquisite joy, Jill suddenly knew. This gift she'd just been given. . .this at-long-last love had been well worth the wait. Her Heavenly Father had not forgotten His lonely daughter. She and Jack had found each other again through God's will, in His merciful way, *and* in His perfect timing. And no matter whatever else happened, she would never cease giving thanks for this miraculous day of thanksgiving.

"You are the love of my life," Jack murmured next to her ear.

"I know, and you're mine. . . ." *Yes, thanks upon thanks.*

DIANNA CRAWFORD

Dianna lives in northern California with her husband, Roy. They have four children and seven grandchildren. Dianna writes full time and is very active in her church, donating much time to various youth programs. She and her husband like to spend their free time travelling, which also allows Dianna to research some of her story ideas. Dianna has written a number of novels and novellas, including a co-authored series for Tyndale with Sally Laity and a **Heartsong Presents** title, *Out of the Darkness*, with Rachel Druten.

December Duet

by Sally Laity

Dedication

As always, thanks so much, Andrea and Dianna,
for your patience and shredding.
You two are the best!

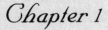

Chapter 1

T hat's it, then, Reverend. Thanks. Take care of yourself." With a good-natured nod, the lanky workman backed out of Pastor Troy Green's office and shut the door after himself.

Cora Dennison caught what might be construed as the hint of a wink as the slightly scruffy carpenter in a flannel shirt and worn jeans passed her desk and strode toward the church's back exit, whistling some nonsensical tune under his breath.

He couldn't have actually winked at me, she thought, dismissing what in all likelihood had been the silly imaginings of a forty-five year old. Why, she barely knew the man. Moments later, she watched his silver and gray Bronco roar out of the parking lot, scattering hordes of golden leaves fallen from nearby trees.

Accustomed to Mike Burgess's presence around the church grounds over the past several endless weeks, Cora had rarely paid the workman any mind. He had his job to do—major remodeling at the parsonage next door—and she, church secretary for Shavertown

Community Church—had hers. Even if she might have been a person prone to romantic daydreams, which she definitely was not, Mr. Burgess was far from the sort of individual she'd weave her illusions around. Though obviously somewhere in her own age bracket, Cora had always preferred tailored, more distinguished types.

Besides, she reminded herself, his project here had finally reached completion, so there was little possibility of their paths ever crossing again. It would be blissfully peaceful without the constant whack of the hammer or the whine of the electrical saw forever interrupting the solitude. No doubt the church staff would all get more work done now.

The minister's door opened and he poked his sandy head in her direction, a hopeful grin making his youthful features appear even more callow. Two years had passed since Pastor Troy had replaced the more staid Pastor Ephraim Walker, Cora's now retired former employer, and it had taken a good portion of that time for her to become accustomed to working for a minister only recently out of seminary. "Ready to go see the finished product at the parsonage? Sharon's baked a cake for us to celebrate." His tie loose and askew around the undone first button of his shirt, he came toward her.

"Sure, why not?" Rising, Cora clicked off her computer monitor and removed her purse from the bottom desk drawer. "Lead the way, Pastor Troy." Standing aside while he went by, she bolstered herself for a possible encounter with the young couple's preschoolers, Chad and Chet, who apparently had no concept of such things as dull moments. Thankfully their older sibling, Tucker, at seven, spent most of his creative mischief on his harried teachers at school. Cora could only surmise what the household next door would be like once the expected new arrival entered the scene. *Please, let it be a girl,* she prayed. *Surely that would make life a little easier. For all of us.*

The four-bedroom, two-story dwelling bracketed by shade trees occupied the adjacent property, its white aluminum siding and brick trim complementing the church's exterior. They crossed the parking lot and entered the well-appointed house where sounds of life preceded them. Cora breathed deeply of the smells of new wood and paint. She never ceased to be amazed at how the minister's slightly frazzled wife managed to keep things tidy despite her rambunctious offspring. No matter what condition the unseen parts of the house might be in, the living room and kitchen always seemed ready for unexpected visitors.

Pastor Troy's dark-haired wife, Sharon, in the late stages of pregnancy, sliced a chocolate cake at the tiled kitchen counter. A smile added puffiness to her expressive face as she looked up. "Oh, hi, Sweetheart. Cora," she sang out, repositioning one of the plates just beyond the reach of tiny exploring fingers crawling like a tarantula toward the rich treat. She gave them a playful whack with the cake server.

"Oww!" a high-pitched voice howled. A freckled face popped up from beneath the breakfast bar, its childish features bearing a strong resemblance to the pastor's.

"Chet," Troy warned. "You know better."

"Yessir." Cherubic lips formed a pout as the sturdy towhead tugged his brother into view.

"Have a seat, Cora," Sharon said, carrying the dessert tray to the next room where the polished mahogany dining table sported matching place mats in a floral print. "Then we'll take you on a tour of our classy new digs."

"Thank you." Just in time she spotted an alphabet block on her seat and brushed it off, ignoring some muffled giggles. "It should be a bit more quiet around here now that the renovations are finished."

"In some ways." Sharon herded the boys to the bench they usually occupied for meals. The imps scrambled into place, where cake and milk now awaited them. Two pairs of huge blue eyes widened in a sweeping arc between one parent's face and then the other. Then, all innocence after everyone had been served, the two folded their pudgy fingers and bowed their heads for grace.

"Thank You, dear Lord," Troy said, "for Your goodness and faithfulness to us all. Bless this refreshment and our conversation and make us better able to serve You. In Your Son's name, amen."

Cora smoothed her paper napkin over the lap of her belted skirt. "How've you been feeling?" she asked the mother-to-be while slicing into the moist chocolate dessert and sampling the scrumptious flavor.

"Getting impatient for the arrival of our new munchkin," Sharon confessed. Sable eyes the same shade as her long shiny curls sparkled against a complexion the exact opposite of the fair minister's. "Sometimes it's so. . . active." She patted the bulging tummy beneath her denim maternity jumper.

Thankfully Cora refrained from blurting the first thought that popped into her mind. Things had changed so much since the days when she'd raised her own younger siblings, after their parents' untimely death during her first term at Bible school. Today's authorities frowned on the strict discipline of the older generation, though it wasn't hard to find instances where some of those old ways were sorely needed. She could not help admiring this young mother's patience, however. Noticing the others were done eating, Cora hurriedly finished her remaining cake and tea in readiness for the ensuing tour.

"This," Troy announced proudly a few minutes later as he gestured into the second-floor boys' bedroom, "was Mike's first project, building all the shelves, the alcove for Tuck's bed and desk, and the other improvements we badly needed. The man was a godsend."

"Really." Assessing the new boyish furnishings in bright Crayola colors, Cora could only admire the first-rate workmanship. Everything she'd seen so far, from the recently added laundry room with all the wonderful cabinetry and built-in ironing board, to the now-enclosed porch that ran the length of the back of the house, all showed the mark of a master craftsman. He'd even made fittings for both screens and storm windows. The fact that he'd managed to accomplish so much with the youngsters underfoot was not to be overlooked, either.

"How'd your new roof do in that last spell of rain?" Sharon asked her as they strolled back toward the side door, the boys occupied in their bedroom.

Cora emitted a whoosh of relief. "First time in ages I felt free to leave the house without setting out a bunch of pots and pails. Of course, the rest of the structure is intent on disintegrating around my ankles, mind you. One of these days I should fix it up and sell it. It's too much for me to keep up anymore."

"Don't sell yourself short," the minister said. "If a few more of our members had half the energy you do, we'd be in the middle of a building program by now."

Cora just shook her head.

"Still," Sharon chimed in, "if you really do need a good carpenter, we wouldn't hesitate to recommend Mike. Would we, Sweetheart?"

"Not at all. He does excellent work. Home restoration is his specialty. And for a guy who only rarely darkens the door of a church, I've found him to be completely trustworthy."

"I'll keep him in mind," Cora said politely, having no intention of actually doing so. Her aging house nestled in the hills outside of Shavertown needed so much work she had no idea where to begin. Besides, nothing was really pressing. She couldn't imagine herself way out in the country all alone for weeks on end with that whistling handyman. Much easier to put the matter off for some future time.

Entering her kitchen door later that afternoon, however, Cora couldn't deny the whole place seemed little more than a collection of musty smells, squeaky doors, drafty windows, and creaking floors. . .especially in comparison to the parsonage's improvements. Even the front porch, the site of so many happy family times, had begun to sag. If not for the treasured memories of growing up here, she'd have dumped the farm ages ago, whether her younger siblings approved or not. They were off living their own lives and making new memories. Not one of them seemed overly concerned that Cora had put aside her personal dreams and stayed home to raise them, then been left behind to rattle around the big old house all alone. Visits were few and far between.

"Yes, well, it does have its charm," she reminded herself, her voice a hollow echo against the cupboards—cupboards with chipped paint revealing layers of color trends. Without too much imagination, she could still envision her crisply aproned mother bustling about the kitchen in its eggshell-blue days, baking rafts of pies and cakes and breads her family adored. Now the whole room bore white enamel, complete with intricate roses and vines her younger sisters Megan and Michelle had stenciled some years ago.

As Cora turned on the faucet to fill the tea kettle, a clunk in the pipes before the water gushed forth quickly banished the sweet memories. Maybe she'd at least see about getting a plumber.

~

"Oh, Cora," Pastor Troy said the following day, "I hate to impose on your good nature, but I'm running out of week. If you could possibly stop by and pay a call on

Nettie Humphries, it sure would help me out. I have three hospital calls to make down in Wyoming Valley today."

"Sure. I don't mind. I'll swing by her place on my way home."

"Thanks. I owe you. And do me a favor, would you? When Sharon gets back from her appointment, tell her I'll be awhile."

"Will do." Returning her attention to the program for Sunday's service, Cora barely heard Troy's sedan pull away. She did notice the quiet and popped a CD into the player for company while she added the final touches to the bulletin. She didn't mind helping out with visitation calls to the shut-ins. The pastor gave her great freedom regarding her schedule and considered the calls part of her working day, plus they added to her feeling of being useful.

Leaving the church a little early, Cora drove to a small, homey, two-bedroom house a mere two miles from her own farm. Nettie Humphries had been a close friend of Cora's parents, and the family had known her forever. Today the elderly widow appeared a touch under the weather and abed in the stuffy back bedroom, her slight form barely evident beneath the half-dozen blankets shrouding her.

"So nice of you to stop by," the pale widow said, reaching a gnarled hand to brush her thin gray braid off her shoulder.

"The pastor asked me to look in on you, see if there's anything you need."

Her small head nodded gratefully. "Oh, I'm gettin' by. Seems I can't get these old crooked fingers to work right anymore, though. Could you maybe help me with a letter to my Ida Mae? Thought she might come and stay with me awhile."

"I'd be glad to, Nettie." Finding paper and an envelope in a bedside drawer, Cora pulled up a chair beside the sickbed and composed the letter as the older woman dictated, then folded the pages and tucked them inside an envelope. "I'll put this in the mailbox on my way home," she said, standing to leave.

"Thanks so much. How's that family of yours?" the widow asked. "I think about them a lot. Any of those brothers or sisters talk about moving back here?"

Cora shook her head. "Not so far. Ted's still active with his mission work in Mexico, Nelson's pastorate in Tennessee is growing by leaps and bounds, and Matt continues his circuit with the evangelistic team he's been providing music for. And the girls are both adding to their own families."

"A pity, that big old place of yours falling to a woman alone. You should have married, too, a nice girl like you. Have a husband and your own kids to take over the farm. Must need lots of work by now."

She couldn't help smiling. "You're right. Lots. Everywhere I turn it's falling apart. But I might fix it up eventually and sell it. Then I could move to some smaller place in town."

"Still, it's a shame. Pretty and nice as you are, living all alone."

"I get by, Nettie. Really, I do. I'm happy in my job, working for the church, making calls. Our congregation is growing every month with Pastor Green's efforts. I don't feel I've lacked much. And you're not so far away that I can't pop over for tea now and again," she added on a teasing note.

"Mebbe. But some nice man's missed out on a real treasure he might'a had."

Cora smiled and bent to kiss the parchment-thin forehead. "Let's just keep that our little secret, okay? Would you like me to pray with you before I go?"

"Yes, that would be nice. Bless you."

Thoughts of the dear woman remained on Cora's heart long after she was in the solitude of her own home, and she breathed another prayer that God would find it in His will to restore her to health again, give the sweet old gal a few more productive years.

Undoing her French twist at the dressing table in her bedroom, Cora brushed out her chin-length blond hair. In curiosity she stopped midmotion and leaned in for a closer look, taking in the admittedly decent cheekbones, the wide mouth with its still healthy teeth, clear blue eyes just starting to appreciate reading glasses. *Pretty*, huh?

A droll smile curved her lips. Maybe once upon a time, fresh out of high school, when a chance meeting with a clean-cut town boy could fill her untried heart with romantic dreams and set her feet to dancing. But that was twenty-five years ago. Another life. All those handsome boys had gone on to college or into careers or some branch of the military, while her own dreams of Bible school were shelved to raise her siblings. She'd been too busy even to stay in close touch with her old school chums as they married, one by one, and relocated. Who even knew where they were now? Likely she wouldn't recognize any of them, nor would they know her. . .this too-thin woman with fading hair who stared back from the mirror.

Better to concentrate on now, on the life she'd inherited. Rising, she turned down the comforter on her double bed and reached to turn on the bedside lamp for her evening devotions.

The bulb sparked and burst, a thin plume of smoke curling upward. A similar puff from the socket emitted a whiff of burnt insulation.

Cora moaned and unplugged the thing, then switched to the lamp on the opposite side. Might not hurt to contact an electrician tomorrow.

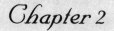

Chapter 2

Mike Burgess signed off the Internet and yawned. Since finishing the renovations at the church two weeks ago, he'd been catching things up around his own place, a story-and-a-half log home he'd built amid the rolling hills of Tunkhannock. Shoulder-high rows of neatly stacked seasoned wood from the tree-studded acreage now lined one side of the house in readiness for the coming Pennsylvania winter. He'd added a new coat of water seal to the raised deck overlooking the small, secluded pond below his property, checked window frames and doors for caulking, and gotten in a supply of heating oil.

Now he could see about the orders for furniture that had been accumulating on his website while he'd been otherwise occupied. Much as he loved making rooms over and seeing the satisfied faces of actual living customers, he itched to get back to rebuilding special order furniture and shipping it all over America to people he'd never met, places he had yet to visit. He derived a certain pride from tacking brass *Built by Burgess* plates on every item crafted by his own hand, knowing those pieces would outlast their owners by several generations. By the time his number was up, he'd leave a lasting legacy, maybe even be immortalized in woodworking journals by some enterprising future reporter. Too bad he didn't have a bunch of sons to learn the business and carry on his name. A few too many years had flown by since there'd been any possibility along that line, though. No point dwelling on past regrets.

After pouring himself a mug of black coffee, he grabbed the orders he'd printed off the computer and started toward his basement workshop, where a wealth of the finest woodworking equipment money could buy awaited his expertise.

The jangling of the wall phone brought him to a stop. He set down his cup and plucked the receiver from the cradle. "Burgess here."

"Hi, Mike. It's Troy. Must be great to be back at the old workshop again."

"Right. What's up, Reverend? I forget something?"

"No, not at all. I was wondering about your schedule, if you have anything pressing at the moment."

"A couple orders for furniture. Why? Something you need?"

"Not me, personally. I might have a customer for you, though, one with an older home in dire need of repair. Interested?"

"Well–l–l," Mike hedged, raking fingers through his still thick hair. "I wasn't exactly looking for another big project right now. . . ."

"Who says it's big? Could you maybe call and set up an appointment? You'd be able to estimate what might be involved before you commit."

Mike didn't respond immediately.

"I do know there's some stuff that needs done before the cold weather sets in," Troy elaborated. "If you can't tackle the job, we'll look around for somebody else. I just wanted you to have the first shot. I've, uh, been kinda blowing your horn over your great work at the house."

A grin spread across Mike's mouth. "Thanks. I suppose it wouldn't hurt to have a look. Where is the place?"

"Back this way, off Demunds Road." He rattled off more detailed directions that pinpointed the location in Mike's brain. "Let me give you the phone number."

"Right." Mike mentally repeated the first three digits after the pastor while rummaging for a pencil, then finding one, scribbled the whole thing down. "I'll check it out. And thanks, Rev. I appreciate the plug."

"Sure thing. When the owner mentioned needing somebody trustworthy, I said I'd find out if you were available."

"I guess we'll see, then. Take care." Hanging up the phone, Mike realized he'd forgotten to get the person's name, but that could be easily remedied. And he did like to keep busy. Could be a relatively quick project he could do in the daylight hours, then come home and work on furniture in the evening. Might as well call and find out what he was letting himself in for. After gulping the remains of his coffee, he punched in the phone number.

Arriving home after work, Cora flipped on the kitchen light switch and smiled. Could be her lively imagination, but since the installation of new wiring, every bulb in the house seemed to burn brighter. She slept more soundly also, with one less worry. Or to be more truthful, two less worries. The plumber she'd hired last week had replaced the ancient corroded pipes that had been causing no end of grief. Added to the brand-new roof from a month ago, the place was being reborn a little at a time. No sense stopping now, when with a bit of sprucing up here and there it could all be set to rights. Perhaps next spring she could start showing the house to prospective buyers.

Setting her purse on the round maple table and draping her fall coat over a chair back, Cora swept a critical glance over the outdated kitchen, the starting spot for a makeover she couldn't begin to envision. Once quite attractive and functional enough to serve three generations of a lively family, its flooring now creaked with soft, uneven spots, scarred and cracked counters looked even more dreary than the chipped cupboards, and as for the big old sink. . . She winced. No amount of cleanser or scouring could make that thing glisten again. What this room needed was *gutting*, pure and simple.

The phone rang, jarring her back to reality. Taming the goofy smile brought on by that extreme mental picture, Cora crossed to the avocado wall unit—itself an antiquated relic with a rotary dial—and picked up the receiver. "Hello?"

A pause. The clearing of a throat. "This is Mike Burgess. Reverend Green asked me to call this number regarding some possible remodeling."

"Oh. Mr. Burgess. Yes. Pastor Troy told me you might phone. I'm Cora Dennison, his secretary."

"I see." Another pause. "What exactly did you want done, Mrs. Dennison?"

Still viewing the kitchen's shortcomings, Cora resorted to complete candor. "Actually, to be truthful, I don't know what all this old place needs. And it's *Miss*."

"I beg your pardon?"

"It's Miss Dennison," she repeated. "I guess what I need to know is how much repair work it would take to ready the house enough to sell, come spring."

"So you're needing an overall evaluation."

"That's correct. And the pastor assured me you'd be fair and honest."

A low chuckle. "Tell you what, Miz Dennison, I'll come by your place and give you my *fair and honest* opinion, say, after work tomorrow?"

"That would be fine, Mr. Burgess. I'll be home by four. Thank you."

Hanging up the phone, Cora retrieved her coat and took it to the hall closet, giving things the once-over as she went. Habitually neat, she'd always kept her residence tidy, but there were a few things she needed to do before Mike Burgess came to tromp through the entire house tomorrow. The man might not be the neatest person around, but Cora set pretty high standards regarding her own appearance and that of her surroundings.

Within moments of arriving home the next day, Cora heard the Bronco rumbling up the lane from the main road. The fact that she'd had a roofer, a plumber, and an electrician here making repairs within the past month had been an advantage, one that helped her through the initial awkwardness of having workmen around. At least this carpenter wouldn't be a complete stranger. Or so she told herself in order to relax. She just hoped he'd act with the propriety Pastor Troy avowed. Surely that near wink had been a figment of her imagination. Middle-aged men weren't prone to such brashness. . . and middle-aged women should know enough to ignore them.

Drawing comfort from that assurance, she detected the sound of footsteps on the back porch and answered the door a second before he knocked.

A faded jacket gaped over the flannel shirt tucked into his work jeans. And as before, he appeared in need of a shave. But his casual stance didn't seem at all threatening, especially with that lopsided smile curving a corner of his mouth. "Miz Dennison."

"Mr. Burgess. Thank you for coming by. Come in, won't you?" Cora stepped aside to permit him entrance. "I was just about to make fresh coffee. Would you care for some?"

"You bet. And it's Mike."

With an uncertain nod, Cora moved to counter and pressed the start button on the coffeemaker she kept in readiness. Turning back, she found his keen gray eyes watching her. They matched the hue of his plaid shirt, she noted. In fact, he had very. . .nice eyes. Kind, observant—perhaps too much so. She blurted the first thing she could think of. "While it brews, I'll show you through the rest of the house." She started to turn.

"Wait a minute." He held up a calloused hand. "What exactly are we talking here? How much of the place needs work? What kind of investment are you prepared to make? Might as well know that up front."

The shrewdness in his expression softened considerably as her shoulders sagged. "I have no idea," Cora admitted. "That's what I need you to tell me. I'm not a wealthy woman, by any means. But I have some savings, and I'll spend whatever it takes to turn the clock back on this place, make it worth buying." She cast a despondent glance around. "I hardly think anyone would be interested with it in this present state. For all I know, a bulldozer might be the better option."

"I wouldn't be too quick to assume that." His gaze followed hers. "I'll have a look. Then we'll talk over coffee. Okay with you?"

Cora gave him a polite smile. "Fine. This way, then. I'll show you the upstairs."

She'd intended for the tour to be fairly short and swift, but he took his time in every room, studying layouts, checking window frames and testing floors upstairs, downstairs, and in the cellar. After perusing the front porch and making a circuit around the exterior perimeter, he nodded. "Okay, we can go have that coffee now."

Moments later, he sat at the kitchen table while Cora brought over steaming mugs and a plate of over-sized homemade chocolate chip cookies. "Do you take cream or sugar?"

"Black is fine, thanks."

She added a little milk to her own cup, then took a seat opposite him. "Pretty bad, isn't it?"

"This place?" He grinned. "Old, maybe. Lived in. Needs some work here and there, but anybody can see it must have been a grand house in its day."

He could see that? A chunk of Cora's usual reserve melted and broke away like snow off a rooftop. Maybe this wouldn't be so bad after all, having this handyman working around the house for however long it took for the repairs to be completed. Which brought up another concern. "What sort of time frame will all this entail?"

"Depends on how involved the renovations are that you're considering. Where did you plan to start?"

"Here. The kitchen."

"Good choice. It needs the bulk of my attention, that and maybe the upstairs bathroom. Most of the rest will be minor, if you want anything else done, that is."

Cora had to agree. "What I'd really like is for this room to be warm and homey. Not old-fashioned, but not overly modern, either. Everything should look. . . timeless, as if it always belonged here." She blushed. "That probably sounds silly."

An understanding smile gentled his features, and he rubbed his chin in thought, his gaze making a slow circuit of the room. "Not at all. The floor's pretty well

281

shot, needs redoing and bracing, which I'm sure you already figured."

Cora nodded.

"You gonna want natural hardwood or vinyl floor covering?"

She thought for a moment. "Probably vinyl. . .with a warm pattern. Like stone or brick, perhaps. More countryish."

"Easy enough. Then with a new sink and fixtures, better quality doors on the cupboards, maybe a built-in oven and microwave, it might look the way you'd like it to. Of course, you'll have to put up with a mess for awhile," he added, one eye twitching with that almost wink she'd glimpsed at the church.

Cora's spine straightened a notch, and she reverted to a cool businesslike tone. "I understand. I'm willing to keep out of your way as much as possible. The pastor suggested a good portion of the work might be undertaken while I'm at the church. I could let you in each morning before I leave, and you'd have free rein most of the time." Her gaze met his straight on. "Since you're *trustworthy* and all."

An amused twinkle sparked in his eye, but he maintained a straight face by kneading his chin again. "Let me take one more walk-through and make some notes, figure out what I'll need to get started, then I'll run some figures by you and you can decide if you want me to do the work." He shoved his chair back with his knees and stood.

"I've already decided," Cora said, determination

evident in her voice as she rose and gathered their cups. "I don't care what the figures add up to, Mr. Burgess. I'd like you to just do what needs done. I intend to sell the place afterward, and most of the investment will be recovered, I'm sure."

He gave a nod of acknowledgment. "Just the same, I'll let you know ahead of time what my plans are, keep you abreast of wood choices, fixtures I'll need to buy. That kinda thing. Wouldn't want to take advantage of a. . .customer. Especially a woman like yourself."

Having no idea what that remark meant, Cora let it pass. She knew she was setting a lot of store by Pastor Troy's high recommendation and assurance of the workman's character. And having seen the quality of his craftsmanship, she had no doubts regarding that. But a large part of her seriously hoped she wasn't biting off more than she could chew by embarking on a project that would put the two of them in close proximity for. . .heaven knew how long.

His voice cut across her musings. "Might as well chuck the formality, since we're gonna be seeing a lot of each other for awhile. As I mentioned before, I go by Mike."

Cora managed a dubious nod but averted her gaze and began clearing the table while Mike Burgess took one more leisurely stroll through the house, the floors creaking from one room to the next with his movements.

This was going to take some getting used to. . . hearing a man's footsteps around the place again. A lot of years had passed since her boisterous brothers tripped up and down the stairs, cracking jokes and filling the house with the sounds of life. She just hoped she didn't let herself become too used to it, because that would make returning to her solitude that much harder.

Even so, it would be far less cumbersome to call him Mike, Cora decided. She'd always liked the name.

Chapter 3

So how're things going out at your place?" Troy asked, setting some signed correspondence on Cora's desk. "Have you decided to let Mike do the restoration?"

Folding the top letter on the stack and tucking it inside an envelope, Cora nodded. "Thanks for calling him. He came by on Friday to look things over, stopped back the next day to drop off some supplies and show me some samples. Flooring, countertops, wood grains, and the like."

"So he'll be starting right in on things?"

"Yes. He arrived bright and early this morning, eager to get going." She licked the flap and sealed it, then went on to the second piece.

"Great. I know you won't regret contracting him. The man really takes pride in his work, which according to my dad is rare these days."

"Sure is." Cora stopped working and smiled. "His optimism is quite catching. I'm anxious to see what he manages to accomplish this time without anybody getting in his way."

Troy chuckled. "Like my two little live wires, you mean?"

She felt a flush creep up her face. "I meant interruptions of any kind."

"Whatever. Well, I—" The phone in his office rang just then, and with a wave, the young minister strode away to answer the summons.

Cora's thoughts wasted no time returning to the house, and she wondered what was happening there. She'd left the coffeepot ready for Mike to turn on, plus set out a fresh apple pie with a note for him to help himself. What would the normally tidy kitchen look like by the end of the day? Would it even be useable? At the rather bleak vision of her having to pick her way gingerly across gaping floor joists for days on end drifted to mind, Cora wondered if she should stock up on convenience food for awhile. Or eat out indefinitely.

Mike hummed to himself as he peeled away the layers of linoleum and dragged the useless strips outside. The newly exposed floorboards appeared about the way he suspected they would. . .rotted in places and totally worthless. Fortunately the lumber he'd ordered arrived shortly after Cora Dennison's departure. She probably passed the truck on her way to the church without even knowing it. And by the time she got home this afternoon, a lot of her kitchen would be only a memory. It would be several days, at least, before she'd be able to start using it. He hoped she was prepared for that.

Refilling the coffee mug she'd left out for him, he sipped the rich liquid slowly and leaned against the edge of the counter, calculating which end of the room to begin ripping up first. With no little relief, he'd discovered the floor beneath the stove to be sound. The unit itself could stand replacing, however. He'd mention the advantages of a countertop range, since he'd be installing a wall oven and microwave. Then, of course, the old fridge would look out of place. Maybe she could take a couple of hours and accompany him to an appliance store to choose things that would match each other and complement the new surroundings. He'd suggest the possibility when she came home.

A lazy smile tweaked his lips at the thought of her ramrod straight back. When something made her go rigid, she looked skinny as a flagpole, the opposite of the type of women he'd always found appealing. No doubt being at the church so much, she probably knew the Scriptures backward and forward, too, and could do a fair bit of preaching about how people should attend services regularly. He grimaced.

She did have a real nice face, though. Downright handsome and gracious to boot. But she sure could get flustered if he dared look at her crosswise. That was one thing he'd noticed while working around the church and parsonage. But after living by herself so many years, perhaps that was to be expected.

Surely she had family. He'd scanned a collection of framed pictures lining the hallways, mostly group shots of her and a bunch of younger people who bore strong fair-haired resemblance to her. How come no relatives had swung by to check out the handyman she'd hired to do such an extensive amount of work? Maybe they would yet.

Mike, an avid reader of people, had detected something else about Cora Dennison, too. She had excellent taste. Even though several spots in this old family home were crumbling around her, all its furnishings bespoke the very quality she yearned for in the kitchen. . .timelessness. He believed he could predict precisely the new choices she would make. He could almost picture the finished kitchen in his mind before tearing out a single board. In fact, he had a few ideas she hadn't even spoken of, additions that would ensure the kind of homey, country room she wanted, like stripping the ceiling paint off and exposing the original wood, adding open beams where she could hang herbs or baskets the way ladies liked to do. He planned to leave this place better than she dreamed. For some reason that seemed important.

Downing the remains in his mug, he determined not to waste any more daylight. He picked up a claw hammer and began yanking nails out of the floorboards.

❧

Cora arrived home an hour earlier than usual. Intending to pay a call on an elderly shut-in, she'd driven to the woman's address, only to find no one there. Likely the ailing invalid had been transferred to the hospital, which Pastor Troy would discover while making his rounds down in the valley. After the fruitless trip, Cora headed for home instead. Exiting her car in the garage behind the house, she could detect some hearty singing from inside the house, accompanied by sounds of work in progress. The back door hung open. She approached it with caution, peering around the doorjamb.

The floor no longer existed! Even though she'd expected it, seeing the actual open gaps between the joists stunned Cora. "Hellooo," she called out.

The singing stopped midsentence. "I'm down in the cellar," Mike hollered. "Watch where you step." Then his work boots clomped up the cellar stairs. "You'd better use the front door for a day or two." He wiped his hands on a rag which he stuffed into a back pocket as he came into view. "I jacked up the joists in a couple of spots to level the floor, then we can start installing the new boards."

Hoping to cover her dismay, Cora managed a nod.

"Actually, I'm glad you're here," the carpenter went on. "Thought we might run down to a couple appliance stores in Wilkes-Barre so you can pick out the replacements. I have an idea of what might go with the new decor, but it should be your choice. You're the one who'll be living with them when all's said and done."

"We need to go today?" Cora asked.

"Sooner the better. By the time they're delivered, the floor will be down. Game? We can take my truck."

Unable to come up with a feasible reason to decline, Cora acquiesced. Surely the man knew what he was doing. "Just let me switch to some comfortable shoes, and I'll be right out."

Soon enough, Cora found herself heading down to Wyoming Valley with a man she barely knew, a most unusual and unprecedented experience for her. Some pair they made, she conceded, with her attired in a fashionable skirt, blazer, and flats, and him in soiled work garb. Thankfully, his vehicle seemed reasonably clean. Obviously he took pride in it. Did he expect her to make small talk, to fill in the silence? But Mike eliminated that possibility by turning on the truck radio. A touch of a preset button, and the strains of a Rachmaninoff piano concerto filled the Bronco's interior.

Cora marveled that his taste seemed the opposite of her preconceived opinion of him and relaxed a notch listening to her favorite composer. She focused her attention on the passing scenery until they turned onto the Cross Valley Expressway toward the large shopping areas on the other side of the Susquehanna River.

"Nice day," he finally said, turning down the volume a little as they crossed the bridge. Patches of autumn's fading glory reflected from the distant mountain ridges that ringed the valley, their blended hues a bright blur against the dark current. "I've always been partial to fall in Pennsylvania."

Cora smiled. "My sentiments exactly. But spring has charms of its own. Everything coming back to life again in all new colors after the long winter."

"Yeah, that's hard to beat." His lips quirked with a suppressed smile. "We could do with less humidity, though, round about August. Don't think anybody ever gets used to that."

"No, I don't expect so."

A busy intersection ahead ended the seasonal discussion. "Might as well hit this place first," Mike said, turning onto a side street and veering into a wide parking lot. "Since it's right near a building supply place, maybe you'd like to check out a bigger selection of floor coverings while you're at it."

"Whatever you think."

He parked not far from the main entrance, and shortly the two of them stood among rows of gleaming refrigerators and stoves in enough styles and colors to boggle the mind. Mike didn't rush her, but Cora listened to his advice regarding the advantages of water and ice dispensers and countertop ranges and found it to be sound. She made choices he seemed to approve, and then they headed to the huge building supply place across the parking lot.

She'd had no idea so many styles and finishes for kitchen cabinets existed, to say nothing of sinks and fixtures. But actually seeing them up close in person did give a much better perspective than merely flipping through catalogs or examining an array of small wood chips linked together on a chain. Cora felt like a kid in a candy store, moving from one full-sized display to the next, awed by each one.

"So these are the cupboard doors you want?" Mike asked, his large hand resting on a definite country-style finish. "You're sure."

"Positive. Don't you think they'll go perfectly with the stone-look flooring?"

"I do. Just wanted to make sure you're happy with 'em."

Cora smiled her pleasure. "I haven't had this much fun in ages. To think I've been putting up with that old ramshackle house for years, when it could have been so much nicer." She wagged her head.

"Don't be so hard on yourself. The point is you're doing it over now. When I'm done, you won't recognize the place. But you will feel at home, I promise."

The jovial twinkle in his gray eyes and the way that open expression gentled the features in his long face made her wonder why she'd ever thought of Mike Burgess as scruffy. He merely looked like what he was: a master carpenter who had an appreciation for quality, old and new. And so did she. Somehow Cora sensed truth in his promise. Already she could hardly wait to see the finished product.

"What do you say we catch a bite to eat?" he suggested. "Seeing as how I've made a royal mess of your kitchen, I'm afraid you're not gonna be able to do much cooking for a couple days."

"Good idea. It'll be my treat."

He looked aghast at her. "Forget that idea. Your treat was that apple pie you left out this morning, Lady. This one's on me. My favorite diner just happens to be up in this area."

Cora knew better than to argue. "Okay. This time. But when all is said and done, and that new range and oven and sink are in place, I'm going to cook you a meal you won't forget."

"You won't hear me refuse an offer like that, Miz Dennison."

"Cora," she said softly.

"Cora." He tipped his chin and smiled when he said it, and her know-better heart did the strangest little. . .dance. She *had* to get ahold of herself.

❦

Mike felt in his element, standing in the middle of the building supply store. Cora Dennison's house was not the first he'd contracted for major renovations. And she wasn't the first customer he'd carted around to look at new fixtures and flooring. She *was*, however, the first customer who made the chore seem more like fun than work. While looking at the various displays, those cornflower blue eyes of hers radiated with childlike delight. Nothing missed her attention. Those slender fingers trailed over the different wood finishes and cabinet doors, stroked the rich Corian countertops, even checked out the smooth vinyl and faux stone floor coverings. He could almost see the various displays taking shape inside her head as she envisioned how one style would look at home as opposed to another.

But most amazing of all, down to the last item, her choices exactly matched his. Almost as if he stood behind her making subliminal suggestions: *Choose this one. This is perfect. Just what I'm looking for.* How many times in the past had he been forced to grit his teeth and make himself install something completely tasteless just to satisfy a determined customer? This was really weird. No wonder he felt the conviction she would be pleased when he added the special touch of open beams, which they hadn't even discussed. He just knew they'd finish off the kitchen perfectly.

Ushering Cora back to the truck and then to a quiet booth at Ned's Diner, Mike had to forcibly banish the enticing mental image of the two of them sharing a delectable dinner in that perfect new kitchen of hers. Already he could smell her cooking, could taste a melt-in-your-mouth roast with mashed potatoes and dark gravy, maybe another one of those apple pies for dessert. Nobody could top that.

When their orders arrived, and Cora bowed her head briefly to pray over her food *in public*, Mike's fanciful musings slammed once more into reality. Sure they had a few things in common in regard to decorating, but he'd had her pegged right all along. Too churchy. Best concentrate on feeding the gal and getting back to the job he'd contracted for. Once it was done, they could simply go their own ways. Life would get back to normal. They'd both be better off.

Chapter 4

Dear Lord, please don't let me walk in my sleep tonight, Cora added as a postscript to her evening prayers. The yawning chasm downstairs in the kitchen was more than a little unsettling. What if she forgot and strolled blithely to the sink for a glass of water, only to end up a crumpled, bloodied heap on the cold cellar floor! The horrors of that possibility sent gooseflesh up her arms. Rubbing them as she rose from her knees, Cora turned down the blankets and crawled into bed.

What an amazing day this had been, she recalled with a smile. Who would have believed such lovely things existed for homes or that a number of them would soon be part of this very farmhouse? If the kitchen ended up half as pretty as she imagined, she would give Mike Burgess carte blanche in fixing up the rest of the place as well.

Replaying the afternoon's events, Cora felt a niggle of guilt creep through her. Mike himself had proved to be the opposite of her first impression. What she'd deemed forwardness in his manner turned out to be mere friendliness. He'd certainly treated her with respect and consideration while introducing her to the wonders of hardware and appliance stores. Likely the real fault lay in her own bent toward being prissy and standoff-ish. What a lesson in humility. *Forgive me, Lord. Help me not to judge people so quickly.*

He had seemed a little more remote after she'd habitually said grace in the restaurant, Cora admitted. But the prayer had been silent and extremely brief, certainly not something that should offend anyone. Just because the carpenter wasn't prone to attend church often, if ever, Cora could see no reason to alter her own lifestyle. She never ate without first thanking the Lord for His provision. Once the renovations were completed on her house, Mike would go his merry way and she'd go hers. . .but that didn't mean she wouldn't pray for his soul in the meantime. A purposeful smile settled over her lips as she closed her eyes.

When Cora arrived home from work the next day, she found the kitchen floor in place, the unfinished wood emitting a fragrant smell throughout the house. Mike was nowhere to be seen, so she yielded to the temptation of testing his handiwork, making a slow circuit of the room, checking for creaky spots. Not a single one! The man really knew his business. After he installed the floor covering and hooked up the new appliances, she would start leaving him home-baked treats again. In the meantime, it was another frozen entree for her. With a resigned sigh, she headed for the dining room, where he'd moved her refrigerator and microwave.

She changed out of her work clothes while the meal cooked, returning downstairs in plaid wool slacks and a sweater. Then, setting up a TV tray in the living room, she switched on the local news to banish the quiet as she ate.

Mike stopped at a diner for supper and ordered the meat loaf special. He'd worked his behind off today making sure Cora had a floor to walk on when she got home, but otherwise that kitchen was still quite useless. Anticipating the steaming food the waitress would soon bring to him, he debated whether he should have hung around Cora's and taken her out for a hot meal. He doubted a woman like her was used to resorting to convenience food. She gave the impression of being a person who'd take the time to put balanced meals together, even if she was the only one there to eat them. After all, it was the proper thing to do.

Yanking an extra napkin out of the booth's stainless steel holder and a pen from his shirt pocket, he made a rough sketch of the kitchen with the new appliances positioned one way, then another. Practicality declared the ideal spot for the unit with the wall oven and microwave to be the one formerly occupied by the refrigerator, where it would be handy to the counter and sink. If he added a right-angle cupboard at the other end and built an enclosure for the fridge, the L-shape would not only give her more shelves for kitchen items but provide the kind of finished look to the room it had previously lacked.

"Here you are," the slim waitress said, arriving with his meal and coffee.

Mike shoved the napkin aside while she set the plate before him and filled his cup. "Anything else I can get you?"

"Nope. This looks great. Thanks." As she nodded and returned to other duties, he pulled the napkin close again. He dunked his roll into the rich gravy glazing the mashed potatoes and meat loaf and bit off a chunk as he eyed the diagram, his mind already returning to thoughts of his project.

The rest of that wall would be more useful if, instead of ending with the refrigerator, a pantry took up the remaining space. Her round maple table could be moved to the middle of the room on a braided rug and look real homey. And Cora liked homey. That much he knew about her. Satisfied himself, he took a gulp of the strong coffee, then delved into the rest of the meal.

"Good morning," Cora said cheerily, letting Mike in the following morning. Her favorite radio devotional was nearing conclusion, but the volume was low, so she didn't turn it off. Only the last song and short closing comments remained before it ended. "How nice it was to wake up and be able to walk on the floor again."

He chuckled. "Figured you'd appreciate that." Chucking his down jacket on a nearby chair, he cleared his throat. "I was wondering something, though. What with the new flooring and cupboards, those white walls are gonna look a tad out of place. Any objections against my stripping the paint off them and the ceiling? Getting back to the natural wood?"

Frowning momentarily, Cora cocked her head back and forth. "Not at all. Whatever you think is best. I trust your judgment."

"That'll be the plan, then," he returned with a nod. "I didn't want to do anything major without checking with you first."

"You're very considerate." She shyly met his gaze. "It already looks so much better not to see the floor sagging. I try to picture all those new appliances in place, but I can't imagine how they'll ever fit. I think I bought too many."

"Nope, not at all. They'll fit. You'll see." That hint of a wink again, and he headed for the corner where he'd left his toolbox.

It's just his way, she lectured herself. *Don't give it any mind.* But a tiny part of her wondered what it must be like when a wink actually did mean something special. . .and how dopey it was for a grown woman to have such childish thoughts anyway. "I'll be off, then. There's fresh coffee in the dining room and some pastries. Please, help yourself."

"Thanks, Cora."

She smiled and nodded, then retrieved her purse and went to the hall closet for her coat. The sounds of Mike's whistling along with "How Great Thou Art" carried through the house, taking her back to when her siblings lived at home, to days when something lively was always happening inside these walls. How incredibly dead the place had been since the others went off to live their own lives.

～

"And so, dear friends," the radio announcer said, "look around at the wonders the Lord has lavished upon us and remember to think on His greatness today. It'll make your day brighter."

"Yeah. Right," Mike muttered. "My day's bright enough, thanks just the same." With the sound of Cora's sedan pulling out of the drive, he turned the dial to a station which alternated between classical music and light jazz and smiled with relief when he recognized Schubert's two-movement Symphony no. 8 in B Minor, known forever as the *Unfinished Symphony*. "Now, that's more like it." As the magnificent piece filled the air, he went to wrestle the ungainly roll of vinyl flooring awaiting his attention.

The appliances arrived midafternoon. Mike had the new stone-look floor laid, plus a section of the cupboards stripped of paint. He'd purposely decided to leave the originals in place because they were roomier than today's pre-fab ones and could easily be upgraded with the new doors Cora had chosen. A huge job still lay ahead, what with installing the new double stainless steel sink with updated faucet, tackling new countertops, refinishing cupboards, and building enclosures for the wall oven and refrigerator. The kitchen wouldn't be useable for several more days. Yet Mike found the hard work incredibly gratifying as the old place gradually took on a glory it never quite had before. Cora would love it.

That conviction brought a grin. She really would love the place when he got done with it, and that was a fact. Mike knew it as though he possessed psychic ability. . .or that of a prophet, he amended, considering the gal he was working for. She probably didn't cotton to that other generic wrong-more-than-right fortune-telling nonsense. Neither did he, to be truthful. A fatalist at heart, Mike believed that what would be would be, no point in setting one's hopes otherwise. People like Cora and Reverend Green might set a lot of store by the Almighty and His intervention in the lives of His people, but they hadn't had those naive beliefs thrown back in their faces, the way he had all those years ago. Still, he didn't plan on being the one to smarten them up. Live and let live, and all that. It was a good enough creed to live by. . .even if it didn't quite satisfy.

Mike's stomach began rumbling in earnest about half an hour before Cora was due home. Considering the likelihood of her leaving him coffee and store-bought baked goods every morning, the least he could do was return the favor by taking her out for a hot meal now and again. He'd at least offer. She could go if she pleased.

He didn't have long to wait. Cora arrived a few minutes early, and when he heard her light step on the porch, he looked up and met her gaze as she came in.

"Oh, my. The new floor is down. It's beautiful!" She gazed around in obvious appreciation.

He just nodded.

"I'm surprised you're still here," she said airily. "Must have taken longer than you expected."

Mike kept his tone casual, noncommittal, while he gathered up his tools and put them into the toolbox. "Yeah, well, since I am, how about joining me for a bite to eat?"

Her even brows rose a notch. "How thoughtful. It's really not necessary, though. I manage just fine."

"I'm sure you do, Cora," he countered. "But seeing as how I'm making your life something you must *manage* around a raft of inconveniences, it's only right that you be treated to a decent meal once in awhile."

She opened her mouth, her features revealing an intent to decline.

"Besides," he quickly added, "I thought maybe we could talk over a couple things, ideas I have for the kitchen, see if they sound reasonable."

"Oh. Well. If you put it that way, sure. A hot meal sounds delightful. Just let me change into—"

"Comfortable shoes," he said right along with her, and they both laughed.

"Okay, so I'm predictable. I admit it," Cora said sheepishly.

"Hey, there's nothing wrong with predictable. I kinda like it, myself. Some guys waste their entire lives just trying to figure out how to please a woman."

Mike glimpsed the barest hint of pink crest her fine features before she turned. "I'll be just a moment," she said over her shoulder.

A short drive up Route 309 took them to The Chicken's Roost, a new establishment gaining rapid popularity. It specialized in fried chicken, among other traditional home-cooked entrees. Mike had eaten there a time or two and found both the food and the service exceptional. As an added bonus, the interior was styled to resemble a really nice barn, something he knew Cora would like.

"I've been meaning to try this place," Cora said. "I don't eat out very much myself."

Why does that not surprise me? "I think you'll like it." He grinned at the pert teenage hostess with a trendy burgundy hairstyle as they approached her.

"A booth for two? Right this way." Snatching a pair of oversized laminated menus from a holder attached to her appointment stand, she led the way through a maze of red and white checkered tables to an uphol-stered vinyl booth along the far wall. "Melanie will be your waitress this evening. She'll be right with you."

After he and Cora shed their jackets, Mike waited for her to get settled, then seated himself.

"Cute place," she said, glancing around at rough-hewn walls and open beams brightened by country-style white curtains at each window. Bluegrass music played unobtrusively in the background.

"They do a considerable amount of business," he told her, "considering how recently they opened. Any minute now it'll start filling up."

"I don't mind the quiet. It makes talking easier, don't you think?"

"That I do. What are you hungry for?"

She made a quick perusal of the huge menu. "Judging from the variety of chicken dishes, I'd guess that's the specialty of the house, right?"

"Yep. Fried, to be exact."

"Then, fried it is." With a small smile, she handed him her menu.

Mike couldn't help but notice how her medium blue cardigan seemed to deepen the hue of those cornflower blue eyes of hers. So trusting and guileless, they contained a rare quality that stunned him, especially in this day and age: Innocence. If a guy wasn't careful, he could easily get lost in them. He blinked and cleared his throat as he took her menu.

"Hi, I'm Melanie, your waitress this evening," a petite blond in a gingham dress and ruffled apron said from the end of the booth, her notebook and pencil in hand. "Ready to order?"

"Yep. Fried chicken, two orders, and we'll both have the salad bar."

"Coffee? Iced tea?" she prompted.

"Iced tea," they said as one.

"I'll be back with your food shortly. Help yourself to the salad." She swiveled on her heel and left.

"How did you know I wanted salad?" Cora asked.

Mike didn't have the foggiest notion. It had just popped out. He blurted the first thing that came to his mind. "You were a farm gal once, right? You must be partial to fresh vegetables."

But her puzzled expression was nothing compared to his own confusion. How *did* he know so many of her preferences?

Chapter 5

After a short discussion regarding Mike's suggestions regarding the kitchen, the carpenter went for a second helping of salad. Cora took advantage of the opportunity to study the tall, lanky man from the discreet distance of their booth. He actually wasn't bad looking, she conceded, and might even be considered attractive behind the stubble on his chin. His neatly cropped mahogany hair showed a touch of silver around the temples, and tiny grooves fanning out from his deep-set eyes only added character to that long, lean face.

Seeing him glance her way as he rounded the salad bar to the chilled fixings on the other side, she lowered her gaze and nibbled a slice of cucumber until he was occupied again, then she continued her assessment. Hard work undoubtedly attributed to his muscled trimness and the lack of the typical paunch sported by many of his peers. But most fascinating of all, she decided, were his hands. Big and square, with long tapered fingers, enough calluses and scars to make them interesting. She liked looking at his hands.

"Ah, this should do it," he said, rejoining her. "They sure have fresh stuff here."

Cora hastily curbed her wayward thoughts. "Yes, they have. The owner must be an old farm boy," she quipped.

Mike's chuckle stopped just shy of turning into a real laugh. "Touché."

Cora couldn't remember when she'd last enjoyed a quiet dinner out with a friend. She knew Mike wasn't exactly a friend yet, but she was quickly growing used to his cheery grin when he arrived each morning and the pleasant comments that fell so easily from his tongue. And who knew, perhaps the very fact they had no designs on each other was what enabled her to relax around him so much sooner than she might have otherwise.

Golden-haired Melanie, a large round tray propped on her slim shoulder, brought their orders just then. She flicked open a portable stand she'd toted in her other arm, then set the food on it. "Here we go, two fried chicken specials. I'll be right back with more iced tea. Enjoy." A flash of a perfect smile, and she turned away.

"Thanks, young lady," Mike said.

Cora eyed the generous portions piled on her plate and released a whoosh of breath. "My goodness. They expect a person to consume all this?"

"Not really," Mike assured her, a twinkle in his gray eyes. "You're allowed to leave the bones."

"Well, that's a relief," she shot back on a droll note.

This time he snickered and she had to laugh.

"Don't worry, they have carry out containers here." He picked up a crispy drumstick and took a healthy bite.

Cora slit open the huge baked potato and added butter, then sampled the first of her three pieces of chicken. "Mmm. It really is tasty, isn't it?"

By now other customers had begun drifting in. The restaurant grew noticeably noisier as numerous couples and groups sprinkled throughout the roomy eating area added their chatter and laughter to the music, which went up a notch to compensate. Cora didn't mind at all. Suddenly she sensed Mike staring at her. She swallowed and checked her blouse, to see if she'd dripped something on it. "Anything the matter?" she finally asked.

He blanched, returning his attention to his meal. "No. I was just wondering if I could ask you a personal question."

"How personal?"

He shrugged. "Oh, like how it is that an attractive woman such as yourself is still running loose."

"That's an easy one," she answered candidly, without acknowledging the compliment. "I had five siblings to raise, and—"

"Five?" His dark brows climbed the ridges of his forehead. "What happened to your parents?"

"They got caught in a blizzard, coming home from our aunt's funeral in Pittsburgh. Their car skidded off a mountain road and plunged over the side. The other kids and I thought they decided to stay with the relatives a couple extra days, at first. Then the highway patrol showed up. I can still see those somber faces."

"I'm. . .sorry. That must have been a rough one."

"Yes. Rough." She picked at the skin of her potato with the tines of the fork. "That's a good word for it."

"And you were how old?"

"Barely eighteen. Fortunately I happened to be home visiting between terms at Bible school. I couldn't go back, of course. I felt it was more important to keep the rest of the kids together, my three brothers and two sisters, make sure they were raised right. That occupied me for a number of years. A few too many, I suppose." A resigned smile punctuated the statement.

He rubbed his chin in thought.

"After our parents died, some neighbors, friends of ours, farmed my dad's land and paid us for the usage. The income kept us going. I still lease it out."

The waitress's airy voice broke into the moment. "Are you and your wife having dessert this evening?" She lowered a huge pastry tray filled with all kinds of delectable concoctions to provide easy perusal of the array.

Obviously amused by the girl's assumption, Mike made no reference to it as he eyed Cora. "Game?"

"You're kidding."

"Look at that Boston cream pie," he cajoled. "It'd go perfect with some fresh coffee about now."

Against her better judgment, Cora agreed, though she knew she'd regret the calories later.

Mike berated himself for dredging up Cora's past. He should have known better than to be so nosy. But a part of him really did want to understand why an appealing and decent woman like her lived all alone out in the country in a big old house set far back off the main road. Life hadn't treated her fair. But then, what *was* fair in life? He took a gulp of coffee.

"It's only fair, you know," Cora said, her voice bringing him back to the present with the exact opposite of what he'd been thinking.

Had she read his mind? He gave her a slack-jawed look.

"For me to ask *you* a few questions," she went on. "After all, you're *running loose*, too. Why is that? Weren't you ever. . .in love?" She sliced a delicate chunk of her cloud-like sweet and looked up at him. Waiting.

He cleared his throat. She'd been honest. No reason he shouldn't be equally so. One side of his mouth curved up in a wry smile. "Once. Her name was Meg. She was everything I ever wanted, my ideal. I thought the world of her, worshiped the ground she walked on. For almost a year we went everywhere together— church and all, believe it or not. Meggie was real active in church things. We both were, actually." Having grated out that tidbit, he exhaled a bitter breath. "Then we, uh, started spending a little too much time together and decided we'd better get married before we did something we'd both regret. So she planned us a wedding nobody'd ever forget."

After a pause, Cora sniffed. "So you married her then? In this unforgettable wedding?"

He snorted in derision. "I was all set to. . .only it turned out the caterer happened to be her old boyfriend from junior high. A week before our wedding was to take place, the two of them decided to fan their old flame. She felt he was *God's will*, you might say."

Cora gasped. "How despicable."

"Good word." He rubbed the back of his neck to ease a kink. "But that was a long time ago. I focused my energies elsewhere, went off to college, earned a couple degrees in business, and then discovered I preferred trade school and working with wood."

"Well," she continued, "they say it's better to find out if a person's fickle before you're committed. Of course, that's small comfort to a hurting heart."

"True. Nevertheless, life goes on." Noticing that Cora had folded her napkin and appeared finished, he stood and offered her a hand. "Thanks for the company. It's. . .different, having somebody to talk to. I usually eat by myself. In front of the TV."

"Me, too," she admitted, accepting his assistance. "This was a most pleasant change." She picked up her carryout container and purse.

"We'll do it again sometime, if you want. No sense in the two of us eating alone every night as long as I'm working at your place."

An easy smile spread across her lips. "I'm bound to be hungry again within a week or so!"

Mike laughed, patting his stomach. "Same here." But

as he paid their tab and walked her out to the car, his more reserved side cautioned him against getting used to this. He'd already let down his guard and dumped more on this lady than he'd ever intended. Worse, he didn't even know why. He only knew one bad experience with a female had been enough to last a lifetime.

⚜

Maybe they'd talked themselves out or something, but Cora suspected the drive back to her house would have been completely silent if Mike hadn't turned on the radio. As an unfamiliar violin concerto filled the void, she cringed at the realization she had actually bared her soul to this guy, this carpenter who out of necessity would be in her life for a limited period of time and then gone. Of course, he'd been great company, pleasant and charming, ever so easy to talk to. But still! She must have bored the poor man silly. She needed her head examined. She'd better use her common sense from now on, remember her place and his, to say nothing of the fact that soon enough neither of them would have any contact whatsoever. If there was one thing she could not afford, it was to start counting on his being around.

Daylight was a dim memory by the time they arrived at the house. Cora opened the Bronco door and hopped out into the chilly night, thankful that she'd left the porch light on. "I must thank you for the delightful meal. I enjoyed that restaurant very much."

"Don't mention it. See you tomorrow."

"Yes. Tomorrow. Take care, now." She closed the

door and headed toward the back porch. Once she was inside, Mike made a U-turn and drove down the lane to the road, leaving a heavy silence in his wake.

Cora switched on the lights and habitually locked the door behind herself—something she'd never had to do in times past—and drew the blinds and curtains closed. Even out in the country a person never knew who might be lurking in the darkness. One had to be cautious these days, especially with the family collie, Pal, laid to rest. She'd never quite gotten around to replacing him. Perhaps the time had come to look for another dog. . .a small one that could stay inside for company. It would be good to feel needed again. Right now, the thing her weary bones needed most was a long hot bath.

The next morning, the air filtering in around the window frame of her bedroom had a definite chill to it, proof that the occasional light snow flurries so common this time of year were a mere prelude to winter's bleakness and heavy blizzards. Though she preferred dresses and skirts in the mild weather, they held little appeal during the short, dull days of late November. Cora dressed in brown wool slacks and a peach cashmere sweater set, adding a fine gold chain necklace with matching earrings. With warm socks and ankle-high leather boots, she knew she'd be comfortable at work. She hurried downstairs to make coffee and have her devotions before Mike arrived.

Last night, she hadn't allowed herself to dwell on the mealtime's pleasantries. Right after her bath, she'd settled in her most comfortable rocker with the new correspondence course on the epistle of Romans she'd ordered from one of Troy's ministerial magazines and focused her attention on that until she grew too weary to think. Then she'd gone to bed and dropped right off to sleep. That worked so well, she planned to continue in the same pattern until the course ended, or the house renovations were done. . .whichever came first. Definitely the prudent route.

The Bronco crunched up the drive at the usual time, just before the radio devotional's conclusion. Seconds later, Mike clomped across the porch and rapped on the door with his knuckle before opening it and coming in, his nose and face rosy from the cold. "Morning," he said casually, looping his jacket on the spindle of one of the wooden chairs, and went right for his toolbox in the corner of the room.

"Good morning." Cora slipped her arms into the sleeves of her coat and picked up her purse, rummaging in the front compartment for her car keys. "There's fresh coffee—oh, you know the routine. Have a good day."

He chuckled. "You too."

With a polite smile, she collected herself and headed out the door for the garage. Her subconsciousness had picked up on some subtle change in Mike on her way past him. . .something she couldn't put her finger on right away. But she had other things on her mind, duties she'd be focusing on at the church.

Halfway there it dawned on her out of the blue.

He looked different.

Younger. Neater. Handsomer. And no wonder his face had looked pink. Mike had shaved!

A silly smile tickled Cora's lips.

Chapter 6

A meeting with a group of deacons occupied Pastor Troy that morning until ten o'clock. When the older men finally emerged from his study into the hallway and left by the side door, the sandy-haired minister brought a pile of notes to Cora's desk for her to type for the file. "No real hurry on these. It's all general stuff."

She nodded and resumed her computer work, designing a brochure for an upcoming area women's conference the church would be hosting early next year.

"So how's everything going out at your place?" Troy asked, assuming a nonchalant pose beside her desk, his cream-colored shirt and tan slacks blending with the neutral colors of the church office.

Cora paused with her fingers still on the keyboard and met his gaze. "Fine. Couldn't be better. Another week or two and you won't recognize the kitchen. New floor and linoleum, new appliances and cupboards. . . . It'll be elegant enough for me to entertain royalty."

"Great." He paused. "And Mike? Is he behaving?"

The mention of the carpenter's name brought back the sudden and unexpected improvement in the man's appearance, which so far she'd managed not to let herself think about. She feigned a small smile and hoped it appeared casual. "Of course. He's been a model of decorum, impressing even me." She debated whether to go on, then opted to do so. "I've. . .started praying for him."

The minister's thoughtful nod preceded his answer. "I'm not surprised. The guy's decent and has a good heart. I don't think he's quite the agnostic he pretends to be. He hinted once at having been disappointed by some Christian he deeply respected. Most likely that's what he's been dealing with. But Sharon and I aren't about to give up on him, that's for sure. We and our kids pray for him during family devotions every night."

Cora basked in that warm ray of encouragement. "Power in numbers, right? Two or more of us agreeing in prayer on a matter, like it says in Matthew."

"Exactly. I might not have half the experience of our deacons, but I've seen enough answered prayer in my life to know God really does care about people and intervenes in their lives." A conspiratorial grin broke free. "Between you, me, Sharon, and the boys, poor Mike doesn't have a chance. He just doesn't know it yet." Giving her desk a playful tap with his fingertips, the pastor turned and went back into his study.

Cora gazed unseeing after him, absorbed in thoughts of her own. Mike did have a good heart, a big one, that was a fact. He also possessed a rare level of decency. How easily he could have taken advantage of her vulnerability, living off the beaten track as she did, yet he went out of his way to keep her at ease. In addition to those qualities, from the first day he'd started working there he endeavored to restore as much order and tidiness as was humanly possible before she got home, regardless of the particular job he'd been doing. He'd brought over a small utility trailer and parked it alongside the house for scraps and refuse. She appreciated those small considerations.

In truth, despite her best intentions, she was starting to appreciate quite a few things about Mike Burgess, and that really unnerved her. So did a peculiar heightened awareness of him. . .an awareness she must ignore at all cost.

Disjointed fragments of their mealtime conversation drifted through her thoughts as she tried unsuccessfully to concentrate on the wording of the brochure. The very idea that some young supposedly churchgoing girl would think of stomping all over the sacred love and trust of a fine man like him! Only Cora's Christian convictions kept her from hoping Meg Whoever-she-was had been utterly miserable all these years.

Cora rolled her eyes and gave herself another silent lecture on maturity and retaining a businesslike relationship with the carpenter. After all, she was not a schoolgirl. She really needed to avoid getting caught up in useless, fanciful daydreams.

Closing the file on the partially finished brochure, she switched her computer over to the Internet and logged on with her password. Maybe there would be some E-mail from her siblings. At least the family kept in touch that way quite regularly, passing on one another's latest news flashes or prayer concerns. Thank heaven for modern technology.

❧

The next couple days passed with a smoothness and swiftness aided by the comfortable routine Cora and Mike established from the start. His arrival time never varied more than five minutes one way or the other, and her return home rarely more than ten. She always had fresh coffee waiting for him, along with treats she purchased in town, a gesture he seemed to appreciate.

Also, Cora conveniently planned her departure before the conclusion of her morning radio devotional every day. Whether he actually allowed the program to finish once she was beyond earshot she could not be sure, but she prayed fervently that the Lord would take the thoughtful insights presented and use them for Mike's good. One could always hope a tiny seed of faith would take root inside him and stir to life the former beliefs he'd once considered sacred and precious.

"Care to go out for a bite?" Mike asked when Cora came through the door after work on Friday. His amiable grin put a sizeable crack in the wall of resolve she'd worked hard all day to build.

A vulnerability in his expression made Cora realize that new friendships were quite rare for people in their age group. If she didn't enjoy this relationship now, however temporary it might be, she might be wasting a blessing, to say nothing of blowing an opportunity for the Lord to use her. A few weeks from now when the pleasant interlude came to an end and they both reverted to their separate lives, she'd adjust to her old predictable routines again and learn to exist without Mike around. But no sense crossing that bridge before she came to it.

"Sure. Dining out would be lovely."

Mike drove them to a little coffee shop at Harvey's Lake, less elegant than the Chicken's Roost but considerably homier and not quite so crowded. Yesterday's golden oldies played in the background while they perused the menus, then ordered fish specials. . .hers with rice pilaf, his with fries.

"Man, I sure hate leaving you with an unusable kitchen for so long," he remarked, buttering his roll after their food arrived. "I could come over tomorrow and do some more work, if you like."

Cora shook her head. "I wouldn't think of imposing like that. Weekends are your own. I'm managing fine with the new sink and countertop stove, and the microwave is still plugged in. And you must have chores that need catching up on." She paused. "Where do you live, anyway? You've never said." Determined not to get caught staring at his angular face—downright arresting now that he no longer hid behind a scruff of whiskers—she gave intense concentration to rearranging the peas and carrots alongside her rice pilaf.

She detected the slight shrug of his shoulder. "I built myself a little place in Tunkhannock."

"Oh?" She flicked a glance up to his eyes, then averted it again. "In town?"

"Nope. Kinda back in the woods. No real close

neighbors, just lots of trees, a pond, and a whole bunch of wildlife."

Cora could easily picture him off by himself secluded by the endless wooded hills so typical of northeastern Pennsylvania. But a tiny part of her wondered if in reality he was hiding from people, from life. "Are you a hunter?"

He grimaced. "Hardly. Can't see killing animals just for sport, and there's no way I could eat a whole deer on my own. The only way I shoot them is with a camera."

She smiled and sampled some rice, then sipped her coffee.

"I fish, though," he added, slicing into his grilled halibut. "Row myself out to the middle of the pond and wait for a nibble. Course, it's too cold to do much of that now. I'm usually too busy anyway."

"Are you? What do you do when you're not remodeling parsonages and other houses?"

He smirked. "What is this, Twenty Questions?"

Flustered, Cora repositioned the napkin on her lap. "I'm sorry. I don't mean to pry, really. I was only making conversation."

"I know, Cora-girl. I'm just teasing." He flashed a grin when she looked up. "Actually, I run a business out of my house, building custom furniture in my basement workshop. I sell it on the Net."

Taking no offense from the nickname her father had used long ago, she brightened. "Oh, how interesting. My dad had a workshop in our old barn, but it was small-scale. He made wooden toys. He was always so proud of those projects," she added wistfully. "I've always been partial to the smell of new wood, paint, glue. . ."

"Must be why I haven't heard any complaints while I've been ripping things out and redoing them," he said, a gentle smile pleating the corners of his eyes.

He had a very nice smile, she realized. It took her a few seconds to find her voice. "You won't hear me grumble. I really like the changes, the new cupboards you're building. . .and I appreciate the amount of work you've taken on in my house. I know this whole project got dumped on you out of the blue."

His grudging nod held no unpleasantness. "I might as well admit it. I've enjoyed myself, seeing that old place coming back to life." His gaze lingered an extra few seconds before he stabbed a pair of fries with his fork. "Too bad it doesn't work that way for people," he muttered, popping the crisp potatoes into his mouth.

"Oh, but it does," she countered softly. "Once in awhile."

A bitter grimace tightened his mouth. "Yeah. Right. Let's see, what'd that radio preacher say is the key? Oh yeah. Forgiveness. We're supposed to forgive and forget, and all our troubles will be over."

So he had listened to the programs! Cora latched onto to the hopeful possibilities that knowledge brought. Her spirit breathed a prayer of thanks, also seeking wisdom and insight for this moment as she ventured a step into the forbidden. "Not all of them, perhaps. But it's a start, letting go of the past, pressing on toward the future. It brings peace."

Mike merely stared at her, his expression unreadable.

Cora tried another chunk of halibut, sensing from her companion's dark look that a change of subject might be timely. "Have you any family in the area, Mike?"

"Huh? No. Everybody's gone now. I did have a brother, but he got killed in Vietnam. It's just me now."

"Oh, I'm so sorry." Automatically, she placed a hand atop his on the table, then embarrassed at her actions, quickly pulled her own away. "My siblings all live out of state," she blurted, hoping to regain equilibrium. "I don't get to see them often. They're all busy with their own lives."

"Guess that's how it goes." He resumed eating, then raised his gaze to hers again. "So I presume you've forgiven your brothers and sisters, then. Being a good Christian, and all."

Cora rose to the bait. "Whatever for?"

An amused smirk curved his lips. "Figures you'd be such a martyr you don't even acknowledge they wasted your life. If not for your staying home and raising the lot, you'd have a family of your own by now, instead of being all by yourself."

"Perhaps," she said evenly. "But I didn't consider it a waste. Besides, what else could I have done?" Even as she spoke the words, Cora felt a twinge of guilt. Lest he see how very close he'd come to voicing inner feelings she had struggled long and hard to accept, she focused once more on her meal.

❧

Watching the subtle play of emotions on Cora's face,

Mike chewed thoughtfully. Maybe she'd spoken the truth about not feeling her family had taken advantage of her. Who knew? A woman like her, with so much to give, probably didn't know the first thing about putting her own desires first, going after personal dreams.

He'd been around Cora Dennison only a short time, barely saw her while he'd been working on the parsonage, and only since he'd been redoing her house had he gotten to know her at all. In truth, he'd purposely steered a wide berth around the fairer sex for a lot of years now. But she was different. There seemed to be an almost tangible quality in those beautiful eyes that he couldn't ignore. A gentleness, a true concern for others that drew a person out, invited complete honesty without fear of being judged. He liked that. A lot. It stirred something inside himself, something from long ago he had buried down deep. . .a need to shelter and protect an individual other than himself.

For all her staunch faith, life hadn't treated Cora much more fairly than it had treated him, yet she possessed something he lacked: Peace. Contentment. When was the last time he'd had a real, lasting measure of either of those things? The house he'd built in the woods hadn't taken him far enough away to escape his own thoughts, his needs. Was it really possible for a person to recapture a sense of true happiness after all these years?

Maybe he needed to give some thought to what that radio preacher encouraged, work on forgiving past hurts. Like Cora said, it could be the first step back to peace. . .and there were a lot of things worse than being completely at peace.

Chapter 7

"Good morning," Cora called breezily when Mike arrived at the house right on time Monday. "Have a good weekend?" she asked while he disposed of his jacket and knit cap.

"Yep, that I did. Finished up an order I'd been working on, then did a couple things around the place. How about you?"

"It's always quiet here on Saturdays," she said, plucking her coat from a chair back and slipping her arms into the sleeves. "And yesterday was rather restful. . .between services, of course."

"Of course." A lopsided smile tipped up a corner of his mouth as he retrieved his toolbox and opened it. "You go to church morning and night, I presume." A twinkle in his eyes belied the hint of disdain in his expression.

Cora kept her tone light, not wanting to sound judgmental. "Always have, weather permitting. It wouldn't seem like Sunday if I didn't go to worship."

He made no comment but nodded. "Speaking of

weather, it's, uh, pretty nippy out. Might even get a flurry or two from that storm up north. Dressed warm?"

His concern, though unnecessary, warmed her far more than her clothes. When was the last time anyone had cared two hoots about whether she dressed sufficiently? Cora smiled her pleasure. "I sure am. See you later." Grabbing her purse and gloves, she headed out to the garage.

Cora anticipated a productive day at the office, one with no interruptions except for the inevitable phone calls from church members and religious supply houses. Pastor Troy's mother was scheduled to have surgery this morning, so he, Sharon, and the boys had left for Harrisburg after the evening service to be at her side in recovery. They expected to return tomorrow. Meanwhile, Cora intended to move mountains, possibly get her whole desktop cleared.

Arriving at the church, she unlocked the office door, turned on the heat, and then started a pot of coffee. Several letters sat in her work basket waiting to be typed, plus a whole raft of sermon tape orders from yesterday. Troy had started a new series on prayer, kicking it off with excellent messages in the morning and evening services. Likely she'd be at the duplicating machine for hours. First, however, she'd see to the correspondence. Surely that would keep her too busy to wonder whether Mike left the radio on.

❦

Although Mike had originally scorned the Christian devotional Cora tuned into every day on the radio, it had quickly grown on him. Now he not only tolerated those last few moments of the program's time slot but actually found himself listening to the inoffensive sound bites of encouragement presented by the pleasant-mannered speaker each morning. Amazingly enough, down deep, he found he agreed with them. But even if he hadn't, he did appreciate the first-rate music and would have left the dial set in that position just to hear the final selection.

This morning's short talk had been a continuation of the topic of forgiveness, and now hours later, Mike couldn't get it out of his head. All the while he worked on the kitchen it replayed in his mind as though the minister stood right there in the room. "Another step to help in forgiveness, my friends, is to begin praying for the one who wronged you," the man had said. "Once you do that, it becomes impossible to hang on to those old feelings of pain."

Begin praying for the one who wronged you. To Mike that sounded a bit far-fetched. He hadn't so much as wasted a thought on Meg since she'd dumped him—and now he was supposed to pray for her? That concept would take some getting used to.

Funny, though, the idea of forgiving his former fiancée no longer seemed as outlandish as before. After all, he'd made a good life for himself, done everything he'd set his mind to. . .even if he had done it alone. If the two of them had married, they might have had a passel of kids to support and educate, and he wouldn't have enjoyed half this level of freedom. Maybe he should *thank* Meg for dumping him. The irony brought a wry smirk.

Reining in his thoughts, he ran a hand over the wood-stained finish on the cupboards, which had dried well over the weekend. No reason why he couldn't screw on all the new doors, make this place look like a kitchen again. Wouldn't Cora's eyes light up then, he surmised, smiling to himself. She'd been real good-natured about having dishes and things piled up in the dining room. Later today she could start putting everything back where it belonged.

After lunch, Mike wrestled the wall oven out of the carton and hefted it to the cupboard he'd built to its specifications, then maneuvered the appliance into place. After he connected the power supply, he stepped back to assess his handiwork. Big improvement, with all the new doors on and the oven and microwave filling in the two big gaps, he decided. Now that the rebuilding was out of the way, Cora would see a lot more progress each day, a thought he found intensely gratifying.

Of course, the ceiling and those painted walls still screamed for attention. Against the redone part of the room they looked almost garish. There was still time to start in on them before Cora came home. He'd go bring in the power sander from out of the truck.

The temperature had dropped alarmingly since his arrival earlier. His down jacket barely offered sufficient protection when he stepped outside into the blast of arctic air that whipped around him, slapping his face with fat, wet snowflakes. He turned his gaze upward, toward where a couple million more flakes of assorted sizes looked like black specks against the heavy clouds. Just as he'd suspected, flurries from that storm up north. Picking up the pace, he hurried to the truck and dug out the sander and some plastic sheeting, then returned to the house to tackle the ceiling.

The chore went slower than he'd hoped. The weight of the electric sander, added to the unnatural position he had to work in and the ungainly perch on the ladder, necessitated periodic coffee breaks—a chance to stretch the kinks out of his back and neck, not to mention enabling him to keep an eye on the accumulating snow outside. No sense hanging around if it looked like things were getting too messy for him to navigate the mountain roads to get home. He'd leave right after Cora came in from work. She probably quit early in bad weather.

Cora hummed along with the tune on the CD player, a happy, upbeat song which had prompted even the staid congregation of this conservative church to smile and tap their feet when the choir performed it a number of weeks ago. The office phones had been incredibly silent, and without so much as a window in her cubicle to distract her, she'd accomplished a rare amount of work. She checked her watch. Heavens, where had the day gone? Still not quite quitting time, but there was no reason she couldn't leave now, since nothing remained to be done in her basket. Perhaps she'd swing by Mrs. Humphries' place on the way home and see how the widow and her daughter Ida Mae were getting along.

When she opened the church door, Cora's mouth fell open.

Snow! Everywhere! This little *flurry* the weather forecasters had predicted from the big storm pounding New England had already dumped snow deeper than the floorboards of her car and showed little indication of letting up in the near future—and all this while, she'd been in her own little world, completely oblivious to what was happening!

A glance toward the road showed no sign that snowplows had been along yet, but that didn't mean that they weren't out and about. And she did have good winter tires. They'd get her home, though it would probably be slow going until she came to a plowed road. Likely there'd be tracks from other vehicles to follow, which would help. At least some daylight remained, though the heavy clouds masked what little there was.

Cora locked the door and stepped gingerly through the deep snow toward her car. What a day to have worn low boots! With each step she could feel biting cold wetness working its way around her ankles. Behind her, in the church, she heard the faint ringing of the phone. Likely it would stop before she got to it, so she pressed on. There was snow to clear off the sedan before she could get out of here. She kept a broom in the trunk just for such emergencies.

No answer. Mike hung up Cora's outdated phone with a frown, then relaxed his facial muscles. She must be on her way home. Maybe coming up the lane already. He shouldn't wait much longer before heading for Tunkhannock. He'd already gone out to put chains on the Bronco's tires in preparation for slippery road conditions, but it still wouldn't be much fun getting up those mountain roads.

Where was Cora?

He peered out the window one more time. No headlights probed the growing darkness. "Come on, Cora-girl. You should've been home ages ago. Or at least phoned." Yeah. Right. The gal was bright enough to figure he'd be long gone by now, what with the storm and all. But why hadn't *she* left early? What was the matter with Reverend Green that he'd keep a woman there in this kind of weather? Maybe it was time to check with him. Cora had the parsonage number written on a small message board by her phone, right along with the church office number.

Rotary dials, he groused, poking a finger into the small holes and turning each digit one by one. If nothing else, he was going to buy Cora Dennison a decent phone for Christmas. A wall unit styled after the old-fashioned ones, to fit with the kitchen's new look, but a touch-tone model in keeping with the day's technology. He'd seen just the one in his travels.

When no one at the parsonage answered by the tenth ring, Mike gave up. "Well," he muttered, "there aren't that many roads between here and church. I'll find you myself, if that's what it takes." Grabbing his jacket and hat, he shoved his feet into his boots and headed for his truck. A little voice inside tried to assure him this was just a normal winter storm for Pennsylvania, not out of the ordinary for December. Some years they had tons of snow by now. And Cora was a grown woman, used to coming and going on her own all year long.

But Mike didn't buy it. Because his *other* side was truly worried about Cora. Concerned that a sweet, lovely woman like her might be stuck in a snowdrift, needing help. He couldn't think of heading home until he knew for sure she was safe. It mattered. . .far more than he expected.

Because truth was, *she* mattered. He'd grown to think of her as a good friend. He didn't want anything to happen to her.

Oh, Lord, his spirit pleaded as the Bronco charged down the slippery drive and he gripped the steering wheel for all he was worth, *I know You don't owe me anything. I turned my back on You a lot of years ago, and it was wrong. I see that now. I had my focus set on a person, instead of on You, and I let her failings cause worse ones in my own life. I regret that now. But my concern is for Cora. She's one of Your own and doesn't need yet another trial. For her sake, Lord, please help me to find her. If You'll do that, I'll make things right between You and me. I swear it with everything I have.*

Somehow the prayer brought the beginnings of the

quiet peace Mike had relinquished so long ago. In grim determination he steered onto the main road, his eyes darting from one side to the other, looking for. . .something. . .anything that might lead him to Cora.

Chapter 8

Well, *this is a fine predicament.* Cora eased herself from the driver's side of the snowbound Buick to the passenger seat so she could tuck her legs beneath her coat and retain body heat. Wrapping her arms around herself, she huddled against the car door.

As fate would have it, falling snow had all but obliterated the tracks of previous vehicles on curvy Demunds Road, leaving her the dubious chore of being a pathfinder. Still, had her sedan not hit an icy patch and started skidding and had she not overcorrected, she probably could have managed all right. Now the car was wedged cockeyed in a wide, snow-filled ditch alongside the road with only its roof, if anything, visible through the bushes.

She had passed the familiar houses of Fernbrook awhile back, where she might have stopped to ask for shelter. Now with the wind whipping the snow every which way along this more rural stretch of road, it was hard to get her bearings. It would be folly to try to seek help on foot and in the dark. She had no idea in which direction the nearest house might be.

How could you be so stupid? Cora asked herself for the umpteenth time, her teeth beginning to chatter. *Leaving the sanctity of the church in this storm without informing anyone of your intentions! Nobody will even know where you are, much less that you tried to get home but never made it!*

Miserably, she started the engine again to emit a few minutes' warmth from the heater. *Was this how Mother and Daddy felt that day, plunging over the side of a mountain, hurt and alone, dying of exposure before some-one discovered the broken guardrail?* How ironic that she might suffer the same fate. Despite her determination to stay in control, Cora felt the sting of tears. How long would it be until a plow came by? Had falling snow already erased the car's tracks? Would the storm soon bury her alive?

Trying to ignore the howling wind outside, she gave herself a mental shake. "Stop it. Concentrate on something else. God knows where you are." *Dear Lord, I need help. If there's anybody out there in this storm, please let them find me.* She turned the key off and strained her ears for the sound of another motor but heard only the buffeting gusts. Obviously the other locals who normally traveled this road had used their brains and headed home much earlier or knew better than to brave the elements in the first place.

She reached over to the controls and chanced turn-ing the headlights on for another few minutes. The car sat too deep for the hazard lights to be of any use, but the brighter glow from headlights could alert passersby. . . providing the battery held out long enough. And providing someone actually came along.

༄

Mike railed against the blowing snow wiping out any recent car tracks on the road. Surely other people had to get home from work. Where in the world were the snowplows? The county had an ample number to keep roads cleared in a blizzard. Jaw clenched, he plunged onward, his eyes peeled for Cora's Buick anywhere within the beam of his headlights. Fernbrook, the tiny hamlet between Shavertown and Demunds, was only a couple miles ahead. Maybe he'd spot her car at somebody's house, or she could have set out for home but changed her mind and returned to the church, in which case he'd find her there.

Rounding a curve, a strange glow caught his attention. . .lights where there shouldn't be any. *Let it be Cora, Lord. And please let her be all right.* As he drew nearer, he made out definite ridges in the snow of the opposing lane. Car tracks—tracks that hadn't quite made the turn! Grinding to a stop, he flicked his hazard lights on and jumped out of the Bronco, leaving the motor running while he all but leaped down the small incline to the dark blue sedan unceremoniously embedded in the snowy ditch.

His heart surged with relief. "Cora!" he hollered, yanking the driver's side door open.

"Mike?" she gasped, her voice small in the darkness.

The waning headlights cast a pale glow over her aston-ished and thankful features. "I've n—never been s—so g—glad to see anyone in my l—life! I was s—sure you m—must have gone back to Tunkhannock by n—now," she managed, her teeth chattering audibly.

"The thought did cross my mind. Come on, let's get you home. We'll worry about your car tomorrow." Turning off the headlights, he noted the inadequate boots on her feet as she moved stiffly across the seat toward him. With a shake of his head he swept her up in his arms, the ends of her scarf buffeting them both in the wind. There was a lot to be said for a gal who watched her weight, he decided, holding her real close, hugging her to his heart. Man, she felt good.

Cora was too cold to put up any resistance against the stalwart man intent on whisking her bodily to the wait-ing Bronco. But resisting was the farthest thing from her mind at that moment. She looped her arms around those strong shoulders and snuggled her head against him, promising to give more thought to proper deco-rum another time. Right now she was too relieved and too busy thanking the Lord for sending a rescuer, in general, and—heaven help her—this one in particular.

Reaching his car, Mike opened the door and set her gently on the seat, then tucked a waiting blanket around her shivering form before closing the door once more against the icy blasts. The warmth pouring from the heater almost made her face burn but felt ever so welcomed.

"Th—thank you, M—Mike," she whispered when he climbed in his side. "For c—coming."

A muscle worked in his jaw as he stared long and hard, the dim glow from the dashboard reflecting in his eyes. He reached over and ran a gloved finger down the side of her face. "I wouldn't have quit looking until I found you, Cora-girl," he murmured, his voice husky.

An indescribably delicious tremor coursed through her whole being.

The chains made the truck jounce a bit on the homeward drive, but Cora couldn't have cared less. Her heart was so full no words could have expressed the way she felt inside.

When they reached her place, Mike again came around to Cora's door and carried her over the drifting snow to the house, where he took her directly to the living room couch and adjusted the blanket over her once more. He then touched a match to the logs in her fireplace. "We'll have you warmed up in a jiffy," he said with that tiny wink she now considered irresistible. "I'll make you some tea."

"Wait," she said, raising a hand as he walked by on his way to the kitchen. "Please. I'm fine now, Mike. Truly I am. Stop fussing over me. You need to get home before the snow gets much deeper."

He smiled and knelt down before her, taking her hands in both of his. "I know you're fine, Miss Self-reliant. But you've just been through a harrowing experience, and I'm not about to run off just yet. According to the radio, we're under a major storm warning for twelve more hours. I might be able to get through to Tunkhannock, and I might not. That's not my foremost concern at the moment. You are. So relax and give me the honor of waiting on you, for once. Okay?"

They stared at each other, old defenses no longer in place and new possibilities, infinitely precious, hovering within their grasp. What could she say?

She released a breath of defeat and nodded.

While Mike busied himself putting a meal together, Cora got up to use the bathroom and freshen her face and hair. Goodness, she looked a mess, tendrils of hair from her French roll going every which way, her mascara streaked, lipstick smeared. . .it's a wonder her hero hadn't run off at the very sight of her. But she took a deep breath and made the necessary repairs, then reported back to her station, rather enjoying the homey sounds of Mike's movements and the pots clanging now and then in the kitchen, wishing they never had to end. Something smelled pretty good, too. It just dawned on her how famished she was. Smiling, she closed her eyes.

"Dinner is served," he soon announced, offering her his arm. "Hope you like spaghetti. . .I knew it wouldn't take long to throw together."

"It's one of my favorites," Cora admitted, accepting his assistance and reveling in the warm feeling of that muscled arm beneath her fingertips until he seated her. "I was supposed to be cooking *you* dinner once you had the oven in and everything hooked up, remember?" A sweeping glance took in the lovely new cupboard doors. Everything looked so homey, so charming. She smiled her appreciation.

"Sorry about the ceiling," he said. "I didn't get as much paint off as I'd hoped."

Now that he mentioned it, Cora thought she detected some flecks of white amid the mahogany strands of his hair and others in his eyebrows. But as far as she was concerned, he'd never looked so. . .perfect. So incredibly perfect. Despite her best intentions of remaining aloof and reserved from this very compelling man, the unthinkable had happened. And at her age, of all things! Could this sweet anguish crimping her heart, this exquisite pain actually be. . .love?

"You'll still have your chance," he promised.

"I beg your pardon?"

"To cook me that meal, like you promised."

"Oh." Cora closed her gaping mouth and swallowed. "Of course."

Mike brought over two plates he'd dished up with steaming spaghetti and crisp salad and claimed the chair opposite her. Then he took her hand and bowed his head. "Dear Lord, thank You for guiding me to Cora like I asked. Thank You that she's home again and safe. Please bless this food You've provided and use it to strengthen us both. . .and I still aim to keep that promise I made. In Jesus' name, amen."

A feather could have knocked Cora off her seat.

So could the gleam in Mike's gray eyes when he opened them and smiled. "Well, eat up. We have some serious talking to do later."

"We have? About what?"

"What else? Rectifying the situation we have here. I might very well be snowed in at your place and have to camp out on the sofa tonight. . .which could besmirch your good name, you know."

Cora felt the blood drain from her face. "Oh, grief. . ."

"Don't worry, though," he went on without missing a beat. "I have a solution for that. Trust me." Another wink, and he ate like there was no tomorrow.

After the meal, Mike escorted Cora to the uphol- stered floral couch again, taking the seat beside her. With a small smile, he raised an arm in unspoken invitation, and she melted against him, the sound of howling winds diminished by the cheerful crackling fire in the hearth. Lyrics from an old favorite song drifted to her mind. *What a difference a day makes. . .twenty-four little hours. . .* For the first time ever, Cora could relate to that thought, though no words of commitment had been spoken between the two of them.

And who would have guessed a woman could derive such intense pleasure from the feeling of a man's heartbeat? So vastly different from a brother's. And from the musky scent of aftershave? She blushed at the thought.

"You know," Mike finally said on a pensive note, "I thought I had everything life would ever offer me. I'd become comfortable, satisfied with the status quo. I never even realized how lonely I was, until I met you."

Her heart missed a beat. She gathered her musings into something she could articulate. No one had to tell her that chances like this didn't come along very often.

"And I had no idea a. . .grown woman. . .could feel like this."

"How's that?"

She shrugged. "All trembly inside. Giddy as a schoolgirl, happier than I've ever been before."

Mike drew her closer. "I'm feeling a lot of things I'd forgotten about too, Cora." He paused, his hand idly tracing a path up and down her forearm. "I know we haven't known each other very long, but there's just something about you that made me realize my life wasn't as full as I pretended it was. Part of that was because I closed the door against God. And I've rectified that now, thanks to you. The other reason was because I didn't know anyone like you existed in this world. Then the Lord brought you into my life. I have to say this. I love you, Cora. I finally admitted it to myself when I was trying so desperately to find you out in the storm."

"Oh, Mike." Cora swallowed against a joyful lump in her throat. "I love you too. To hear that you've made peace with God and that you actually love me. . .it's just. . .overwhelming."

"Couldn't have said it better myself." His smile broadened into a grin. With his free hand, he cupped her face and raised it to meet his lips in a kiss so tender, yet so promising, Cora decided even a word like *overwhelming* hardly did justice to these new sensations. How had she existed before Mike came along?

"So, about that dilemma you mentioned before," she ventured upon regaining her breath. "You said you had a solution in mind?"

He nodded, the glint in his eye partly teasing but mostly serious. "It's like this. Here we are, two people who've been living solo all these years. Now God's brought us together. I think He wants to blend our lives into a duet of praise to Him. Would you consider marrying a guy like me, Cora? Would you become my wife?"

Losing herself in the silvery depths of Mike's eyes, she felt a tingle spiral all the way to her toes. God was giving her a desire she had never even thought to ask for. Maybe it was never too late for love. She smiled at the wonderful man who held her in his embrace. "I would consider marrying *only* you, Mike Burgess. Yes. A thousand times yes!"

"Of course, we don't have to rush," he assured her. "If you prefer, I could court you proper. We wouldn't have to get married until spring or summer. What do you say?"

"On the other hand," she whispered, "we've already wasted half a lifetime. Christmas is coming. Wouldn't that be the perfect time for a wedding?"

"It couldn't be more perfect," Mike said, hugging her tighter.

A log broke in the fireplace as their lips met in another kiss. But Cora was sure that the burst of glowing sparks cavorting up the chimney paled in comparison to the glorious hope dancing inside of her. At long last. . .love.

SALLY LAITY

Sally spent the first twenty years of her life in Dallas, Pennsylvania, and calls herself a small-town girl at heart. She and her husband Don have lived in New York, Pennsylvania, Illinois, Alberta (Canada), and now reside in Bakersfield, CA. They are active in a large Baptist church, where Don teaches Sunday school and Sally sings in the choir. They have four children and twelve grandchildren.

Sally always loved to write, and after her children were grown, she took college writing courses and attended Christian writing conferences. She has written both historical and contemporary romances and considers it a joy to know that the Lord can touch other hearts through her stories.

Having successfully written several novels, including a series co-authored with Dianna Crawford for Tyndale, three Barbour novellas, and six **Heartsong Presents** titles, one of this author's favorite things these days is counseling new authors via the Internet.

A Letter to Our Readers

Dear Readers:

In order that we might better contribute to your reading enjoyment, we would appreciate you taking a few minutes to respond to the following questions. When completed, please return to the following: Fiction Editor, Barbour Publishing, Inc., P.O. Box 719, Uhrichsville, OH 44683.

1. Did you enjoy reading *Autumn Crescendo?*
    ❑ Very much. I would like to see more books like this.
    ❑ Moderately—I would have enjoyed it more if _____
    _____

    _____

2. What influenced your decision to purchase this book?
    (Check those that apply.)
    ❑ Cover   ❑ Back cover copy   ❑ Title   ❑ Price
    ❑ Friends   ❑ Publicity   ❑ Other

3. Which story was your favorite?
    ❑ *September Sonata*   ❑ *November Nocturne*
    ❑ *October Waltz*   ❑ *December Duet*

4. Please check your age range:
    ❑ Under 18   ❑ 18–24   ❑ 25–34
    ❑ 35–45   ❑ 46–55   ❑ Over 55

5. How many hours per week do you read? _____

Name _____

Occupation _____

Address _____

City _____ State _____ ZIP _____

E-mail _____

If you enjoyed

AUTUMN
Crescendo

then read:

Once Upon
a Time

*Four Modern Stories with All the
Enchantment of a Fairy Tale*

A Rose for Beauty by Irene B. Brand
The Shoemaker's Daughter by Lynn A. Coleman
Lily's Plight by Yvonne Lehman
Better to See You by Gail Gaymer Martin

Available wherever books are sold.
Or order from:
Barbour Publishing, Inc.
PO Box 721
Uhrichsville, Ohio 44683
http://www.barbourbooks.com

You may order by mail for $5.97 and add $2.00 to your order for shipping.
Prices subject to change without notice.

If you enjoyed

AUTUMN
Crescendo

then read:

TAILS
of LOVE

Pets Play Matchmakers in
Four Modern Love Stories

Ark of Love by Lauralee Bliss
Walk, Don't Run by Pamela Griffin
Dog Park by Dina Leonhardt Koehly
The Neighbor's Fence by Gail Sattler

Available wherever books are sold.
Or order from:
Barbour Publishing, Inc.
PO Box 721
Uhrichsville, Ohio 44683
http://www.barbourbooks.com

You may order by mail for $5.97 and add $2.00 to your order for shipping.
Prices subject to change without notice.

If you enjoyed

AUTUMN
Crescendo

then read:

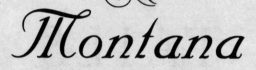

Montana

A Legacy of Faith and Love
in Four Complete Novels by Ann Bell

Autumn Love
Contagious Love
Inspired Love
Distant Love

Available wherever books are sold.
Or order from:
Barbour Publishing, Inc.
P.O. Box 721
Uhrichsville, Ohio 44683
http://www.barbourbooks.com

You may order by mail for $5.97 and add $2.00 to your order for shipping.
Prices subject to change without notice.

If you enjoyed

AUTUMN
Crescendo

then read:

🌴

FLORIDA

FOUR INSPIRING LOVE STORIES FROM
THE SUNSHINE STATE

A Place to Call Home by Eileen M. Berger
What Love Remembers by Muncy G. Chapman
Summer Place by Peggy Darty
Treasure of the Keys by Stephen A. Papuchis

Available wherever books are sold.
Or order from:
Barbour Publishing, Inc.
P.O. Box 721
Uhrichsville, Ohio 44683
http://www.barbourbooks.com

You may order by mail for $5.97 and add $2.00 to your order for shipping.
Prices subject to change without notice.

$\mathcal{H}$EARTSONG ♥ PRESENTS

Love Stories Are Rated G!

That's for godly, gratifying, and of course, great! If you love a thrilling love story but don't appreciate the sordidness of some popular paperback romances, **Heartsong Presents** is for you. In fact, **Heartsong Presents** is the only inspirational romance book club, the only one featuring love stories where Christian faith is the primary ingredient in a marriage relationship.

    Sign up today to receive your first set of four never-before-published Christian romances. Send no money now; you will receive a bill with the first shipment. You may cancel at any time without obligation, and if you aren't completely satisfied with any selection, you may return the books for an immediate refund!

    Imagine. . .four new romances every four weeks—two historical, two contemporary—with men and women like you who long to meet the one God has chosen as the love of their lives. . .all for the low price of $9.97 postpaid.

    To join, simply complete the coupon below and mail to the address provided. **Heartsong Presents** romances are rated G for another reason: They'll arrive Godspeed!

YES!   Sign me up for Hearts♥ng!

NEW MEMBERSHIPS WILL BE SHIPPED IMMEDIATELY!
Send no money now. We'll bill you only $9.97 postpaid with your first shipment of four books. Or for faster action, call toll free 1-800-847-8270.

NAME _____

ADDRESS _____

CITY _____ STATE_____ ZIP_____

MAIL TO: HEARTSONG PRESENTS, P.O. Box 721, Uhrichsville, Ohio 44683